"James Kelman

—Douglas Stuart, au

"Probably the most influential novelist
of the post-war period."
—*The Times*

"Kelman has the knack, maybe more than anyone since Joyce, of fixing in his writing the lyricism of ordinary people's speech.... Pure aesthete, undaunted democrat—somehow Kelman manages to reconcile his two halves."
—*Esquire* (London)

"The greatest British novelist of our time."
—*Sunday Herald*

"A true original.... A real artist.... It's now very difficult to see which of [Kelman's] peers can seriously be ranked alongside him without ironic eyebrows being raised."
—Irvine Welsh, *Guardian*

"A writer of world stature, a 21st century Modern."
—*The Scotsman*

"The real reason Kelman, despite his stature and reputation, remains something of a literary outsider is not, I suspect, so much that great, radical Modernist writers aren't supposed to come from working-class Glasgow, as that great, radical Modernist writers are supposed to be dead. Dead, and wrapped up in a Penguin Classic: that's when it's safe to regret that their work was underappreciated or misunderstood (or how little they were paid) in their lifetimes. You can write what you like about Beckett or Kafka and know they're not going to come round and tell you you're talking nonsense, or confound your expectations with a new work. Kelman is still alive, still writing great books, climbing."
—James Meek, *London Review of Books*

"The greatest living British novelist."
—Amit Chaudhuri, author of *A New World*

"What an enviably, devilishly wonderful writer is James Kelman."
—John Hawkes, author of *The Blood Oranges*

Keep Moving and No Questions

Books available by the same author

NOVELS

A Disaffection

How Late It Was, How Late

Mo said she was quirky

Dirt Road

God's Teeth and Other Phenomena

SHORT STORY COLLECTIONS

If it is your life

A Lean Third

That Was a Shiver

NONFICTION

Between Thought and Expression Lies a Lifetime: Why Ideas Matter (with Noam Chomsky)

The State Is the Enemy: Essays on Liberation and Racial Justice

All We Have Is the Story: Selected Interviews, 1973–2022

Keep Moving and No Questions

stories

James Kelman

Keep Moving and No Questions

ISBN: 978-1-62963-967-3 (paperback)
ISBN: 978-1-62963-975-8 (hardcover)
ISBN: 978-1-62963-982-6 (ebook)
Library of Congress Control Number: 2022931970

Cover by Drohan DiSanto
Interior design by briandesign

10 9 8 7 6 5 4 3 2 1

PM Press
PO Box 23912
Oakland, CA 94623
www.pmpress.org

Printed in the USA.

Acknowledgments

James Kelman thanks Other Press, Canongate Books and Tangerine Press for permitting the inclusion of stories from the collections *If it is your life*, *That Was a Shiver* and *A Lean Third*.

Contents

Even in Communal Pitches

I had arrived at the following conclusion: even in communal pitches people will claim their portions of space; he who sits in the left-hand corner of one room will expect to obtain the equivalent corner in every room. This is something I cannot go but I felt obliged to conform to standard practice. It was a kind of community I was living in. A veryrichman owned the property. He allowed folk to live in it at minimal rents; the reason was to do with Y being equal to C plus S or I. It was quite noisy but no worse for that, for somebody like myself, just in from country travels. A party had been in progress for the two days I was here; it seemed to move from room to room; those desirous of sleep but without permanent quarters were having to grab a spot here and there, preferably keeping a room ahead all the time. In its own way that was fine and a nice camaraderie always seemed about to exist, although for some reason people only spoke to me in reply to questions about tea and coffee and where was the bathroom etc. It didnt annoy me, I could just lie on the floor and listen to their conversations. Next to me a guy kept going on about medieval conventicles on the southern tip of England; he was with another guy who was having to conceal yawns. Then I noticed they were irritated by my presence. What's up? I said. But they ignored the question. At this stage I would definitely have been entitled to get annoyed, but I didnt, I was too tired, far too tired; all I wanted to do was sleep. But could I get a sleep! Could I fuck. Then this woman; up she comes: Are you John Myatt?

Who's that? I says.

Never mind, came the reply, and she moved off on her stocking soles.

That was the kind of place it was. There was this other woman who was friendly, but I made a blunder by introducing the business of that conclusion I had arrived at. And she looked right through me. I was beginning to think: When did you last change your socks?

Gradually it dawned on me they were waiting for something; it was a bloke, he turned out to be a kind of Master of Ceremonies. A get-together had been organized in a semi-official way so that for this night at least, the party would be taking on a structured form. You were expected to do a turn. Somebody shoved a bunnet under my nose, he was looking for a donation, presumably for a carry-out, some booze. I was skint unfortunately but when I explained he got all fucking annoyed and went off in a huff. Eventually I saw he was sitting not far from me, about six or seven spaces away, and he was pointing me out to his neighbours in a really underhand manner. Who cares.

The entertainment began with a series of monologues, one of which was delivered by the guy who knew about medieval conventicles. It was so totally boring you werent sure if you had missed the overall irony but when you looked about you could see no one at all was grinning, it was meant by him as dead serious. Other speakers were concerned with recent events in the world of politics. A woman with a big hat got up and sang a song and this was the best so far. But then another woman got up and she recited poetry. Well, it has to be said that she was not brilliant although I dont know but something in the way she did it plus the good hand she got at the end made me think it was all her own stuff she was reading.

Meanwhile the carry-out arrived, such as it was, and it was being guarded jealously; even so but it was finished in what seemed like a matter of moments and everybody began looking at each other as if secretly laying the blame on certain members of the company for drinking more than their fair share. I wasnt involved. I had taken some of the drink but without overdoing it. I was more concerned with retaining the portion of space. And with a bit of luck I would snatch a couple of hours' kip. A guy got up on the floor with a guitar then a lassie joined him and everything was fine and going good till they started on these songs with choruses and we were all to join in: Farewell to the Trusty Rover and so on. What made it hopeless was the way if you werent joining in you felt it was being noted. The only ones okay were couples, it being assumed as valid that your attention could be total elsewhere so long as it was being concentrated on your partner. But not too much later a couple of folk began smoking dope and passing the joints about, then out came the plates of grub—grated carrots and turnips and cabbage, with wee dods of cheese and onion. And that was fine because although the quantities werent up to scratch the actual health-factor made you feel satisfied.

Then one by one people were getting up from the floor, making the move to a new room, a few having a laugh and trying to get everybody to do one of these snake-dances where you hold the person's waist to the front and somebody holds yours to the back. I had grabbed my stuff immediately and without making it too obvious was keeping into the wall and bypassing folk, heading out of the room and onto the landing where the vanguard had made it already, glancing at each other for signs of where to go, whom to follow, whether it was best to say fuck it and just shoot off in the offchance you would get to the correct room under your own steam. I waited a couple of seconds, not looking at anybody, then strode to the staircase and went on up to the next landing. There were scuffling noises behind but I didnt look back. I didnt mind at all if people were following me; I just didnt want to give the impression I knew where the fuck I was going, cause I didnt, I was just bashing on, hoping for the best. In situations like this the proper method of action can seem to trigger itself off on you without any deliberate thinking beforehand and sometimes I really go for it, setting all the conditions and so on. I wasnt wrong. On the next landing the door on the far side seemed familiar; it was the bathroom. I had been in using it earlier. It was a good bathroom, very spacious, to an L-shape design and I have the feeling it had been used as a small bedroom in years gone by. When I closed and snibbed the door I could hear the sounds of a couple of folk outside on the landing, as if they had been following me and had now realized it was a wild goose chase. Obviously I was a bit sorry for whoever it was but in a sense this was it about claiming your portion of space and I was only fitting in with the conventional wisdom of the place.

I sat down on the toilet-seat and began thinking about the whole carry on, in particular the woman who had recited the poetry. But that other woman kept butting in, her who wanted to know if I was John Myatt. I find it really really irritating when something like that happens. Another thing: it was so long since I had slept with a woman. Aye, gradually that was creeping up on me as well, and I dont know but sometimes you can enter terrible fits of depression for no apparent reason. And this other kind of daydream was beginning to butt in: there I was bashing my way into room after room and then by a fluke I would find myself in this wee closet where the elderly owner would be raking about in his moneyboxes. Aw christ, I dont know, I began opening the bathroom door and was walking downstairs in this really slow slow step by step by step way, with noises of folk coming from somewhere, and muffled laughter as well. And just at that moment came an explosion in my head and I knew there was a change in me, a change in me for keeps. Something had happened and my life had altered in a way that might never have appeared significant to an onlooker but as far as I was concerned, having to live this life, I knew it could never hope to be the same again, and I started to smile.

Keep Moving and No Questions

It was my own fault. My planning never seems to allow action of an intentional nature. I can always bring myself to a point where a sort of precipice is odds-on to be around a corner. But this bringing-of-myself appears to be an end in itself; nothing further happens, not as a direct effect of my own volitions. Terrible state of affairs. I had arrived back in London fine, as conceived, was ambling around the King's Cross Area quite enjoying seeing the old places. Next thing a publican was calling Time Gentlemen Please and I was stranded. Nowhere to go. Nothing fixed. Never anything fixed.

This fixing business ... I dont know about this fixing business at all. Obviously getting here was sufficient otherwise something further would have been transpiring. And something further could easily have been a straightforward sign-in at a cheap bed & breakfast of which the King's Cross Area has more than a few. The money right enough. The money could have been one subliminal motive for my lack of the leap forwards.

I was watching this drop of water on the tip of an old woman's nose. It didnt quiver. We were sitting on a bench at a busstop outside St Pancras Station. The rain had stopped some twenty minutes ago. I got a bar of chocolate from a machine. The old yin took the piece I offered and chewed on it for a long time. She had no teeth and was probably allowing this chocolate to slide back and forth over her gums, wearing it down while increasing the saliva flow. She never spoke. Stared straight ahead. I was to her right. I doubt whether she knew I was watching her; doubt whether it would have bothered her anyway. She didnt smoke and I found this surprising. I lighted my own. Although she moved slightly her gaze never altered. The drop of water had gone from her nose. Then the rain again, a slow drizzle. I rose from the bench, making more noise than necessary when I lifted my bag; for some reason I reckoned a quiet movement might have disturbed her.

Along towards Euston I walked. Night lights glinting on the pavement, on the roads and on the roofs and glass fronts of office buildings. And on the moon as well; a moon in full view, to be beheld during this drizzle. I was no longer ambling now. And a good thing this; it was somehow sending me on ahead of myself. Yet at the same time I was aware of the possibility of missing out on something a more leisurely stroll could perhaps have allowed me to participate within. On up, Tavistock way. Nobody about. A brisk pace. My boots were fairly able; no misgivings about stepping into puddles. Across and towards the British Museum and around the back in the shadows, and around the front and back around the back and back around the whole thing again for Christ sake.

Onwards. Figures appearing hailing taxicabs, going home to their places out the rain. More lighting now, brighter on the main road. Through into the rear of Soho where my pace lessened. Smaller buildings, narrower pavements, railings and basements; rain drops plopping off the edges of things; occasionally sharp lighting giving out from windows where folk would be gathered, snugly. One basement in particular with its iron gate at the top lying ajar. Downstairs I went slowly. A sign on the wall: two quid to enter. Music. One please, I said to this guy inside the lobby who gave out no ticket and stuffed the money into this pocket on the breast of his shirt, buttoning the flap down on it.

The push door made a creaking sound. The lighting dim. A girl singing in this English voice. An English traditional song she was singing in this icy voice. An odd voice; not a voice without feeling. A direct voice, and reminiscent of a singer whose name I couldnt quite rake out although I used to hear her fairly often at one time. All the people there; a lot sitting down on the floor with their backs to the wall, others lying with their hands clasped behind their heads or sitting cross-legged. Couples with arms about shoulders and heads on shoulders. All listening to the girl singing her song.

I sat down in a space next to the back wall and after a moment closed my eyelids. When I opened them again the space to my right had increased to around five yards and a girl was kneeling on the floor with her arms folded. She was alone—but in this direct fashion. Her head stiffly positioned, the neck exactly angled. Only her shoulders twitched. The position must have been uncomfortable. The small of her back there—I can make the curved motion with my hand. And yet only her shoulders made any movement whatsoever!

I closed my eyelids. Footsteps. It was a man making towards her, his manner of moving was only to her though he walked loosely as he threaded the way between people. And now the girl's shoulders were not even twitching. She had edged her feet from her shoes. Her toes seemed to be maintaining a sort of plumb point—and her arms!—folded in this direct fashion. Jesus.

He paused a fraction when he arrived, then dropped to his knees, his hands placed on the floor to balance, fingertips pointing to the side of her limbs he was facing her. But she continued to stare at the singer. Poised there, only her toes working.

He could kneel by her all night but it would still be finished. I could have told him that. She half turned her shoulder and said about three words; her eyes had remained in the direction of the singer. Then the shoulders returned to their former position. His time was up. Your time's up I said without opening my mouth.

He left, but he was not making a retreat. He was just making his way away from her. Eventually the girl swivelled her knees to stretch out her legs, moved to rest her back against the wall. She opened her handbag but after a brief glance inside she closed it over. She placed it to the blind side from me. I could see her toes now exercising, her knees, and her neck; until finally she relaxed. A bit later I rose to see if they served coffee; I left my chattels lying on the spot.

I bought two and back inside I handed one across to her. Put it to the side of her. Look, I said, all I'm doing is giving you this coffee. Nothing else. Just a coffee. Just take a drop of this coffee.

She didnt reply.

I'm leaving it lying there, I said. You should drink it. I'm not doing anything. Just giving you this coffee to drink.

She lifted it. The eyes passed over me. She took a little sip at it.

Jesus Christ; well well well.

Pardon, she said.

I didnt answer. I lighted a cigarette and inhaled deeply. Too much for me. Everything. The way she could do it all. Even the man. He could do it all as well. Jesus. It was bad. I had the arrival for a plan. An arrival! Dear God. Hopeless. It was bad.

Pardon?

What ... I glanced at her. I must have spoken aloud. Maybe the bad or the hopeless.

Nothing ... I said. I was only ... Couldnt even finish the sentence. With a slight nod she looked away from me. I closed my eyelids. But they opened immediately. Look, I said, will you take a smoke? I saw you footering around in your handbag and I was going to offer then but decided against it—not a real decision—not something I . . . A cigarette. Will you take a cigarette from me?

She nodded. I passed her one.

My coffee was lukewarm. It had never really been hot either. I shuddered on draining the last third of it. I dont mind lukewarm tea but never seem to have got the taste for lukewarm coffee. The singer had stopped for a breather and her band were playing a medley of some kind. Some of the audience had risen and were moving around on the floor.

I glanced at the girl. She was smoking in a serious way although she let out big mouthfuls of smoke before inhaling; and when she exhaled this last stuff she did so making an O shape of her mouth so that the smoke came out in firm columns. Food. A meal, I said, fancy a meal. Nothing startling. Just a plate of chips or something in a snackbar. Nothing else involved. I just feel like a plate of chips and taking you for one as well, eh? Fancy it. That coffee was murder polis.

Pardon?

That coffee. Terrible. Lukewarm to begin with I think. No chance of enjoyment from the start. Fancy a plate of chips?

Scotch?

Aye, yes. What d'you say?—you coming?

She hesitated, another cloud of smoke before the inhaled lot emerging in its fixed shape. She said, To be honest I . . .

Nothing else involved. I'm not doing anything. Look, I said, all I want to do is get a plate of chips and take you for one as well. Too much for me. All of it.

What?

Ach. Fuck it. What a carry on. I dont know . . . can never really get it all connecting in an exact manner. Out it all seems to come. She was not bothering though. Knew what I was saying, she knew it fine well. I was just . . . Passes the time, I said. Keeps you warm—plate of steaming chips and a piping hot cup of fresh tea.

You'll have to wait till I collect my things, she answered; I'll meet you at the door.

The guy with my two quid in his breast pocket was standing pretending not to have noticed me there hanging about with my bag. She came along carrying an enormous suitcase. Jesus, must be emigrating or something.

Pardon?

Your suitcase—looks like it contains the life possessions.

O. I was staying with friends over the week. Just got back this evening. She pointed at my effort.

I nodded: Deceiving bag this. Takes everything, all of the chattels. Good buy. Got it in a sale a couple of years back. Strong stuff it's made out of.

I held the door open and we went upstairs. The rain still drizzling down. I could not think of where to go for all-night snackbars. There is one, she said, not too far.

Suitcase—it looks heavy. I'll take a hold of it for you, eh?

No, I can manage.

What a surprise.

Pardon?

Nothing ... I was just ... I'm starving. While since I ate anything.

While she was walking she looked straight ahead, and always somehow half a pace in front or behind me. Buildings and basements and the rest of it: none of this interested her whatsoever. On she went. A place near Charlotte Street. I ordered the grub. No words spoken during the eating. I made to get another two cups of tea but she said: No—not for me.

There were other people in the snackbar, many were chatting and she must have been aware of this in relation to herself and the situation because she began glancing at the door.

Well, I said.

I better be going home.

I know that. Nothing else of course. I wasnt worrying about that.

We're not supposed to be out late, she said.

Late by Christ it must be near ... But then I stopped. Anyway, what did it matter.

Outside the snackbar she was set to go off alone. Half turning to me she said: Thanks.

No bother. I smiled, kind of hopefully, I suppose. Hang on and I'll get you home, I said. And dont worry. I'm not eh ...

Honestly, I'll make it all right on my own. I dont live far from here.

I sighed. It was too much for me. Far too much. Plate of chips and a cup of tea I mean that's that, precisely that, nothing else was involved. Same as the walking home, I said, it passes the time. I'm not eh ... Jesus, I said.

But I'm only round the corner.

Fuck all to do with me where you are. I'm not doing anything. Just hanging about till it all begins this morning. Still dark as well, you're best taking no chances, a woman, know what I mean who's around, ye dont know, ye never know.

She nodded: Alright then, thanks.

Back along in the direction of the British Museum till she halted outside of a place, the place where she lived. It's run by nuns, she said.

Aye.

I must go in.

Yeah.

At the top of the short flight of stairs she half turned but without actually seeing me. She said: Bye.

Aye.

When she closed the door after her the light went on in the hall. I hung about waiting for a time.

Nothing whatsoever happened. The light went out. But no other light came on upstairs. Maybe she lived at the back of the building or in the basement.

More than quarter of an hour I stood there until eventually I caught myself in the act of taking a seated position on the second bottom step. I walked off. Returned to St Pancras Station where I sat on the bench. No sight of the old woman. Nobody about; nothing at all. The rain had gone off. Maybe for good. I checked my money. The situation was not fine. I concentrated on working out a move for morning. And already there were signs of it; a vague alteration in the light and that odd sense of warmth the night can have for me was fast leaving.

A Wide Runner

I was in London without much cash and having to doss in the porch of a garden shed; it lay behind the shrubbery section of a grass square which the locals referred to as a park. The man who maintained it was called Kennedy. When he found me asleep he didnt kick me out but wanted to know what was what, and he left some sacking for me that evening. Next morning he brought John along with him; inside the shed he brewed a pot of tea. It was good and hot, burned its way down—late autumn or early winter. He got me answering the same questions for John's benefit; when I finished he looked to him. John shrugged, then muttered something about getting me a start portering if I wanted, interview that afternoon maybe. With a bit of luck I could even be starting the following morning.

Christ that's great, I said.

If he cant do it then nobody can, chuckled Kennedy. He's the blue-eyed boy in there!

John grimaced.

Yeh. Kennedy winked at me. Gets away with murder he do!

John shook his head, moments later he left.

At 8 a.m. next day I was kitted out with the uniform then being introduced to the rest of the squad in the porters' lodge. The place was a kind of college and the duties I performed were straightforward. For the first few days John guided me round; we pushed barrows full of stationery and stuff though in his position—Head Porter—he wasnt supposed to leave the vicinity of the marble entrance hall. He also fixed me up with a cash sub from the Finance Office, one week's lying time being obligatory. It was a surprise; I hadnt asked him to do it. That's great, I said, I'll buy you a pint when we finish.

He glanced at the clock in the lodge and shrugged, Just gone opening-time Jock, buy me it now if you like.

Kennedy was on a stool at the bar. I ordered pints for the three of us and he nudged me on the ribs. Yeh, didnt I tell you? Blue-eyed boy he is!

Leave off, muttered John.

But Kennedy continued chuckling. You'll be moving to a new abode then?

Aye, I said, thanks—letting me use the shed and that.

He laughed. Us sassenachs arent all bad then eh!

Silly fucker, grunted John.

After work they showed me to a rooming house they reckoned might be suitable. The landlady was asking a month's rent in advance but they had prepared me for it and eventually she did settle for the same sum spread over the following four weeks. It was an ideal place for the time being. The college was less than ten minutes' walk away. Round the corner lived Kennedy and his family while John rented a room farther down the road, in a house managed by a middle-aged Irish couple who tended to make a fuss of him; things like doing his laundry and making a point of getting him in for Sunday dinner every week. They were a nice couple but John got slightly irritated by it. Yeh, he said, you're into the position where you got to go; you're letting them down if you dont.

It turned out his wife had been killed in a road accident several years ago. I didnt discover the exact details but it seems to have been an uncommon kind, and made the newspapers of the day. One night he was drunk he told me he could never have married again, that she had been the greatest thing in his life. To some extent this would explain why people reacted to him as they did. Kennedy was right, John did get away with a lot.

Inside the college an ex-RAF man had overall charge of the porters and all the rest of the hourly-paid workers. An officious bastard, he treated those under him as though they were servicing the plane he was to pilot, but he shied clear of John. Our dinner hours were staggered between 11:45 a.m. and 2:45 p.m. Unless totally skint John spent the entire three hours in the pub. If the ex-RAF man needed to contact him he made a discreet call to the lodge and sent one of the older porters with the message.

Not surprisingly a few people resented this special treatment. Yet nothing was said directly to John. He was in his mid-sixties, as thin as a pole, his skin colouring a mixture of greys, greens and yellows. He could be brusque, short tempered, he ignored people who were speaking to him. I got on fine with him. I was young, I still had it all to do. So that was that, plus I liked the horses. Once he realized my interest in horse-racing wasnt confined to the winning and losing of money we got on even better.

Money was probably the main reason why he affected people. John had won and done vast sums of the stuff and while I was hearing many stories from him himself, I was also hearing a few about him. Not always to his credit. A fair amount of respect was accorded him but it could be tinged by that mixture of scorn and vague annoyance which nonpunters and small punters can display whenever the exploits of heavy gamblers are discussed. Kennedy was an example of this. Although he genuinely liked John and enjoyed recounting tales of his past wins, he would finish with a wink and a snort . . . Yeh Jock, then me and the Mrs had to feed him for the next bleeding month.

A couple of weeks into the job I was given additional duties in the college refectory. I was appointed dish-washer. Being the last porter in the job I had no option. But it suited me. I loved the job. A woman managed the place and three other women worked there. I was the only guy. They were all old but it was a cheery place. In return for rinsing the pots and the pans I could eat as much free grub as I wanted. It meant I didnt have to worry about eating in the evening. Also I was escaping from the porters' lodge. Portering can be an extremely boring job. Much of the time was spent in and around the lodge, just giving information to people; most of time just yawning and moving from foot to foot. When John was there it was okay but if not the only chat was job-gossip, last night's television. It was the kind of job people either stuck for a month or remained until retiral. Most of them had been there for years, even the arrival of some nice-looking female didnt seem to interest them much. One of the morning duties involved the distribution of mail; this entailed journeying in and out of all the different offices. It seemed the kind of job the porters would want to work on a rota-system just for the chance of walking about and having a laugh with the office-women but they werent bothered at all. Anybody who felt like doing the mail or the stationery rounds could go and get on with it. That suited me. The college employed a temporary staff from the office agencies and seeing the new girls was something to look forward to.

The woman who managed the kitchen and refectory was another to make a fuss over John. She nagged him about eating and she made sure that he did. She wrapped left-over food in tinfoil and sent it across to the lodge in time for him coming back from the pub. At this stage of the day John's actions were erratic, absentminded. He stuck the tinfoil packages in his uniform pocket and forgot all about them. You could be sitting having a chat with him and out one would come, the tinfoil unwrapped, John continuing the conversation while he munched on a couple of rashers of bacon. One time in the lodge a porter went into silent hysterics at the window. The rest of us crept over to see what was what. Out in the marble entrance hall John, with a piece of steak-pie in one hand and a clutch of mashed potato in the other, and a visiting dignitary inquiring direction. John was gesticulating various routes between bites, bits of gravy and potato flying about.

Too much brown ale was the chief cause but added to that was his preoccupation with the afternoon's racing results. John bet daily. And nightly, when possible. He had a credit account with the bookie over the road. Either he used the phone in the lodge or sent me. I placed quite a few bets for him. Not too many on my own behalf. Only because I wasnt too interested at the time. This was the winter and horse-racing had come to a complete standstill. Not because of the wintry weather. An unknown virus had swept through horse stables up and down the country. There was no end in sight. In an effort to check the spread the authorities had postponed racing indefinitely. People were betting on greyhounds, the virus being strictly equine.

In his day John had been a regular round many of the London tracks and whenever he was holding a few quid he still liked to have a go. But at the time I started in the job nothing was going right for him. Everything he touched fell apart. It was the kind of spell any punter goes through. With John it was bad though because he bet heavy and he was tapping dough from everywhere and from anybody. And the way things were with John it became common knowledge. People talked about him. I got irritated when I heard gossip in the lodge with the other porters. The same in the pub. But there was not much to be said because he was tapping them. And by tapping them he gave them the opportunity. It is very unusual to meet somebody with the credit he had. He had a tab with the bookie never mind the pub. He could be skint on a Wednesday morning but filling his place at the bar by lunchtime, having a bet in the afternoon and meeting you in the pub after work.

He had sources all over the place. Yet even so, gradually, he was returning early from the pub during the day. In the evening he would mutter an excuse and go home early. If making a bet he would do so only in cash and get me to carry it to a different bookie because he was in for too much with his regular one. He was taking a real hammering.

The equine virus caused great deprivation. Before Xmas, as a special treat for starved horse punters like myself, an enterprising television team crossed the English Channel to screen back three races from a race-meeting in France. It was a Saturday and the British bookies were offering a complete race by race service. Me and John worked overtime in the morning. In the pub afterwards I loaned him another tenner and we walked to another betting shop. He knew the manager in the shop here but only bet cash with him.

Although race punters knew next to nothing of the French form some of us did know the good jockeys and trainers and the rest of it. John laid the £10 on three crossed £2.50 doubles and a £2.50 treble. My own bet was identical except I chose a different three horses.

Back in the pub we watched his first two runners win. And then we watched his third runner win.

That third winner is the magical side of life. According to the betting forecast the horse was a 7/2 chance. But the French tote, the pari-mutuel, returned a dividend amounting to slightly more than 25/1.

Twenty-five times your dough!

When the price of the winning horse flashed onto the television screen John sat forward on his stool, he frowned then snorted. He glanced round at me, as if to say: These cunts think they're kidding me.

Then he got down off the stool, and me with him, we rushed away to the betting shop for confirmation.

It was true. His winnings amounted to more than £1,200. There wasnt enough hard cash on the premises to pay out in full. John was quite happy to wait until Monday morning.

While the guy behind the counter was getting the cash together John walked to study form at a greyhound meeting taking place that afternoon. He scribbled out a bet on the next favourite for £300. The man had to phone his head office to have it okayed. I was watching John. He was shot through with nerves and yet I doubt whether a stranger could have noticed. At the best of times he got the shakes but here in the betting shop he was making a conscious effort to control himself. He stood with his hands in his trouser pockets staring up at the results board. Usually his shoulders were rounded but now he was holding them as straight as he could. The greyhound he backed won at 7/4.

When the result was announced he hesitated, he glanced at me then back to the board; finally he nodded. Yeh, he said, that'll do.

On the way back to his house we stopped off at the licenced grocer where he purchased a crate of brown ale, plus two bottles of gin which he passed on to the Irish couple. It was the only occasion I was ever in his room. There were a few knick-knacks and family photographs, and a big pile of old Evening Standards heaped in a corner. A fusty smell hung about the place. He noticed my reaction. Fucking pong, he said, open a window if you like. Then taking two cups from a cupboard he passed me one along with a bottle of brown ale, and continued talking.

He was defending greyhounds. It wasnt that I didnt like them, just that it was almost impossible getting a line to their form without visiting the actual track to see them race. He admitted this but went on to tell me about an old mate he used to have. He had told me about him before. It was in connection to a system he worked. According to John, his old mate worked it so successfully that the bookies refused to deal with it across their betting-shop counter.

The guy was forced into going to the track to make his bets with the on-course fraternity.

The system is quite well known, nothing startling: it's called the stop-at-a-winner and in principle consists of a minimum one bet with a maximum of four. You select your four dogs and back the first to win; if it loses you back the second; if it loses you back the third; if it loses you back the fourth; if it loses you've done the money.

The cash outlay on the first leg of the bet doubles on to the second then triples on to the third, quadruples on to the fourth. If your initial stake was £10 and you chose four losers then you wind up doing £100 i.e. bets of £10, £20, £30 and £40.

The beauty of the system lies in this stopping-at-a-winner: as soon as a dog wins the bet stops automatically. Only one solitary winner from four is required and a profit is almost guaranteed. In theory to choose one winner from four is not too difficult. It is not certain and by no means easy but still and all, it should not be too difficult—and one thing is certain, if the bookies dont like the bet then it cant be bad.

This is all fair enough but like anything else it applies only under normal circumstances. When somebody is on a losing streak everything goes crazy. Odds-on shots run like 100/1 chances. All these stonewall racing certainties that should win in a canter, they all fall at the last fucking fence. The one thing they have in common is that you've backed them. That is the one thing: *you*. It reaches the stage where you feel guilty about choosing a favourite because of the disservice you're doing the rest of the punters, them who have laid down their dough.

I was reminding John about that kind of stuff. He smiled briefly then he sniffed and got up off his chair; he walked to the corner of the room and lifted a bunch of the old newspapers. He produced a quantity of various coloured pens. Jock, he said, I been wanting to have a go at this for years. While he was speaking he sorted through the back editions, opening out their respective dog-sections, spreading them along the floor. You got to play it wide, he said, that's all; you just got to play it wide. What you do Jock, you cut out the fucking middle man. Yeh, he said, the fucking middle man. You know who that is? It's you, you and me, we're the fucking middle man. Yeh, he said, open another couple of bottles.

He halved the quantity of pens. That old mate of his, the guy he was telling me about, eventually went skint for different reasons but the most important one was his method of selection: he didnt really have one, he just chose the dogs from his own reading of the formbook.

What you had to find was a genuine method, so that the four dogs would be chosen for you. So it wasnt you. The deal had nothing to do with you. You were keeping yourself out of it. And then there was another thing to consider: which races to work it on. It would be pointless using a system that forced you to hang about the track all night with money in the pocket. At most greyhound meetings there are between eight and twelve races. Probably the best way out the bother is to work it on the first four races of the night. In that way you get in and get out; in fast, out fast. You arrive for the first race and make your bet, then leave as soon as you back the winner. And if you dont back a winner then you leave after the fourth race, and try again the next night.

Yeh, said John, you got to screw the nut.

Plenty of selection methods were available. For the following couple of hours we set about testing as many as we could think of, using the old back editions, working on the past meetings at all the London tracks. Some useful information resulted. Many dog punters use methods and one of the most common is acting on the advice of racing journalists, they bet the journalist's selection. Some bet on particular trap numbers. They have "a lucky trap." In every race there are six dogs and each goes from an individual trap, numbered 1 to 6. We tested that and we found that Trap 6 was the most successful. On one occasion this draw had provided the winner of seven consecutive races. Imagine that was your lucky trap, you would have won a fucking million. But for the stop-at-a-winner system that kind of consistency is irrelevant. All it required is one winner out of four.

It was me who came up with the right method. The time-dog. We were both a bit surprised, and I was also a bit disappointed. The time-dog is the greyhound to have recorded the fastest time of the six runners in their most recent races. To the nonpunter it may seem obvious to say that the dog who runs the fastest will win the race because it runs more quickly. Well it does seem obvious but it never works out that way as most punters know. Too many variables exist and recent times are only a guide, like everything else in the formbook.

But the fact remains that dog punters who reckon themselves expert on the subject will set more store on time than any other factor. And this is why I was disappointed with what me and John discovered when we checked everything out. We seemed to be proving them right. And if they were right then how come they were usually so fucking skint!

John just shrugged. Well yeh, he said, but like I say Jock, most of them the cunts're looking to back eight winners out of eight fucking races.

Aye I know but still and all.

Open a couple of bottles.

Aye but John . . .

Look Jock, listen to me now: see I been watching this for years and I know what I'm fucking talking about. You got some important things here. Now what you got? you got a system, you got the stop-at-a-winner, right?

Aye.

So you know what you're doing for a fucking kick-off. Most of them the cunts they dont even know that, they dont know what the fuck they're doing! right? Now what else you got? yeh, the fucking dogs, you got them chose for you, you got them selected, right?

Aye but . . .

Right?

Right, aye.

Okay, so what else you got?

The time-dog.

Yeh yeh, the time-dog, that's how you got them chose—but what else you got?

Eh.

Come on Jock! He grinned and reached for the bottle I had passed to him. He began pouring the brown ale into the cup, his hand trembling. Then he sniffed, What else you got?

Well you need a lot of fucking luck.

No you dont! Leave off! You dont need no fucking luck. Why d'you think we got the fucking system! Jock, you got to play this wide.

Aye.

Now you take me, I'm a cunt. I'm a cunt Jock, no two ways about it. You go down the pub and ask any of them and they'll tell you, I'm a cunt.

I snorted.

And you, he said, you're a cunt. We're both cunts—you know that—so what we got to do, we got to cut out the fucking middle man, right?

I shrugged.

Right?

Aye, right.

Okay . . . John took a mouthful of the beer, refilled the cup. What we do Jock we work it together. Now we both know the score, we got to make the same bet and we got to take the same dogs. John shrugged and he glanced at me. Look at this afternoon? Yeh, now I aint criticizing, in your place I'd do the fucking same. But I lift a grand and you go skint.

Yeh but.

You go skint.

I shrugged.

Yeh. John peered at me, then grinned suddenly. Fucking froggies, always did have a soft spot for the cunts.

First thing on Monday morning he disappeared from the college to open a bank account. The day before he spent out of the district, visiting his family but also repaying a few debts, I think. He was allowing £400 for the system, that is, £200 apiece. Our initial bet was to be £10 so we needed £100 each for the stake; the extra £100 was for emergencies. I kept mine planked in my room. Whether John did the same I was never sure. A lot of punters go about with their life-savings in their pockets just because you never know, if something turns up, you dont know, so you're ready.

That first Monday went well although we saw little of each other till the late afternoon when we resumed chatting. Previous to this it seemed as if we werent chatting by some unspoken agreement; almost like we were avoiding each other. It could have brought bad luck on the system to talk about it all the time. John survived the day without one solitary bet. Even during his midday break he made a point of drinking less than normal.

His dayshift had started earlier than mine and so he clocked-off before me. We met in the pub for 7 p.m. I just had time to swallow a pint and then the taxi was there and we were off.

An hour later we were back in the pub. The first runner had won a short head at 9/4, throwing us a profit of £22.50. Next night to another track where the first two runners got beat but the third won a length at 7/2, giving us a profit of

£75 each overall. This was almost twice the weekly wage I was paid as a porter. It was very nice. And the obvious problem arose: how to continue going to work every day with all that cash in the pocket. Not that it bothered John. Put it this way, he said, at my fucking age what else I got to do?

During the next couple of weeks the time-dog missed on two separate occasions; then came a losing sequence of three consecutive evenings. It was a bit of a bombshell. There's a funny sense in which you expect one to be followed by two. In the gambling world you know better than that. Since the time-dog had failed on individual evenings the worst I expected was that it would fail twice in a row. We went along for that third evening and I doubt whether I truly thought about what would happen if it failed again. But we stuck with it. The dough was there and that was that. As it turns out we had enough in hand to attend for the fourth night and the time-dog won the second race at 6/1. Gradually we recouped the losses without having touched the emergency fund.

We werent winning a fortune but it was paying.

Then the equine virus vanished, as mysteriously as it had struck. This came as an anticlimax. Horse-racing remained at a standstill. This was the winter and the ground either was waterlogged or bonehard.

But on went the greyhounds chasing that parcel of fur. Some of these nights were freezing cold and making the trek across London could be a slog; especially knowing you might be on the home journey half an hour later.

One night John had to go a message on behalf of his family and we arranged to meet in the track bar. If he came late I was to double up on the bet to keep his side going. It was the old Wimbledon track. I made the journey by rail. But I forgot there were two Wimbledon stations and I wound up getting off at the wrong one. It was only evens and that was me, beat as usual.

The station where I got off was in the middle of fucking nowhere, just all these houses with gardens and I had to hoof it for miles, not a taxi in sight. I missed the first three races. But there was John, he had arrived in time and doubled up on the bets for me. What if he hadnt made it on time? What if the time-dog had won and we missed it, all because of my stupidity? John didnt say a word but he knew the same as me. He just gave a wee shrug and that was that. We just got on the gether. He was forty-five years older than me but we were pals.

To be honest, I could have done with a night off now and again but I didnt broach the subject in case I hurt his feelings. Weekends were the worst—Fridays and Saturdays had come to resemble Tuesdays and Wednesdays. A lot can go on in London and it doesnt all take place at the dog track. A new shorthand typist had started in one of the college offices. When I brought in the mail we had reached the stage of avoiding each other's eyes which I thought was good if it meant—whatever it meant. But if I asked her out it had to be a Sunday, if not explanations were called for. I suppose I could have arranged to meet her after racing some evening but explanations would still have been called for. The routine me and John were in meant leaving the track together and taking a cab or a bus back to the local pub. Once I had swallowed a couple of pints in there I could rarely be bothered moving.

It was different for John, he was enjoying the life. Almost every night somebody at the track spotted him and came over to ask how he was doing and where he had been hiding. The company was good as well, the doggie-guys, all with their yarns, and it might have been nice hanging on for the chat, but we couldnt. The essence of the system's success was this stopping-at-a-winner. And once we did we had to leave the track—immediately. Anything else was a risk. We would have wound up making another bet; just for an interest but that would have been that. Systems have to be regular otherwise they arent systems.

Oddly enough that side of things would have given us status. In fact it isnt odd at all. In any racetrack in the country there is nobody more respected than the punter who comes to back one dog and one dog only. Whether it wins or not is fundamentally irrelevant. That is somebody with the head screwed on. A guy like that is a professional.

We told nobody about the system but these doggie-guys John knew must have become aware something was going on—as soon as we cheered home a winner we vanished.

At college and in the pub we said nothing either. A little minor hostility occurred early on, towards me. The pub regulars were seeing us go to the track and return from the track and because it was all being accomplished within an hour or so they assumed we were continually doing the money. Kennedy acted a bit coldly, as if I was responsible for John's welfare. Maybe he reckoned I was just tagging along for poncing purposes, just taking his money. It was pointless explaining anything. It was still pointless when they realized we were backing winners. Occasionally a kind of daft undertone was there, as though we were wasting time and money. Why fork out cash on taxi fares and entrance fees when you dont stay to watch the whole night's racing. That was just stupid.

It's difficult to say what people felt. Nonpunters dont really know. It was all guesses. One of the daftest statements I ever heard came from Kennedy on that very first Saturday, the one when John turned the £10 into £1,200. It was unusual to find Kennedy in the pub at all that night because it was a Saturday which was the one night of the week he went out with his wife. If they came to the local they didnt come into the bar, they sat through in the lounge. But that first Saturday evening he was on his stool at the bar when we entered. John was playing it very cool, knowing everybody in the district would've heard the news.

The regulars were doing their best not to let John see he had been the main topic of conversation since opening time. I got the pints in for the three of us. Kennedy didnt speak for a while but he kept on grinning and shaking his head, nudging me on the ribs. At last he winked and chuckled. Yeh Jock, we all got to start backing them French horses. Yeh, he said, we got to start backing them French horses. Kennedy laughed and swivelled on the stool giving a wave to the regulars. Hey lads! he called. We all got to start backing them French horses now!

The laughter was loud. John reacted by raising his eyebrows and studying the gantry. The guvnor came through from the lounge to see what was what and he grinned, and after a moment he said: Alright John?

John continued to study the gantry. When the laughter subsided he muttered, Silly fucker, but it went no further than that.

I think he felt sorry for Kennedy. The man had a lot of good points but he had that bad habit of playing to the gallery, no matter at whose expense. His nights were rarely complete unless John unwrapped one of his tinfoil packages. Yet John was friendlier to him than he was to anybody else in the place. I saw him do something in the lodge once which would have crushed Kennedy. He had asked one of the porters for a match and the porter cracked a joke while passing him a boxful. This porter was known to be tight with his cash but still and all, I was there when it happened, and there didnt seem any genuine malice in the remark. He was just being daft. It had something to do with people who gamble huge sums of money but neglect to spend on the petty essentials. John turned and stared at the man for several moments. That is all he done, he stared at him. Then he placed the box of matches on the table unused. He started talking to another man as though the one who had cracked the joke had left the room. The atmosphere was terrible after that. Nobody was able to look at the guy. Eventually he left the lodge without speaking. If John had done that to Kennedy he would never have recovered.

The bad side of it was how John left himself open to criticism because he borrowed dough so indiscriminately. It was a thing about him I couldnt understand. During the bad losing spell he must have tapped everybody, everybody, in the pub and in the college, and not just the porters' lodge but the women in the refectory, the kitchen and probably the upstairs offices as well. Once I knew him better I dug him up about it, just that idea of leaving himself so wide open. It's cause people who dont gamble, they dont really know, they dont know what it is. So then they think there's some kind of—whatever, just something, they dont know what it is. Then you get a win and you pay them back and they're just, Aw great, but there's a wee bit where it's different, and it's just . . . I shrugged.

Yeh, you're right, he said.

The second time the method failed three nights on the trot it coincided with a general thaw. Horse-racing resumed on a regular basis. Three nights' loss on the trot was a hard one to take. The first time we had enough in the funds to see it through but this second time we had to go into the emergency fund. But again we managed it, the time-dog scooshed in on the third leg and we shouted it home, we shouted it that night. So we had fought back, we had recouped the losses. It took a while but we were doing it and we were still in the game. That was something. That was big.

Although the horse-racing had resumed I was happy to ignore it. Because of the long interruption the formbook would've been as well chipped out the window. It was a bookie's paradise, impossible to pick a winner. When a favourite actually won a race you were expecting to see it headline news. Better just holding off until things started evening out.

The game was tough enough without the elements against you. We were discussing this across at the dog track one night—Catford I think it was—we were in company with a couple of guys John knew. The sanding machine was out on the track. The snow was in heaps in the middle. For the past two nights snow had been falling thickly then melting during the day. The officials declared the going "heavy" but according to the doggie regulars this was an understatement, it was like a bog, particularly on the inside.

The inside of the track receives more of a pounding than the outside. On really heavy going the dogs who favour the inside can race at a disadvantage, as though they're trying to run through thick slidey porridge. In an effort to correct it the track authorities had strewn straw round the inside. But the early results were bad and according to the doggie-guys it was the straw to blame. Contrary to expectations the dogs drawn on the inside were not simply holding their own, they were getting what amounted to a yard and a half of a start. The first three favourites all got beat without having been in the hunt. The dogs on the inside were romping home. The same thing applied to the first three time-dogs, two of whom had been favourites. It was pathetic. Normally we at least got a cheer but tonight we had hardly been able to raise a shout.

Down in the bar the conversation went on among the doggie-guys, with John taking his part, listening and occasionally nodding, rarely talking. As the merits of each greyhound was discussed for the fourth race I could hear the time-dog being rejected mainly on the basis of its draw, it was to run from Trap 6. This dog was also an uncertain trapper which means it sometimes started fast and other times started slow.

The dogs were parading before the start of the race, all with their coats on and they needed them on a night like this. I liked the way they walked. The doggie-guys were watching them, making their comments. Greyhounds have their own ways of racing. Some start slow and finish fast, or start fast and finish slow. Some race inside, some outside. Some look at the other dogs, the best ones just chase the rabbit. Also about this Trap 6 dog, it liked to run its race on the wide outside of the track. But in this particular race so did Trap 5, the dog in the next trap. The other complication here was that this Trap 5 dog was always fast out the traps. And because of that it was more or less guaranteed to steal the ground from Trap 6. It started quicker than Trap 6 so then that was it in front. So it was up to Trap 6 to try and pass it. But if they were both racing on the wide outside then that was difficult to do. So what with this, that and the next thing Trap 6 wasnt reckoned much of a bet at all, it wasnt even guaranteed to get past Trap 5 never mind the other four runners. That was how the conversation was going among the doggie-guys and fair enough, it was all grist to the mill. And then the warning bell sounded for the end of the dogs parading and the company dispersed to lay their bets on the outcome. John sniffed, then shrugged: What d'you reckon Jock?

How d'you mean? I said.

Them big wide runners, they're doing fuck all tonight. What d'you reckon? Reckon we should leave it out?

How, what d'you mean?

John shrugged. No use fucking throwing it away.

Ach! I shook my head and we left the bar, hurrying along to the betting-ring. They were making Trap 6 an 8/1 chance and as we stood there they moved it out to 10/1. See what I mean? he said, a no-hoper Jock—save the dough.

I looked at him. You must be joking.

He pursed his lips and paused then made to say

something but I shook my head and stepped over to the nearest bookmaker and took the 10/1 for the £40. I held up the ticket for John to see.

He indicated a bookie a few pitches along the rank who was making Trap 6 a 12/1 chance. He shook his head at me. I shrugged. I left the betting-ring, went up to our place in the Stand. We always went to the same spot, high up in line with the finishing post. Everybody waiting, the nerves, jangle jangle. The whirr of the rabbit along the wire, intakes of breath and whoh up go the traps. John was there beside me, just before the off, and that instant prior to the traps opening he told me he had backed the favourite.

Trap 2 was the favourite. The punters had gambled it off the board; from an opening show of 6/4 the weight of money going onto the thing had reduced its odds to 1/2.

John didnt tell me how much he had stuck on the dog but at that kind of price he must have done it for plenty, and I mean plenty. According to the doggie-guys up in the bar Trap 2 was a certainty to lead at the first bend and get the best of the going up the back straight; by the time it hit the last bend the race would be all over bar the shouting.

But there was no shouting. Trap 6 shot out the box and led from start to finish. Who knows what happened to the two dog. This was the kind of race where the crowd goes so quiet you can hear the dogs puffing and panting. The punters are stunned by what they're having to witness. Bang goes the wages. I was also watching in silence. When you back a winner in a race like this you dont want to broadcast the news. I collected my winnings and met John in the bar. He had a drink ready for me. Apparently he was too engrossed in his racecard to make any comment. I just sipped the beer. It was the first time we had ever been there beyond this fourth race. Not a word was passed.

I footered about with my own racecard then had my pen out and marked in my comments on the previous race.

It was something I did for future reference, and it helped pass the time.

John was watching me.

What's up? I said.

He shook his head.

Ah well John ... I smiled. You've got to mark in the form and that.

Mark in the form! you cunt. Mark in the form! Dont make me laugh.

Ach come on for fuck sake. I've backed a winner and you've backed a loser, it's as simple as that.

As simple as that! As simple as that! you cunt! John's hand was shaking on his glass and I thought he was going to knock it over.

He left his drink on the bar and strode out of the place. I stayed where I was. Before the start of the fifth race I walked up to the Stand and stood where we usually stood but he wasnt there and he didnt arrive back in the bar afterwards. Outside the track I had a quick look in a nearby pub but he wasnt there. I didnt go back to the local that night, I took a taxi up West.

I didnt bother going into the college on Monday or Tuesday. I phoned in sick. I also stayed away from the local pub. On Wednesday I was back at work but we kept out one another's road. Along at the refectory the woman in charge of the refectory gave me the tinfoil package for him. The way she did it was just her usual cheery self so I knew John had kept what happened a secret. He came looking for me later. I was way along a corridor pushing a stationery barrow. He apologised immediately. What a cunt, he said, always have been. You ask anybody Jock, they'll tell you. I just ... he shook his head.

Och ... one of these things.

Several days later I was handing in my uniform to the ex-RAF man who was in charge of the store. I stopped by the porters' lodge to say cheerio. Even without the incident I would still have been leaving. It was just time. I had a good few quid gathered and the weather progressed; a nice hint of spring in the air.

John was back hitting the betting shop every afternoon, horses or dogs, whatever was going. He was taking a real hammering, as far as I heard. It was totally daft, the results were still erratic after that long shutdown. Leaving that aside, there was only about a month to go before the start of the new flat-race season. John was like me in that respect, things like steeple-racing and greyhound-racing only helped fill in the winter gap.

Ascot was his favourite course and Royal Ascot his favourite meeting. Without fail that was when he took his holidays, every year he took his holidays in June and went to the track for as long as the money lasted. Well you got to, he said, them's the best racehorses in the world Jock.

He was superstitious about it. He told me how on occasion after occasion he had been skint and June rapidly approaching. Then at the very last possible moment, the very very last, he would get a turn, and everything would be fine. Yeh, he said, you believe it or you dont believe it—it's all the same to me—but I've seen me in it right up to the fucking eyeballs, cant show my face or the cunts, they'll be taking swipes at it, yeh—then bingo! right out the fucking blue Jock and I'm down there. Go on Lester! Go on my son!

That punters' dream from the old days, the summer sunshine with strawberries and champagne, and Lester Piggott going through the card.

the same is here again

My teeth are grut.

What has happened to all my dreams is what I would like to know. Presently I am a physical wreck. If by chance I scratch my head while strolling showers of dandruff reel onto the paved walkway, also hairs of varying length. Tooth decay. I am feart to look into a mirror. I had forgotten about them, my molars; these wee discoloured bones jutting out my gums and lonely, neglected, fighting amongst themselves for each particle of grub I have yet to pick. Jesus. And my feet—and this mayhap is the worst of my plight—my feet stink. The knees blue the hands filthy the nails grimy, uneatable. What I must do is bathe very soon.

One certainty: until recently I was living a life; this life is gone, tossed away in the passing. I am washed up. The sickness burbles about in my gut. A pure, physical reaction at last. I feel it heaving down there, set to erupt—or maybe just to remain, gagging.

It is all a mystery as usual. I am very much afraid I am going off my head. I lie on pavements clawing at myself with this pleasant face probably on the countenance. I have been this way for years. More than half my life to present has been spent in acquiring things I promptly dispose of. I seldom win at things. It is most odd. Especially my lack of interest. But for the smile, its well-being, the way I seem to regard people. It makes me kind of angry. I am unsure about much. Jesus christ.

Where am I again. London is the truth though I was reared in Glasgow. In regard to environment: I had plenty. But.

The weather. The hardtopped hardbacked bench concreted to the concrete patch amidst the grass. My spine against the hardback. My feet stuck out and crossed about the ankles. My testicles tucked between my thighs. I am always amazed no damage is done them. I have forgotten what has happened to the chopper. The chopper is upright though far from erect. It lies against the fly of my breeks. And now uncomfortable.

Explanations sicken me. The depression is too real. A perpetual thirst but not for alcohol. Milk I drink when I find it. Smoking is bad. Maybe I am simply ill. Burping and farting. All sorts of wind. I should have a good meal of stuff. But even the thought. Jesus.

My hand has been bleeding. I cut it while entering a car, an old one. A stereo and one Johnny Cash cassette. My life is haunted by country & western music.

I have no cigarette in my gub.

And yet this late autumnal daylight. The spring in my step. Grinning all the while and wishing for hats to doff to elderly women. I am crying good-evening to folk. I might have been in the mood for a game of something. Or a cold shower. When I settle down to consider a future my immediate straits are obliged to be conducive. I am grateful for the clement weather. Facts are to be faced. I am older than I was recently. And I was feart to show my face that same recently. Breakfast is an awful meal. If you dont get your breakfast that is you fucked for the day.

I cannot eat a Johnny Cash cassette.

Breakfast has always been the one meal I like to think I insist upon. When I have money I eat fine breakfasts. One of the best I ever had was right in the heart of old London Town. A long time ago. So good I had to leave a slice of toast for appearances' sake. I was never a non-eater. Could always devour huge quantities of the stuff. Anything at all: greasy fried bread, burnt custard or eggs. Even with the flu or bad hangovers. A plate of soup at four in the morning. I cannot understand people scoffing at snails' feet and octopi although to be honest I once lifted a can of peasbrose from a supermarket shelf only to discover I couldnt stomach the bastarn stuff. So: there we are. And also food-poisoning I suppose. If I ever get food-poisoning I would probably not feel like eating. Apart from that

but not now. Not presently, and this is odd. My belly may have a form of cramp.

Immediately my possessions include money I shall invest in certain essentials as well as the washing of that pair of items which constitute the whole of my wardrobe in the department of feet viz my socks. For my apparel excludes pants and vest. An effect of this was my chopper getting itself caught in the zipping-up process that follows upon the act of pissing. Normally one is prepared for avoiding such occurrences. But this time, being up an alley off one of her majesty's thoroughfares, I was obliged to rush. ZZZIPPP. Jesus. The belly. Even the remembrance. For a couple of moments I performed deep breathing exercises aware that my next act would of necessity be rapid. And this was inducing vague associations of coronary attacks. My whole trunk then became icy cold. UUUNZZZIPP. Freed. It would not have happened had I been wearing pants. If I was being cared for pants would pose no problem, and neither would vests. Vests catch and soak up sweat unless they are made of nylon. In which case the sweat dribbles down your sides and it's most damp and irritating.

My face looks to be ageing but is fine. A cheery face. It laughs at me from shop windows. The hairs protruding from my nostrils can be mistaken for the top of my moustache. The actual flesh, the cheekbones and red-veined eyeballs, the black patches round the sockets. Every single thing is fine. I am delighted with the lines. On my left—the right in fact, side of my nose has formed a large yellow head which I squeezed until the matter burst forth. I am still squeezing it because it lives. While squeezing it I am aware of how thin my skin is. I put myself in mind of an undernourished 87-year-old. But the skin surrounding the human frame weighs a mere six ounces. Although opposed to that is the alsatian dog which leapt up and grabbed my arm; its teeth punctured the sleeve of the garment I was wearing but damage to the flesh was nil.

I bathed recently; for a time I lay steeping in the grime, wondering how I would manage out, without the grime returning to the pores in my skin. The method I employed was this: I arose in the standing position. The grime showed on the hairs of my legs though and I had to rinse those legs with cold because the hot had finished. I washed my socks on that occasion. They are of good quality. I sometimes keep them stuffed in the back pocket of my jeans.

The present is to be followed by nothing of account. Last night was terrible. All must now be faced. It has much to do with verges and watersheds.

Taxis to Blackfriars Bridge for the throwing of oneself off of are out of the question.

I have the shivers.

Reddish-blue blisters have appeared on the soles of my feet. They are no longer bouncing along. I can foresee. Nothing of account will follow. For some time now the futility of certain practices has not been lost on me. I shall sleep with the shivers, the jeans and the jumper, the socks and the corduroy shoes. I can forecast point A or point B: either is familiar. All will depend on X the unknown (which also affords of an either/or). The A and B of X equals the A and B that follow from themselves, not A and not B being unequal to not B and A. And they cannot be crossed as in Yankee Bets. Yet it always has been this way and I alone have the combinations.

I was planning on the park tonight. I left a brown paper bag concealed in a hedge near the Serpentine for the purpose. It will have been appropriated by now.

The trouble might well be sleep. I had a long one recently and it may well have upset the entire bodily functioning. This belly of mine. I must have slept for ten hours. Normally I meet forenoons relatively alert.

Sheltering in an alley the other night, the early hours, in a motionless state. I should have been smoking, had just realized the cigarette in my gub was not burning where it should have been burning. As I reached for a match I heard movement. Two cats were on the job less than twenty yards distant. The alley banked by high walls. The cats should have been free from spectators and yet here was me, jesus. In a film I saw recently there was this scruffy dog and a lady dog and he took her out for the night down this back alley to meet his friends and these friends of his were Chefs in an Italian Restaurant, one of whom was named Luigi if I remember correctly. He brought out a table and candlesticks and while the dogs sat down the other friend came out with an enormous quantity of spaghetti and stuff. While they were tucking in out came Luigi again with a stringed instrument and him and his pal began singing in an operatic duet.

The grass grows in a rough patch and cannot have it easy. The blades are grey green and light green; others are yellow but they lie directly on the earth, right on the soil. My feet were there and the insects crawled all around. A fine place for games. They go darting through the green blades and are never really satisfied till hitting the yellow ones below. And they dart headlong, set to collide all the time into each other but no, that last-minute body swerve. And that last-minute body swerve appears to unnerve them so that they begin rushing about in circles or halting entirely for an approximate moment.

I have to clear my head. I need peace peace peace. No thoughts. Nothing. Nothing at all.

Here I am as expected. The shoulders drooping; they have been strained recently. Arms hanging, and the fingers. Here: and rubbing my eyes to open them on the same again. Here, the same is here again. What else.

I aint got no stories

There was a panel of frosted glass near the top of the trailer window and I saw a shadow. At last the door opened. The old guy stood there pistol in hand, half in half out its holster like he had caught me in the act but stared upwards, noting how dark was the sky, how ominous. In a matter of moments I would be drenched. He sniffed then allowed the gun to drop back down the holster. His hand remained on the butt and he looked at me for quite a while. What is it people do with these looks? Process information is what they do. His next comment would include the offer of coffee. I would have bet on that. He would remove his hand from the gun altogether; he would spit on the gravel, then he would do it, he would offer me the coffee.

One thing I've noticed, I said, is how blue is the sky in these parts. The rain comes suddenly, and the sky can be clear when it happens—it seems like that anyway. Ye would gamble yer shirt on a wonderful blue sky, talking about early this morning, and you wouldnt be wrong. Except it is gone in five minutes and there you are, from dry as a bone you're drenched to the skin.

He glanced upwards. Me too. I was only doing it to be polite but for him it was a meaningful activity. I engaged with that, moving my head a little, as though seeking clues. Rain falling from a clear blue sky, I said, that's kind of rare. I thought I saw red earlier. I havent heard of that before. Is that what you get round here?

Yeah, he said.

Not always.

Yeah, hereabouts. Always you got the red. It keeps outa sight. Sometimes it dont. I guess it makes this place unique.

More like a phenomenon.

That's about right.

A gift from God.

Aint no gift from God, he muttered. He squinted at me almost surreptitiously, although maybe that almost is misplaced. He had that particular manner you find in old folks, especially men maybe, a combination of wariness, and the consequent commitment to violence, that pragmatic take on life. Whatever it takes. They dont care, not really. A certain kind of old folk, any gender; to survive that length of time takes a genuine toughness of spirit, something most people lack. I always respected the elderly. This yin would have shot me soon as look at me.

By the same token, I would say yes, he was wary. But I was leading the way and fair enough. I pulled up my coat collar, rubbed my hands together, shivering a little. Did you say something about coffee? I said.

Me?

Yeah.

No sir I did not.

I must have been dreaming. I smiled.

How come you knocked on my door? You looking for a direction? You aint asked for no damn direction if that's what it was. You looking for something else? People dont go knocking doors for that sort of information. Not anymore, unless they living in the mountains and this aint the mountains. You selling something?

I'm lost.

He sighed, looking about—for my car I think. I came on the bus, I said.

Oh you came on the bus?

I think I got off too soon. The busdriver said that to me. He said, You sure this is where you're coming?

Well that makes sense. He glanced sideways and roundabout, checking the other trailers. Far off a couple of small kids were dancing about in a circle. How come you came to my door?

I just came in the compound, by the entry sign, and yours was here, so I knocked the door.

Now you're asking me for a coffee?

I thought you offered me one.

I didnt offer nothing to you.

I thought you did.

You asking me for one?

I shrugged, reaching forwards a little, to peer up into the trailer.

What you gawking at?

Nothing. I pointed up the steps. This your place?

He stared at me, still holding the pistol; waving it in my face like an index finger. You scared of this?

Maybe not.

Maybe not . . . He nodded, eventually, pushed the door back farther, still with the gun in hand.

It was an evil-looking gun and reminded me of the old slug guns you saw years ago; military-style. I didnt want to say it to him.

Did you see the dogs?

I never saw any dogs.

They're out back. The old guy sniffed then reached behind the door to lay down the gun someplace. How's that? he said. You coming in or what?

Thanks. I followed him up into the trailer. The television was on but with the sound turned down. He shut the door behind me. You like dogs?

Dogs are okay, what breed ye talking about?

Dont matter the breed, you like dogs you like dogs. Dobermann.

Are they dopey kind of animals?

He glared at me. Why dont you ask them.

I was joking.

Not much of a joke. Doper dopey, is that what you mean? All I know is you get up close you see their eyes flashing: you see their eyes flashing it's time to leave.

Honest, I was only joking.

People make the same mistakes with them other ones, not the German shepherds, them other kind. They see this placid old thing with the big ears, the unclean coat and weary-looking snozzle and they think that dog there is only fitting for lying under the table. You dont want to make that mistake too often. You trust your own eyes, dont make that mistake. Dont mess with them dogs.

I dont mess with dogs at all.

You are wise if you aint kidding.

There was a three-quarters bottle of whiskey on the table. It aint mine, he said, stepping into the kitchen area where there was a long coffee pot, looking full almost to the brim.

He watched me checking things out. From previous experience I might have expected a cramped room with smelly boots and unwashed dungarees; unwashed cups, unwashed plates, old newspapers and sacking but this had a shower-room, and a good size front room. It was a great place. Sure it was an old guy's place but nothing wrong with that. It didnt smell. If it did it blended. This is no home from home, I said, this is a heaven from heaven.

What d'you say?

No home from home.

He sighed.

It's better than that.

Where's your bag anyhow, I dont see no bag.

I had two bags but I dont know where I put them.

So you aint got none, so you had to get out fast. Cops chasing ye? You on the run? What was in your bags? You talking life's belongings? So you're on the run?

Hey, I said, too many questions.

If you got yer life-belongings in them bags then you're on the run. You think I dont know about life? Cause I live here I aint got no life-experience? Folks make that mistake.

I dont make that mistake.

So what you got in them bags?

I just told ye what happened, I left them on the bus.

Dont make me laugh. You come off the bus and set down here out of nowhere and here you are in nowhere. And you got nothing. You think I'm a lonely old guy here so you just come walking in and take everything! No sir you cant take nothing less I want to give it to you.

You're just being hospitable.

Hospitable. That is what it is. You aint feared. You know my dogs and you see my gun. Yeah, and in you come.

I smiled.

Maybe you know some of them old buddies of mine? Yeah?

I didnt know what to say here. It was a difficult question because it seemed to come from nowhere and in situations like this it is best just to leave a gap and see what fills it. He was waiting for me to answer. When I didnt, he spoke. I see it now, he said.

There's always a consistency. If you can find it. He found it, he connected the line and here I was.

They was buddies, he said, and they had to be. Me too. There was no choices back in them days. The guys with you were with you or not at all. You got down off a bus you had the life-belongings, that's what you had.

In your day. Not now. Nowadays mainly it's just stories.

Stories?

Yeah.

What stories? You aint old enough for stories, what stories you got? You talking about Billy Parkes? Huh? You think I'm gonna tell ye about Billy Parkes? Soon as you opened your mouth he would have laid you out cold. Whoever you think you are, you aint nobody. He was a real mean guy. One cold fucker man that was Billy, he would have shot you dead. You take care if ye got anything to say about him. Archie was stupid. He didnt know the difference between sun and rain. He looked out the cabin door and thought the heavens had opened. Archie got annoyed and he got real angry too but he was stupid. Now Billy Parkes was huffy. Things got to him. That's how he did them things. Some say he let them, like a cover-up for how he was. You had to be careful with Billy. You thought he was pally, he was not pally, next week he'd be somebody else altogether. That was Billy, that's how it was with him. Some guys take as ye find. Dont take him, never. You want to take me?

Not at all.

I got this, he said, reaching for the pistol. You know what this is?

You showed me it before.

You think I cant use it?

I know ye can use it. I grinned. I thought ye were goni open fire!

You did . . . ? Yeah. The old guy nodded, he squinted at me. Me and Billy didnt get on too well and that's the truth so help me God it's not something I would lie about, not at this stage. It is my life, this is what you call it. Archie was just his sidekick. He done all what Billy said. If he wanted you dead then you were dead. Archie made sure of that. Because ye never ever knew how Billy was going to be, that is the whole point of what I'm talking about. Like some folks say about sex past fifty, like we all got to go. They do not care to think about them pretty-looking fifty-year-old women. You know what age I am now? Fifty is young to me. I never felt old and I aint too old now. No sir, I'll take a sixties woman. Sixty aint nothing to me. You think that you are mistaken son you are very mistaken. I got my dogs and

I got this gun and I got a whole bunch of other stuff. What you got to say about that?

Nothing at all. I'm just listening.

I heard them old stories and they aint the thing. People's people and that's how it is.

Equal?

Equal, yes sir. That old stuff boy it was bullshit of the worst kind. Billy Parkes made it seem like we spent our whole lives in that den of iniquity. No sir. Is what I called it, the den of iniquity, I hate every inch of you, that was the old song and I could sing it. Archie could sing it too and it was we three had to team up and if we didnt how you think we gonna survive? We never would have survived. We did it all and we didnt have no choice in that. So, you are giving me a most sore head, a heavy heavy pain in my head.

I'm sorry about that.

You aint sorry.

Yes I am.

Two bags, he said. What did you have in them?

Stories.

Aint stories son, these are my life. You think you are the one. You aint the one. I am the one and old Rory the father. He took care of us. I didnt have no mother later on. I can tell you one thing, and how wrong you can be. That little kid got knocked down and killed by a car, yeah, sure she did, but old Rory wasnt driving that car, was me driving that car. So you want to say stuff you say about me and leave him outa that, dont say nothing about him. You want to believe me you should, you should, and if you dont why then you do what you think. Old Rory was a strong-willed man, he was a worker, he worked all over everywhere; down the valley and across the desert. You give that man a chance and he would snaffle it, right from under. He drove trucks for thirty years. It was never the driver's fault anyhow, only the damn county for failing to provide a place. You want safety you pay for it.

This aint no welfare state. How she would have laughed at that, my mother, wherever she was, settled someplace. You know about her? Huh? She took off, she went east.

Nothing unusual in that.

What d'you say?

Women split from men.

Women split from men? Mothers from boys?

Boys are men too.

No they aint.

They can be.

No sir. He looked at me closely. You aint no boy.

I'm young. You're an old man to me.

Sure I am. That's about the first true thing you said since you came looking.

I didnt come looking.

You came looking for me.

I didnt.

He shook his head. I got dobermanns and them what d'you call thems.

There was a pack of cigarettes on a small table and he reached for it. I smiled.

Yeah you smile, he said, you're the smiler, that's what I call you. You like to see folks smile?

Sure, of course.

What about fighting?

Fighting and smiling.

Yeah? The old guy studied me. He was weary and I wished he would relax. He was a good old guy and I liked him. And this place he had, it was good. I was just glad to sit down. I glanced about the place. Although he was no longer studying me he was still watching like I was up to mischief.

You thinking coffee?

Coffee would be good.

I aint making it, he said, taking a cigarette from the pack.

I could.

Yeah you could, sure you could. He shook his head. Dont make me cry, he said, and after a moment he smiled, flicked the Zippo. He blew out a cloud of smoke. His eyes closed momentarily but that was all, that was enough.

Getting there

I stayed with the lorry and bypassed the city. Down the A74 the driver was turning off into the weird Leadhills so I got out. I remained on this side of the road. A van. The driver wasnt going far, not beyond Lockerbie. I went. I spotted an inn in the distance and told him to stop, I felt like a beer, or two. Four customers including myself. Moving to a table within earshot I tried to concentrate on what they were saying but it was difficult, worse than difficult.

I still had money. I had enough to rent some accommodation in the inn for the night and get rid of the beard and the grime and the old skin before heading south.

The man refused me a room. Full up, he lied. I was truly surprised. I had expected a refusal, of course, but at the same time hadnt. I assumed I was exaggerating but I wasnt. He said the rooms were all taken. May his teeth fall out and his hair recede even farther, lying bastard that he was. I was only drinking the beer to be sociable. I only felt sorry for the other four customers, not wanting to hurt their feelings by making too quick an exit.

Enough. I had to vanish in England. I left the place and headed out of town. I was walking. I felt like walking. I didnt fucking have to fucking walk. I just fucking felt like it. I had enough for a fucking bus. Or train. Or buy a fucking bike man I was not skint, do not think I was skint. No sir, I was not without funds. I had dough. I'm talking dough. But the lift came almost at once. I had barely stopped walking at the motorway slip road and here it was and there was me, crossing the border line, bidding Scotland farewell, farewell, should auld acquaintance and so on, adieu sweet thorns, thistles and jaggy nettles.

The Appleton Arms. Pint of bitter and a Cornish pastie with that bright yellow mustard, English mustard, tasty as fuck man I've always said so. A husband and wife team ran the bar. No bother the bed and breakfast sir.

One could only sigh. An outside lavatory. An ancient bicycle was parked against the washbasin. This thing was made of wood. I could only have sold it to an antique dealer.

Upstairs to immerse for twenty minutes in the grime and old skin then out for a smooth shave, then back into the bath again till finally emerging in the pink, collecting the freshly pressed linen underwear and silk pyjamas; the valet awaited to aid the donning of the robes, the smoking jacket Jobson, yes the velvet, and hock shall do ably with the old veined cheese & water biscuits and fly invitations to the chambermaid.

The bed was soft, sagging in the centre, but I slept amazing and woke in fine fettle, in plenty of time for breakfast which was sadly meagre but good cups of dark red tea with plenty of toast to atone.

Waiting halfway up the slip road onto the M6 I allowed three lifts to go by, attempting to explain that it had to be London or bust. Springtime in old King's Cross. But I could see the drivers' faces tightening into huffs at the perceived rejection. I feel bad about that; three probables vanishing from the paths of other wayfarers. I felt lucky. This is a certain feeling one gets on the road. I aint taking any old lift, I want some guy to drop me off within walking distance of Old Kent fucking Road.

No sooner that than the rain the rain.

The rain alters everything, everything. Just huddling there. I was lucky to get a lift at all now and these ones I had let go! Why was I such a damn fool? What was that a question? Did I have to ask it of course I didnt. Hell mend me. I was my own

I was going to say "worst enemy" but it was not true. Here I was on another track, another road, another route. This was a major stroke of luck. The next lift along would bring me to the centre of all that is, that fate hath so determined. So aye—Bristol?

Aye, yes, Bristol. Bristol's fine mate. I like Bristol. Boats. I always liked boats. Boats is good.

Very snug inside the big artic, the driver's music blasting it out and no need to gab but just enjoy the ride down the safe inside lane, the drone of the windscreen-wipers while the rain, battering hard down on the cabin roof. Fuck the M6.

I liked Bristol on sight. Something about the place. Yet I couldnt remember passing through it before. Last time along I maybe missed it. But I had been heading thataway, northward, detouring via Wales and according to maps the passing through Bristol is inevitable for that selfsame detour. That is a strange thing. Soon enough I called a halt to this. Let me out let me out. Fuck Bristol. Weymouth ahoy!

Windswept Weymouth. I wanted to sing a song of good cheer, of ocean swells, green fields and blue skies.

Nothing to add except I still had money.

A bad time aboard. Pounding waves. Passengers having to heave out their guts here, there and everywhere. The mess on the saloon floor, it was streaming about, bits of meat and veg amongst the Guinness-type froth but the grumpy barman stood me a pint when he saw I wasnt getting affected. I told him a yarn about working on the boats off Cromarty—in fact it must have been down to the time spent plying Glasgow buses over cobbled streets, those boneshaking old efforts probably ensuring I can never be seasick again. And so pleased with myself I might have ordered a three-course meal if the cash had stretched.

Later, an old guy had been tethering a group of rowing boats, down on the beach, to the side of a wee pier; then he sat on a deck chair up by a green hut which was advertising fishing tackle for hire. Going over to him and saying: I want your job ya old bastard.

This land. So long it took to accept the warmer weather as a fact. I had no trust.

A great many people on the promenade, all young-looking for some reason maybe to do with the summer looming ahead. The jeans, the shorts, the T-shirts, vests, sandals.

The clouds were not in sight.

In a delicatessen I could buy two ounces of cold garlic sausage and rolls. Narrow streets and pavements and all of the tiny shops. The promenade is very long and straight. Word of an old castle. The rest of it to be explored. In a pub later on I was sitting at the bar eavesdropping on the chat of three girls who were sipping at blackcurrant & Pernod

and the sensation of being offered the opportunity, I could have explained the present predicament

but there was nothing to be said then till finally it was too too late, too late, it getting dark, and the rain drizzling, drizzling.

Staying there in the bar, my back to a partition wall—yet still content—the feet outstretched beneath the table and tucking them under when someone walked by, with apologies articulated that I might reasonably be understood. Clearing the accent to please, in other words; in a good way but.

The barman roused me. It was around half past midnight.

I knew all about the police hereabouts. Throw you off the place at the slightest excuse—unfixed abodes the especial cause. Twice in ten minutes I had to go down an alley to piss. Yet I still wasnt too worried, it was so very dark, so very quiet, and neither strollers nor stray animals. A patrol car rolled by. I had the smoke cupped in the palm of my right hand.

Again the rain, against the rain.

Out onto the promenade I cut smartly across, down the stone steps to the sands immediately below the big stone wall; fast along to the farthest point and up, retracking to the third last shelter. I had to take this chance I think though well aware it was obvious, unsafe. I sat on the bench in the side exposed to the Sea, elbows on knees and hands propping up the head. The rain belting down, like a storm, the incredible noise. I was trying to sort out certain things about my life and being here instead of there and then instead of now but I dont remember doing any of that at all, just entering a kind of daze, a kind of numbness; literally, having to get up and hop about to regain sensation proper.

And the rain blowing in, having to huddle into the side of the wall, escaping the wind but the draughts, the draughts were just not, they were too much—not too much, just, they were just, they were like the wind, sudden blasts, oh and through you, the very marrow of the bones and the being all the beings oh man and this strange experience hearing a clock strike. I had no idea of time, and money in my pocket, what I had, nothing.

Later, through the blackest greys a little red showed in snatches; enough for the luck to be hitting on. I knew it was.

A certainty. No need to hop.

The tide was out. I walked the sands a furlong or so, the boots squeaking then squelching. Sand worms. Red veins. So so tiny, thin. The first time I ever saw them though I had often looked at the mound of twirls they left dotted about.

Amazing.

What are they like at all. The red things.

And sitting on my heels gazing back to the promenade, the row of villas, guest-houses and hotels. And back at the Sea, two boats an inch apart on the horizon.

The House of an old Woman

The hedge was tall but so scrawny we could easily see through it. A huge place. Standing in a jungle of weeds and strange-looking sunflowers, big ones which bent at the top and hung backwards to the long grass. It seemed deserted. I hesitated a moment before pushing open the rusty gate. It grated on the cement slab underneath. Freddie and Bob followed me along the narrow path and we stopped at the foot of the flight of steps. I went up and banged the door. And again. Eventually the door opened still on the chain. An old woman gaped out at me. I explained.

Ten pounds a week pay your own lectric! she roared.

I looked at her. She glared at me: Right then, eight and not a penny less! Well? Do you want it or not!

Freddie spoke up from below, asking if we could see it first. But she glared at me again as if I had said it. I shrugged. She pointed at my suitcase and squinted: What did you bring that for if you didnt want to take it? She pursed her lips and added: Right then, but just for a minute because my daughter's coming to get me! She told me they were wanting to take the place—nothing about wanting to see it! Who did the telephone?

Me.

Huh! The door shut and shuffling could be heard, and what sounded like a whole assortment of chains being unhooked. Then the door opened fully and she beckoned me in. She about turned and, with her skirts held in either hand, she walked with a stoop halfway along the enormous and empty lobby. Opening another door she indicated we were to follow her. It was the lounge. The wallpaper reminded me of the fence surrounding the patchwork hedge outside. Above the big mantelpiece a picture had been recently taken down leaving a space which displayed the original design and colours of the wallpaper. An immaculate television set squatted on an orange carpet but apart from that the room was empty. Pointing to both the carpet and television she said: Somebody might come to collect these but you can use them meantime. The bathroom's on the first floor and the big one and the smaller one and above that there's three other rooms all sizes you can make bedrooms out of and in the attic it's a great big room and down here you've got the kitchen next door and the other room and you cant go into it. There's the W.C. next to that then the back door leading out to the garden and you should start doing it up. There's fruit out there! She breathed deeply for a bit then cried: Ten pounds plus lectric. And you'll have to pay in advance you know because my daughter'll see that you do.

Turning abruptly she walked to the door but bounced roundabout as though expecting to catch us sticking our tongues out. Freddie muttered something to do with it being good value for the money.

Course it's good value! And just you remember about that garden! She said it all directly to me. Once we had wandered about the place we came back downstairs to find her waiting impatiently in the lobby. She wore a fox round the neck of her black coat and a charcoal hat with a large brooch stuck in its crown. Her trousers were amazing though they were probably pantaloons; they had elastic cords fastened at each cuff which were looped round her sturdy walking shoes, to prevent them riding up her legs maybe. These pantaloons were light brown in colour.

Has your daughter not arrived yet? I said. But although I had spoken politely she ignored me. We stood there waiting for her to say something. She acted as if we were not there. It was an uncomfortable feeling. Freddie was first to move. He entered the lounge, and Bob followed. I felt obliged to make some sort of gesture. Eventually I said, Fine—that's fine.

I moved to the door of the lounge and through, and then the door closed firmly behind me. For some reason I let my arm swing backwards as if I had closed it myself.

We sat on the carpet and discussed the situation, but quietly, aware of her standing sentry out in the lobby. Later on the outside door opened, then the lounge door. The daughter appeared, a tall woman who dressed plainly and reminded me of a matron. They left after we paid the advance rent money. Freddie cracked a joke and we laughed. I shuffled the cards and dealt three hands of poker to see who was to get first choice of rooms. I won. I decided on the big one up on the first floor and the other two settled on adjoining ones on the second. It had been a good day. Never for one moment had I really expected to get the place at a rent we could afford. Great value. As I unrolled my sleeping bag I noticed the linoleum was cracked in places and not too clean either. It occurred to me that we should buy carpets before anything else.

Next evening we met in a pub after finishing work. They mentioned they had spent last night in the downstairs lounge. I laughed, but later on, when we were playing cards and drinking cans of beer back in the house, I felt a bit peeved. It was noticed. I passed it off by making some crack about folk being afraid of the dark etc. They laughed with me but insisted it was great having a carpet beneath the sleeping bags. It kept out the cold. They asked if I fancied coming here as well to sleep but I said no. I couldnt be bothered with that. It somehow defeated the purpose of it all, getting a big house and so on. They wanted to carry on with the discussion but I didnt. After a bit we cut for the first bath. I lost. Bob won and when he had gone Freddie said he couldnt be bothered waiting for one and undressed and just got into the sleeping bag. He began exaggerating how cosy it was and soft compared to a dirty cold hard floor, and also how you could chat with company if you couldnt get to sleep.

Rubbish.

I played patience till Bob came back by which time I think Freddie was sleeping. Upstairs in the bathroom I smoked a cigarette while waiting for the tub to fill. Once the taps were turned off I was very aware of how silent everything was. I wished I had been first to think about sleeping downstairs on the lounge carpet. It was a good plan, at least till we started buying stuff to furnish the place. Yet I couldnt really join them now. It had gone a bit far. And it was daft saying that about being scared of the dark. I had meant it as a joke of course and they had taken it the right way. But why had they not come in and got me last night? They said I had been sleeping when they came downstairs but never even looked inside to check, just said they had listened at the door and said my breathing was so regular I couldnt be awake. And the light was off! As if I could somehow wait till I was asleep before switching it out!

I must admit I didnt fancy the idea of sleeping alone the sole occupant of two floors and an attic in a run-down house owned by an old eccentric. But she was not crazy. She had acted the way she had. But old women are notorious. Old people in general—they do odd things.

The bathwater had cooled. No hot left in the tank. Bob must have used more than his fair share. In fact the bathwater was actually getting quite cold. There was a draught coming in under the door which was causing the sleeves of my jumper to sway where it hung on the back of the tall stool. Then the creak! It was terrible hearing it. My body tensed completely. The big cupboard in the corner it came from, and its door moved ajar slightly, and in the shadows I could make out what appeared to be a big coat. It was. I half raised myself up from the bath but I couldnt see it fully. And there couldnt be anyone inside. Otherwise they would have come out. Getting up from the bath I stepped over the side, gathering my clothes without looking in its direction, making my way to the door out. Before opening it I had to relax myself. I stared at my right hand, getting it to stop trembling. I raised it to grip the door handle but did not touch it. My breaths rasped through my teeth. Then I managed to close my fist on the handle but my shoulders had stiffened and I tried to halt my breathing an instant. I could hear nothing but my breaths. I tugged on the handle then the catch released with a sharp click and throwing the door open I dashed forward, cracking my knee against the jamb. I dropped a shoe but didnt stop. I bolted across the corridor and into my room crashing the door shut behind me.

I had suggested clubbing together to buy the largest second-hand carpets we could find, the cost to be borne individually or divided equally, or whatever else they suggested. But no. Objections raised by both. They preferred earlier ideas about buying furniture for each room as each person thought fit. And anyway, they said, they would need at least another fortnight before starting to think about buying anything. To help save I suggested eating in and watching more television but they hummed and they hawed and I could tell they werent too interested. At this point I resolved to bring down the sleeping bag but I could not openly declare it. I hinted the room was freezing cold, it was too big, draughts came in beneath the door and through the patched-up window joints. Neither bothered to comment. One evening I happened to ask whether they still felt the place was good value. Bob grunted something or other and Freddie gave an "of course"—but in such a way I was made to feel as if I had asked something stupid. Upstairs I went without saying anything further. That same quiet pervading the place. Bob was going for a bath. Now and then the loud crash of the tap being turned on startled me and again startled me when turned off. And these gurgling noises as the water filled the cold-tank.

The sleeping bag was fine, snug enough. Yet if something were to happen my legs would obviously have been restricted. I turned onto my side a lot, a position I could maintain for short periods only because my shoulders ached on the floor, while when lying on my front I would soon become aware of my knees jarring on it. Carpets were definitely essential. A bed would have been even better. And yet I appeared to be the only one interested in buying anything. The draught beneath the door turned an empty cigarette packet halfway about. I was weary. It was not easy to sleep, every bit of me felt exhausted, and the thoughts flying about my brain. And yet things had definitely changed since we had come, there was a coolness being directed against me—in the pub, the bus going to work.

The bathroom door opened and closed then silence for a second before the pitpat downstairs, and later the sound of the lounge door opening and shutting quite firmly. I was honestly glad to be up in my own room, glad not to have succumbed for the sake of a carpet and some sort of safety in numbers. A coat in the cupboard! Felt covering the water tank. What a joke! Laughs all round.

In the cafe one Saturday morning for breakfast I again suggested getting the carpets, maybe starting off buying one at a time and if they liked I would pay it and we could sort out the details later on. They refused. Said it was best I did buy it but just to go ahead and kit out my own room. When we went back to the house the daughter was waiting for us. It surprised me at the time yet it was the end of the month and she obviously had to have a key of her own. When I asked after the old woman she replied, Same as ever.

Is she comfortable? I said. It was daft to ask that but too late to retract. The daughter nodded without speaking and I noticed the other two exchanging grins. If they had been prepared to open their mouths then I wouldnt have had to say a word, but they always left me to sort out the business stuff. It was me who got this place. If I hadnt have made the phone call they would never have bothered. After she left with the rent money I told them I would be happy to stay in and watch the sport on television. Immediately Freddie jumped to his feet saying he fancied a pint and then Bob was on his feet saying, A good idea. Off they went, right away. That was definitely that. Something up, no doubt about it. Neither had even given me the opportunity of refusing. Yet I might not have refused. How could they know without even asking? It was as if they were waiting for me to say what I was going to do just so they could go and do something else. They lacked the nerve to come right out with it though. And when they suggested a game of cards later in the day I said no. Bob muttered something about where was I going, was I going out or what? I shrugged. Ten minutes later I went out. To hell with them.

The place was in darkness when I came home. A bit eerie in some ways. I walked along the hallway and flung open the lounge door, but with too much force, and it rocked on its hinges. Of course the room was empty. They had probably gone out as soon as possible after me. I switched on the television and tried to concentrate on it. Past 11 o'clock. The pub was less than ten minutes away. Normally we would have returned by then. Perhaps they had gone to another pub. Yet surely they would have gone there knowing it was where I would have gone? I hadnt gone there of course, but they werent to know that.

I had decided to wait up for them. I changed my mind. Why bother? They could have gone anywhere, they could have gone into the centre of town. Maybe even gone to the dancing somewhere. Why had they not even thought to mention it earlier? They could have said something. And if they hadnt truly known at that time they could at least have mentioned probabilities. If I had known they might be considering the dancing I would have gone out with them. Anywhere at all for that matter as long as it wasnt to the local pubs. Obviously my company was being avoided. And the way my suggestions were never picked up. They said there was no problem about sleeping. Neither there was, for them. Sleeping downstairs on a thick carpet! What's up? Did they lack the guts to sleep in empty rooms!

No point staying up any longer. I switched off the television, the light too. Then in the hallway I couldnt find the switch for the light there. Not that it mattered because of the moonlight coming through the window on the first landing upstairs. Why had the old woman insisted on locking that door downstairs though? It was a question the three of us had discussed on a few occasions. Just as I approached my room I heard noises from outside. It was those two. Then the door had opened. They walked inside, the door closing as if they had only thrown it back instead of actually shutting it properly. They went into the lounge, one of them laughed at something the other must have said.

Yet the following morning was good! Freddie cooked a great breakfast. The first genuine meal we had prepared on the oven. From then on it was agreed we would eat as often as possible in the house and save on the money. I suggested we take turn about with the different things but Bob said since Freddie's cooking was fine he should stick to that and we could do the other bits if it was okay with everybody? Freddie agreed right away so I cut the cards with Bob. I lost. But fortunately he preferred to dry the dishes rather than wash them. I prefer the washing because it gets it over and done with. So it all worked out fine. The early part of the evening we went to the local but they agreed almost immediately when I suggested going into the town. Back home they preferred watching television to setting up a game of cards. By the time Bob came back from what seemed like his daily bath the credits for the late night movie were just coming on. I was lighting a cigarette and getting ready to settle down for it but then he made a display of unrolling the sleeping bag and generally busying about the place. I ignored it. But Freddie was wanting to know if he was getting ready for a kip? Yes, he said. To be fresh for work in the morning, apparently. I kept staring at the screen. He yawned and got into the sleeping bag. Silence for maybe five minutes then Freddie also yawned, a really big one. I got up and left. It was pointless.

My own sleeping bag was lying as I had left it that morning. In the corner was the pile of socks and stuff I had ready for the launderette. I would go straight from work tomorrow. Also I decided to buy a carpet right away. In fact a bed would be better. Why not? With the money a carpet cost it would probably be just the same to get a secondhand bed. I could even buy both. Without bothering about those two downstairs. Why should I? They could look after themselves. And I was sick of making decisions anyway. They never had a clue about that kind of thing. Even this area of the city was unknown to them. They would have had no chance of getting a place on their own, without me. Why on earth did they go to bed when a good film was starting? But why not. The lounge was perfect for a good genuine sleep with that carpet blocking out the cold hard floor. Bastards. Things would have to change otherwise. What? Otherwise what! It was my place. It was me found the house. It was me had to convince them it was great value, that it wasnt too good to be true—that it was at least worth the price of a phone call!

I picked an old newspaper from the floor and wedged it beneath the door to secure it and combat the draught. Whenever I forgot this it banged all night—gently right enough, but a bang nevertheless, especially when you are trying to get a decent sleep. And also the bits of fluff and oose, they would go breezing about the linoleum, and occasionally I felt as if it was landing on my face, getting into my hair—that's the trouble with sleeping on the floor. I laid my shoes on the newspaper to secure it. There was no question that a good carpet was the first necessity.

I was hardly sleeping at all now and my timekeeping was beginning to suffer. Occasionally I worked a little overtime to compensate but this day I returned home to find the old woman's specially locked door lying ajar. An ancient sort of smell hung everywhere. A kind of storeroom it looked like, furniture stacked against walls, faded photographs in frames. If the daughter discovered what had happened she would be well within her rights to order us out at once. Why had they done it? They never thought. How could the lock be fixed? It had obviously been forced. How could everything be put right so she would never notice? The kind of questions that never seemed to occur to those two. I went upstairs immediately and attempted to concentrate on a book. It was hard going. It seemed like hours until at last the outside door opened. When the lounge door closed I rose quietly and switched off my room light, muffling the click by holding a sock over the switch. I wanted them to think I had been asleep for ages. Back in the sleeping bag I lay awake for a long time, just listening, but not hearing anything unusual. What maybe I should have done earlier was to go right into the lounge and see what was going on. But what would've happened if they had found me there? Nothing. It was the lounge. I had as much right to be there as they had. Because they slept in the room didnt mean it wasnt a lounge. But what was going to happen about the old woman's room? Surely they hadnt searched the place? What would there be to find? It was just a kind of storeroom!

They admitted breaking into the old woman's room. Purely out of curiosity. They said they had taken nothing whatsoever, and hardly glanced at what was there. And promised to have it fixed by the Saturday in case the daughter arrived. Yet I doubt whether they would have spoken about it unless I had broached the subject. They showed no interest in the door to my room. It had blown open the night before. A gale was blowing outside and this might have been the cause. It seemed unlikely at the time and no more so now. But possible of course, but just unlikely. It was pointless talking about it to them. As I lay soaking in the bathtub the cupboard door squeaked as usual, revealing the felt round the boiler. And what seemed to be a black hat perched on top, on the spot it would have been had the boiler been a body. I slid under the warm water, enjoying the sensation, but then I came up. Surely it was a hat! And coupled with the felt it really did resemble a body. It might have been a wrapped-up towel made to look like a hat. It was definitely a hat. I got out the bath and strode across to open the door fully. It was a hat of course, perched on the top by having been balanced against the back pipe. And who had done the balancing? Some joke. Let's have a big laugh.

I dried. Maybe they were expecting a scream! I rushed downstairs and grasped the handle of their door but paused, just to control my anger. The light was out when I entered. Bob had sat up straight, he showed relief to see it was me. He muttered something, not loudly enough to waken Freddie who seemed to be sleeping. Their sleeping bags lay end to end in front of the fireplace. I wanted to know who put the hat on the boiler? I asked him again. Still he didnt answer. I shook my head. It was pointless. Outside in the hallway I paused again, wondering if I should stay there and find out if Freddie actually was asleep. But what difference did it make?

I stayed clear of them. That business about eating in had never taken on from the start. Humming and hawing about the time it took when you come back from working all day etc. Rubbish. The Saturday morning the daughter was certain to arrive for the rent I went down to wait but she never appeared. I saw Freddie through the open lounge door and he came out and asked if I was going out? Yes. Where? Ha ha ha. When will you be back? I told him I would be back eventually and let it hang as if I was going to be gone for the whole weekend or something. In fact I went up the town and intended going to a movie that evening, though I ended up in quite a good pub which had entertainment on Saturday nights. Once home I strolled along the path and stood at the door for a few moments then I opened it and strode down the hallway whistling, I had let the door shut itself by shoving it. I went straight into the lounge. They were watching television. I took out a can of beer and opened it, then I left. Loud noises woke me next morning.

It was midday by the time I went down. When I walked into the lounge the place was full of furnishings and fittings. A sideboard at one wall, a table near the window, some chairs. They were lying on the carpet reading the Sunday papers. Without saying anything I went out and along to the old woman's room. It had practically been cleared. What was the point.

They were standing in the doorway behind me. One of them indicated a couple of musty carpets and suggested I take them. The other said what about the big trunk in the corner, was that any good? Ha ha ha. I couldnt believe it. There could be no question that the daughter would notice next time she came. Freddie muttered something about sticking the stuff back in on the Friday night. What happened if she came unexpectedly? Well they could stick the stuff back in every Friday night to be on the safe side. Some idea that! What happens if she decided to look in on another day altogether, just to check up on us? Silence.

They both shrugged. What about me? Oh great, two ancient carpets and a big trunk. Exactly what I need for the room!

Rubbish.

But the crux had taken place. This was it. The lounge was now theirs. It belonged to them. It didnt have anything to do with me. The television set and the orange carpet just happened to be in the room they now used as a bedsitter. I had the rest of the house. I could go anywhere I wanted. The only snag was there was nothing in it. Oh well, not much of a snag!

I went up the stairs and got ready to go out. That was it now. All the plans to decorate the place from top to bottom. All finished. And the garden. Getting the stuff growing properly, seeing the fruit would come out right. The whole lot. All finished. Yes, I could stay in an empty room and they would stay in the lounge. And we would all continue with an even three-way split of the rent. Yes. Fine! Exactly fair.

The door opening was becoming more frequent. It usually seemed to occur in the small hours. Then the silence. Because of the situation I was lying there anticipating anything. Anything at all. But I couldnt even hear their footsteps. It was possible they crept up to the attic to wait a while in case I got up to investigate. One morning I managed to get the early bus I told them people who went about pulling stunts in the middle of the night should be locked away in a kids' nursery. It was Freddie who spoke. He muttered something about my room, a smell. That was good. Freddie. As far as I knew he had never taken a bath since coming to the house! He showered in work, apparently. There was a smell in my room. I knew there was. I hadnt been to the launderette for a while. But I always opened the window for a bit during the early evening if I was home. The real smell belonged to the room itself. In fact the whole house had a smell of its own. Musty. I mentioned it to the daughter on that Saturday morning. Eventually she told me it was a while since it had been aired properly which was fair enough considering the way her mother was. It is doubtful whether she would have done it for years! The daughter picked up the rent envelope and left but I went down the path after her and asked if she had happened to take a look in the lounge recently. She said she was a bit pushed for time. I told her about the furniture. It was unintentional. It just came out. But she just said she was pushed for time again and that was that. I was glad but at the same time not glad. And then I saw she was gazing at the lounge window when she passed on the other side of the big scrawny hedge. Very possibly she would be back to check. And no wonder. Who wants strangers poking about in your mother's room? I had forgotten to mention the television set into the bargain. As far as I had been aware it was only in the house temporarily. Had the old woman not said both it and the orange carpet were going to be collected? What if she had forgotten about them? It could be she had. Being an old person she might well have remembered them but not known where they were. What would happen if it was a rented set? She might end up having to pay the full price as if she had had it stolen. Those rental firms are notorious. But the daughter would see it there in the lounge and know right away it was the one belonging to her mother. It would be fine.

I had to work part of Sunday because of this sleeping in. The man in charge was continually berating me about it and though he was justified to a large extent it was not as if I wasnt trying. At times it got so bad I would rather have taken the whole day off rather than go in and face it all. But I had to! What would have happened if I hadnt? There wasnt much could've happened. I could have been given the sack but I was good at my work. The man in charge obviously knew this. Where would they have got a better worker? Probably they could have—eventually, not right away. I didnt feel like going home when I got off the bus. It had been a long drawn out journey. Sunday bus services. I hardly had any energy left. I went to the chip shop and ate a meal, half expecting to see those two but they were probably off for the day somewhere, at least into the town. I hadnt been to the local pub for some time. It was packed full when I got there and the way I was feeling I had to get a seat. I was obliged to sit at a table where a group of people were. They were regulars. Although I didnt know them well enough to talk to I didnt feel too much of an outsider. Later on I saw them. They were at the bar and looked to have been there for ages judging by the position they had towards the side of it. How could I have failed to spot them before? And how did they not see me? They maybe had and ignored me. It would have been unlikely they could have missed me. Normally when someone enters a pub the first thing is to gaze about for familiar faces. Habit. Everybody does it. If they hadnt been standing to the side I would definitely have seen them earlier. And they probably hadnt even been there when I arrived. What would they do if I ordered a drink at a place where they had to notice me? They could scarcely pretend not to see me—especially with the big mirror on the wall. The pub was busy but so what, they would still have to see me. What would happen? Would they buy me a drink? Ignore me? How could that happen! Impossible. That would be going too far. Even if they wanted to. And of course they would want to. But they couldnt. They werent in a position to. It would be a sort of confrontation. Right out in the open and in a public place. And what could they do? Nothing. Nothing whatsoever! There was nothing they could do except say hello or something, buy me a drink maybe and ask about my job. No chance of them doing anything else. And they could never force me into leaving the place. That was probably the real plan, get me to leave the house altogether. Ha ha ha. And if I hadnt phoned nobody would have. I saw Freddie exchange words with a person next to them at the bar there and they laughed briefly. It would remain to be seen. Things change. Because things are as they are it's no guarantee they have to stay like that. A very different story if I was to go up and start talking right now. Very different from two to one in the downstairs room. No pretences. Simple comments only. That'd be all. And they would have no option but to answer. What else could they do? They couldnt do anything else. The barman happened along just then and he lifted my empty glass. I sat on for a moment. I could get myself another drink right now. What would happen? I didnt have to order at their side of the bar. If I did I would have to be ready. There was no point rushing in without having the thing prepared otherwise I couldnt keep the advantage. It had to be something direct. An opening comment to leave them floundering. Yet one more was also required in case they managed a quick reply. And it had to be short, brief. It was necessary to think things out. I left quickly but waited outside on the pavement for a moment. No, it would have been pointless at this stage. It had to be right. No sense to go rushing in and blabbing something. It had to be that nothing more could be said after such a confrontation—otherwise what was the point? No, time spent on details would not be wasted. I wondered if they had seen me leave but this was unlikely. I strode home as quickly as possible and went straight into their room and folded up their sleeping bags, I stuck them into the boiler cupboard in the bathroom. Then I got their shaving stuff and stuck it inside beside them. But it was too much. It was ridiculous. What would happen when they found it there? They might not find it at all. Of course they would. They would search the house. They would find it. What would they do? They would know who was responsible right away. What did it matter? It didnt matter. I left it all there. Another idea. I got a chair from their room and took it to behind the staircase to climb onto, to switch off the electricity at the mains. I stuck the chair back in the room and left the house. I went back to the chip shop and sat in the eating-inside area. But it was daft. Who else could have done it? There was nobody else. They would know who was responsible right away. Of course they would and I could just deny it. What could they do? Nothing. There was nothing they could do! All they could do was say, It was you! Ha ha ha. I ordered something to eat. It wasnt as if it was anything bad. Irritating at first but it would all be found. Maybe it already was. In fact it might well have been. They didnt like staying out too late to do a thing even if I'd wanted to. They could have found the stuff and be sound asleep at this very minute. It would have surprised them and they would know who was responsible but so what, this was the best thing about it. Enough to let them see how things shift. I strolled about before going home at last. Maybe I shouldnt have tampered with their belongings. So far they hadnt actually done that to me. Yet compared to other things it was really nothing. If it upset them what on earth would they have done if their door had been kicked open in the early hours of a working morning? Even the hat!

The place was in darkness. Inside I crept up the stairs and undressed as quietly as I possibly could. I decided against using the bathroom until much later when it was certain they would be in and sleeping. But they would be in. It had to be after midnight. I listened. I heard nothing unusual. I continued to listen and then on impulse I got out the sleeping bag and used a sock to muffle the click of the light switch. The light came on. I switched it off.

That was that!

They had missed the bus next morning. When I passed along the hallway they appeared from the room. It was unexpected but I didnt find it totally surprising. Bob muttered something about having read any meters lately? I walked on. They spoke to each other. I could feel the anger getting up in me. I was about shaking. It was coming to the head. But it was the wrong time. I wasnt ready. I turned and stared at them. I didnt speak, I just looked. Then I went out. And even if I had been prepared it would have been pointless. Very different in a place like the public bar of a local pub. That would have been a real confrontation. Yet even then I would have to see everything was right, prepared.

The man in charge was at the window of the office when I arrived. I didnt want to go in. I wanted to get back to the house. It was pointless not to.

Everything was neat in the room. Their sleeping bags were folded, one lying on a chair and one lying on the big trunk. A poster covered the blank spot above the mantelpiece. But if the old woman's stuff had been shoved back into her room what would be left? Nothing. Sleeping bags and a poster you could buy anywhere. I lit a cigarette. Then all of the furniture including the television set and the orange carpet I carted straight through into the old woman's place. I could close the door but not lock it. How did they do it? Maybe they didnt even lock it at all! Maybe they just stuck the stuff back and hoped the daughter wouldnt check to see if the actual door had been broken open! I stayed in the house until an hour before they were due off the bus. I didnt come back until much later. Of course they would have known. Who cares? But the daughter could have done it. She could have come in unexpectedly to check in the lounge. And how could she be asked to stand by and let her mother's belongings be used by a couple of strangers? And what about the television and carpet? She had every right to take them as well. They didnt belong to them. They were only temporary. I had as much right to them as they did. In some respects even more. Turn and turn about. They had their turn and surely I should have mine. My room would have been a great place with a carpet and a television set. Even just to have borrowed them once or twice. We could've cut the cards to set the nights. Everybody would've wanted Saturday but it could've been worked out fairly.

The front door had slammed. When I got to the window I saw them disappear along the street.

A padlock had been fixed onto their door. It was brand new. I hadnt heard it being put on. They must have done the job while I was out and I missed seeing it when I came back. Why did they do it? They didnt have to. They could've let things come to a head and that could've been the confrontation. It would've all been sorted out. They didnt even know for certain it was me. It was obvious. But it wasnt certain. It could easily have been the daughter. And she had every right to do it. They couldnt know for certain it was me. But what would happen if they did? Nothing. Nothing could actually happen. They would have to speak perhaps. And they would have to be speaking soon anyway because I hadnt left my share of the rent out at the weekend. It wasnt on purpose. I just overspent. My wages havent been too good recently. I only had enough for getting to work and getting by on food for the week. But if they wanted the lounge as a bedsitter an agreement had to be worked out. The television and the carpet could be sorted out side by side otherwise—what? Otherwise what?

The padlock was a problem. The only alternative to forcing it was to go in through the window but maybe the thing was bolted down. Knowing how the old woman had been this was very likely. I went into the kitchen and looked about and then I saw a metal rod near the sink. It was long and sturdy enough. But still the snags about after. What would happen after? Who cares. Nothing to worry about—after! The padlock glinted, sparkling new. I struck it over and over but it wouldnt give. I wedged in the rod to use it like a crowbar but this wasnt working right either and I began battering it again and again then wedging it again till finally it creaked and came away, the whole apparatus including the screwnails, bright and shiny new. I booted the door open. The orange carpet was back in position but the television wasnt. Neither was anything else. Not even the sleeping bags. What happened? Had they left it all in the old woman's room? Or packed up and left? Packed up and left maybe. They hadnt been carrying anything going down the street. They could have done it earlier on. I turned to leave and made out the big writing on the wall. HA HA HA, it said. I could check the other room or just go up the stair. It was cold in the hallway. And that musty smell.

Charlie

Charlie had one suit and he wore it all times. He worked for a stone-cleaning outfit travelling throughout England and Wales, and in his situation this was perfect. He owed a fortune in maintenance back payments for a wife and three weans he had left up in Lanarkshire somewhere. He was self-employed. In theory he subcontracted himself out to the stone-cleaning outfit—something like that. What it did mean was that he was more or less untraceable. I was living in digs in Manchester at the time, had just survived a lean spell and now moved into this lodging house paying a week's cash in advance.

Not a bad place. Long-distance lorrydrivers inhabited it mostly. During the weekends few people were around and until Charlie arrived I had the lounge and dining room virtually to myself. Charlie seldom went anywhere except to his work. Friday and Saturdays were the only ones he would not stay for overtime beyond 7 p.m. He worked the other five for as long as they needed him. Before entering the house on Friday evenings he spent an extra couple of minutes slapping the grey dust from out of his suit. After the evening meal, he stepped down to the local pub. He rarely drank more than five pints of bitter. He was always back in the house before closing time. I doubt if he particularly enjoyed drinking beer.

Having received my girocheck* on Friday mornings I was normally skint by Friday evenings. Charlie began taking

---

* Unemployment benefit check.

me along to the boozer where he would buy me pint for pint the same as himself. He seemed glad to make the move back to the house, sit and watch television then up the stairs. I think he just needed company occasionally and also to get rid of a couple of quid in a bona fide sort of manner—before making it into the betting shop on the Saturday afternoon. I tagged along with him to watch the performance. It was dismal.

Once or twice I had gained a few bob on the Friday afternoon and could have a go on my own but that was rare. The usual thing was me being skint and watching Charlie. He never won. Never. Never whatsoever. He did not receive one solitary return during the weeks I knew him.

He bet in permutations to the precise extent of what lay in his pocket. If he had twenty-two quid his bet was a £2 yankee which at eleven bets would amount to the full £22.00. Twenty-six quid and he would place a £2 canadian to equal the £26.00. If he had twenty-nine quid in his pocket then he would make out the line as a 50 pence heinz amounting to £28.50 and toss in the extra 50 pence on the accumulator bet. It had to be that his pocket contained nothing bar pennies after the day's business. Anybody happening to observe his bets would say something like: When Charlie knocks it off, he'll do it in a Big Way.

Women liked him. In the betting shop the young one behind the counter used to give him a nice smile. Nothing to do with his being a loser because she had no percentage in the take, she was only a counter-hand. The landlady also liked him, so too the wee lady who helped her. Charlie was always punctual for meals, said a good morning, washed before getting to the dining room table. And the ladies delivered him up the largest portions, the choicest cuts, the additional rashers of bacon and the rest of it. If he was aware of this treatment he never acknowledged it that I knew about. All the lorrydrivers had noticed though. They could be seen weighing up the number of spuds they had in comparison to Charlie, but nothing was ever said—even in a joke. All he ever did was smile politely.

His total failure to get a return on his betting-shop outlay was no failure in this sense: he planned it. He bought weekly travel-passes and hoarded the dowps of each cigarette he smoked though he didnt give this as a reason for smoking plain cigarettes. I used to mix these dowps in with my own tobacco and roll him a decent smoke because he never managed to learn how to handroll himself a cigarette. And he never bothered buying any of these rolling devices you can get, and some are cheap. He said: I've thought about it. I just cant get round to it. Then he shrugged.

What did that shrug mean? Whatever it was, I think that is how women liked him. A man would have wanted to give him a shake, except he was strong as fuck and ye would never have tried it. He was a mild kind of guy but ye would have been mad to take him on.

The way he lost his money depressed me. Yet only in retrospect. There was something about those bets he made. They always seemed to show promise. That was something about them. That was how people thought if ever he wins he'll do it Big.

The majority of his selected runners would be going in televised races but he made a point of leaving the last horse to be in an event scheduled to run late in the afternoon—once the televised races had finished. This was for the sake of his nerves. Imagine having four winners, he said, and having to watch that fifth yin run its race out on the telly. Naw. I couldnt stand that. That would finish me.

There was no danger of this ever happening. The nearest he ever got was one afternoon when his first runner romped home at 16/1. And before the runners came under orders for the next he was up and downstairs from his room to the lavatory about ten times. Thereon one by one they all went down the tubes: fukt, fukt and fukt again. When it was eventually revealed to him that his bet had lost as usual he said: Bastard. Fucked again.

And we settled down to watch television or read books till the following Friday, tapping smokes from the lorrydrivers and the wee lady who helped out in the kitchen, once my tobacco and his dowps had finally run out.

Considering the amount he was punting I told him it was best to stick it all down on a single horse—possibly spending the whole of Saturday morning just studying form to pick out one stonewall certainty. That's a thought, he said.

Look what happened with that 16/1 winner! If you had just bet that by itself ye would have won a right few quid.

Charlie nodded.

The trouble is he didnt really have a clue about what he was doing. It was like he chose them with a pin. I tried to give him a hand. I was pretty decent on the formbook. The following Saturday I spent the whole morning huddled over the racing papers to come up with three possibles, any one of which I fancied strongly, and I mean strongly. If I had had enough to make a bet of my own I would have hammered it. No question. When Charlie came back from work he agreed about the chances of the horses I had chosen, and eventually he chose one. But only to include it in a permutation. There was nothing to say. That was just a sort of compromise. The horse ran in the first race, and finished second, only beat by the favourite. The thing had definitely been unlucky not to win, and not just in my opinion. But Charlie said: See what I mean? That would've been me fucked before I had even really started—just about!

No matter that his next four selections all finished well down the field. He reckoned the point had been settled.

I never made a similar suggestion. It did depress me though. He was the epitome of it all. It was like all the bad bets of a lifetime were walking about in that old good suit.

He knew nothing about horse-racing. Nothing. Yet week in week out there he was punting to the limit of his pocket. And considering the maintenance money he owed back in Scotland he was also punting to the limit of their pockets, his wife and three weans. He would not speak about that side of it. After the fourth pint one Friday evening I asked him about his family. Closed book that, he said, shaking his head.

A few weeks after his arrival he invited me for a game of snooker instead of crossing the road to the boozer. I had told him I liked playing and he did too, although he had not played for a while. We went to that good old club along Oxford Road. And without ever having seen me play, after we had tossed a coin for the break, which I won, he said: Make it for a pound eh!

I told him no. As usual I was skint. Apart from anything else I was relying on him to pay the cost of the table. Doesnt matter, he said. You can pay me when ye get the giro.

Next week, I said.

Okay, he said.

Charlie broke the balls and I won easily, that game and the rest. He was a very bad player. Five games we played in two hours which meant I had won myself five quid. I told him it was hopeless. I'm too good for you Charlie, I said.

He shook his head: Not really. I'm just an unlucky bastard.

Well I need to give you a start.

Get away, he said, I've never taken a handicap in my life. I'll win it back off you next Friday.

Next Friday I took him for another fiver, and each successive Friday was the same, until he left on a new sub-contract down in Folkestone. He played a mad game. Mighty swipes. No positional play. No potting ability. No nothing. Whenever he sunk a red this red would have cannoned off maybe half a dozen other balls and all of the cushions. It was pathetic.

And my own game soon degenerated to his level, although never quite enough to lose. But for the first time in my life I was beginning to consider throwing a game on purpose. I didnt though. It would have been too embarrassing—maybe even shameful.

On each break of each new game Charlie was setting out with this real possibility of winning. It was apparent in his approach to the table. When he messed a shot badly—and this meant not only miscuing but jumping the cueball off the table altogether through the unchannelled force of his damn shot—I was beginning to find it difficult to keep from laughing. This was the worst. While bending to retrieve a ball from beneath the table, or somebody else's table, I was having to remain below for an extra few seconds to set my face straight. It was becoming too much. Charlie just shrugged. His explanation was: Some fucking luck I'm carrying the night!

But I think he knew I was concealing the laughter. I was ashamed of it although there was nothing I could do so how come I was feeling like that. I gave him an ultimatum. Three blacks of a start, I said.

Never taken a handicap in my life, he said. When I do that I'll know it's time to chuck it.

Two Saturdays before leaving for Folkestone I landed quite a good turn in the betting shop. I passed him a tenner without saying anything. He promptly lost it on a further permutation. And next Friday he returned me the money. What's this? I said. That tenner wasnt a loan. I just gave you it.

He gave me a look. How to describe it? I dont know. He folded the tenner and stuck it into my pocket. Come on for a game, he said. I'm due to take you for a few quid.

Two hours later, with the weekly fiver tucked away in my hip pocket, I told him I was guesting him into town for the rest of the night. Maybe go up a casino or something, I said, fancy it?

Not me.

Fuck sake Charlie you've been buying me drink and keeping me going since you got here.

Doesnt mean I've got to go into the town.

The following day I gave him a tenner after the last race but still he wouldnt go into town so I went in by myself. I think it was because of his clothes. I kind of assumed he had some new good suit planked away someplace. But now I think that was all he had, that old one he wore to his work.

During the coming week I was inventing methods for not taking his money. On the Thursday night I had finished my tea and was sitting reading a book when he arrived back from work, a day earlier than expected. Off to Folkestone the night, he said. The job's finished here. A guy's coming to collect me.

Upstairs he went for a wash and a shave. He returned carrying a small suitcase plus the bag with his tools. After eating his meal he bade cheerios to the ladies and stuck his head round the lounge door, he tossed me a ten-pound note. I enjoyed playing that snooker, he said. Years since I had a go at it but. A wee bit costly.

Bellies are Bellies

It couldnt last much longer. I checked my pockets again, discovering the same two coins that had haunted me since Monday night. A two-pence and a one-pence. What could you do with them? Nothing. I also had the usual fruitless search for half-smoked cigarettes and butt ends and nothing. I went back to bed. How I had managed to survive the past four days! I needed a job I needed a job.

Calm down. I needed a job. This no money was a problem. How was one supposed to eat? God, how is one supposed to eat? I mean fair do's and all that pish.

I spoke out loud, that is how bad it was. Depression depression. Lying there staring at the ceiling then thoughts about that hotel up west; one I heard about that served meals to all their employees, plus all the ones working in these other hotels in their chain. There was a chain of them. You just walked in and that was you, you got served. No questions or raised eyebrows. No doubt when I got there it would have changed. Usually these things turn out to be shite, fairy tales.

But why not take the chance. Of course what it meant was having to leave this lovely, warm and tender, dirty, scratchy kip.

Still, it was worth it. I got out of bed.

It was so cold. Man. This was terrible. Why do landlords never supply proper central heating? Always these shitey old gas efforts needing coins to make them fucking work. Why not huge roaring logs burning and hot toddies. Danish blue cheese and french bread. Twenty smokes and a lassie. Oh man. They definitely did not care about their lodgers in this place. You could starve or freeze to death.

I was going to do a moonlight, that would show the bastard. Of course he would hang out the flags, old John, that was the kind of guy he was, miserable fucker.

My belly. Bellies are bellies. There was a cafe two streets away, the Rumbling Tum they call it. What a name!

Christ imagine having a right few quid. Maybe get a good place, a real good one, with fitted carpets and whatnot, refrigerators and TV sets. Easy to get a lassie then with a bit of comfort around. That's all you need, just a bit of damn comfort, instead of freezing all the time. The towel was like plywood. I lifted it and walked to the sink.

No, on reflection, why wash? The water would be ice cold. Could die of heart failure when it splashed the face. Why take the chance? Nobody would know the difference anyway.

I walked back and dressed fast before I froze to death. It must be great being able to put on a fresh pair of pants, maybe a T-shirt, a clean one, one that doesnt smell. Still, at least I can dress quite respectably on the outside. Thank God I couldnt find a pawn shop that accepted clothes. Imagine that, you'd be nude.

I had to get down to the launderette shortly, the socks too were beginning to crack.

I needed to look okay for this hotel. Imagine getting a knock-back? You get to the door and you walk across and some cunt graps you and chips you out man that would finish me, I would fucking kill him except except they are always big bastards, they just fucking sit on you. Worth it but worth it, chicken fricassaise or something, imagine that. Curried chicken with all the etceteras oh Christ man cups of tea, one during and two after. Perhaps somebody will offer a polite smoke afterwards, who knows, wanting a chat or something, like a cigarette? yeah thanks, dont mind if I do. Imagine it was a woman!

My hair was all over the place, seeing it in the mirror, Jesus Christ, screwing up my face and doing tricks with my eyebrows. I wet my hands and smoothed the hair down then left the room. I locked the door. One of the other tenants happened to be climbing the stairs, old Reilly, carrying a brush and shovel.

Well son, he said, got a start yet?

Why, no Mr Reilly. I have not got a start yet.

Why dont you try building sites. Ha ha. Always plenty of work going there eh?

I smiled. Yeah, that's a great idea, thanks, building sites, right. Might just do that.

Help get you back on your feet again, eh? Ha ha.

That's right, ha ha, it would put me back on my feet again. Ha ha.

Yes well, anyway, he smiled uneasily, got some cleaning to do eh! No rest for the wicked eh! Ha ha ha. He kept on walking.

Yeah hurry away ya miserable, Oh Mr Reilly . . .

He stopped and turned.

Eh could you spare a cigarette eh just I mean I havent had a chance to eh . . .

He frowned and then gave a long sigh but he took out a pack and gave me one of these ones with the long cork tip. He didnt say anything.

Thanks, ta, thanks Mister Reilly, thanks a lot.

He nodded and carried on. I waited a moment then went downstairs. I saw the piles of mail, piles of it. It was all shite. I left without checking. No point. If there was any it was bad news.

The Rumbling Tum. No toast please. Sorry, changed my mind plenty toast. Hot buttered, yes please, thick. Coffee or tea? One on top of the other. I'll balance the fucking cups.

I realized I had cheered up. How come I dont know. The smoke from old Reilly maybe. I would keep it for later. At least it was dry, supposed to be rainy. A rainy day. What was the day? Rainy. Ray-ni. Strange word, ray-ni, it is rainy, a rainy day.

Later later later. So too the bellies, one thinks of bellies. Bellies I have one. Imagine being a camel.

I enjoy walking.

Anyway, money was too scarce. Buses and subways, trains, fucking airplanes man boats, ferries and steamers. Rickshaws, fucking rickshaws. You push about a bogey. This big fat millionaire cunt sits on the bogey and you push him about. That is the job.

It was busy, people everywhere rushing about with all their places to go, here, there and everywhere scurry scurry. I was hungry too. One thinks about grub. The old grub. Imagine the grub. I know a place sells crispy rolls with mustard. What a combination! With coffee too it is something else, it is fucking something fucking else man. The sausage egg and bacon but one imagines the scene. No toast thanks just eh

Oh God please let me find a wallet lying on the pavement.

Hey look at the state of him man this guy coming along the road! Jesus Christ! Look at the gait, the gait, I wonder if that's the only nose he's got. If I had a nose like that man I dont know what I would do.

Take one look at me ya bastard and you'll need a new one.

Oh quite a nice looking lassie, hullo she's looking across. Wink wink, hey, wink wink. No response. Wink wink. Less of the wink wink shite man that is shit shit shit.

No response, no wonder. Thank you anyway thank you thank you thank you for not acknowledging it with a quirk of the lips, a friendly smile. Actually you are a hackit-looking bag, so there. Ha ha ha.

Jaysus look at the walk on her
do do do do,
do do do do,
the girl from Ipanema goes walking.

Good morning Astrud, I called.

Startled, hurrying away. Ah well at least you noticed me. The crack was a bit above your level anyhow. Sorry darling but there it is. Not your fault. It's me it's me it's me. It's me. I'm a slug, apologies apologies, slug.

Oh God. Oh. Thought that was a coin there, a pound. Couple of scones, packet of crisps. Ah never mind. Still though imagine having lived on Britain's green and pleasant land for twenty years and not a tosser to show for it, apart from the faithful three pence. No man, I definitely have to change my ways. I mean it.

And this time I did mean it. Really and truly I did. Get a job and a nice apartment man. Really go to town—do it all up—get a cocktail cabinet, that is a must. Cocktail cabinets. People talk about them. You see it in the fucking movies. Look at the cocktail cabinet! What is a fucking cocktail cabinet?

Bottles of Dimple and Drambuie, all the best gear. Brandy of course, vodka too and Bacardi for the women. One of those boxes containing at least a hundred cigarettes, all in their wee columns. The fridge of course, cheese and steak and ice cubes, crates of beer. Christ imagine it, ninety-six tailored jackets, thirty-four pair of the finest shoes, trews and Levis jeans, and Wrangler shirts—didnt have to be Wranglers, or Levis, man who gives a fuck I would take whatever, just a good-looking kind of . . .

I stepped off the kerb, right into a puddle for FUCK sake! And I shouted it loud, this deep deep hole in the road fucking puddle Jesus Christ man and stepping back out seeing the startled expressions of the shocked passers-by. God love us all, you step into a puddle the size of a loch, dirty filthy water and dogs' pish man getting over the tops of your fucking trainers soaking your feet and you cant even shout fuck in case you get fucking arrested. Ach. I'm sick of it. So so sick of it just sick of it really sick sick sick of it, all of it. I am talking about the fucking lot of it, just everything, everything, and my belly too, oink oink, that's the sound it makes, a pig searching for grub, a packet of crisps, a couple of biscuits.

It would never have happened if I could have afforded a bus. If I could afford a bus I would buy crisps instead, or a sandwich, bacon and fried egg.

Must get a job a job man a job, must get a fucking job, I needed one bad bad bad oh man what a life. Oh man, man man man this is really bad. I would be squelching and sliding in my shoes all day now. Even a pair of socks. How far was it to Blackfriars Bridge?

A woman!

Excuse me miss, how far . . .

But she walked on hurriedly. Women walk on hurriedly. What a look she gave me! An honest simple question. What is it with people?

A little crowd ahead. Waiting to cross the road. Traffic lights. You see the faces. Some of them are scary and some of them are

I dont know what they are.

God love us. At least my face isnt out the question. Imagine having one of these kind of—ugly, just fucking ugly, pot ugly. A guy in the place I stayed had one of the worst coupons you ever saw. He should have been on the fucking telly. With one like that I would jump out the window. Course he'll have money but that's the difference. God makes up for it. Ugly bastards get the dough. That's the balance. What do you want to be son, pot ugly or skint? I would go ugly in a minute if the money went with it.

Hell with it man.

Personality—ugly cunts have interesting personalities. That's what they tell ye on the fucking television.

Crossing over the road and a guy was smoking. Quick quick. I called to him. Hey, hey!

He looked at me like he was going to take a lunge. Big guy, he would have flattened me, if he had caught me. He fucking wouldnt have caught me but man I would have been offski, look at that flash, see him go, that would have been me. I had the cigarette in my hand and he spotted it. You got a light?

He stared at me. He wasnt used to people asking him for stuff. He passed me a lighter and stood watching.

Aw thanks mister thanks, thanks a lot. Thanks. Ta. Thanks an awful awful, that was eh thanks …

So grateful I nearly bloody kissed him. He carried on walking. Just as well. I took a big drag on it inhaling deep deep and into a fit of coughing, really coughing, snotters and fucking fucking knows what, uncontrollable man causing looks of concern from the onlookers and when I spat this lump of catarrh was so green and thick it bounced off the ground like a fucking golf ball.

Disgusting. The usual but it was just the usual. Maybe it was more than that. Maybe it was a warning. Maybe it was a sign of something, something worse. I would have to see a quack, fucking doctor quack. Quack quack quackety quackety. Jesus Christ but imagine dying of cancer at twenty-three it would make you sick. My old Grandpa died of cancer. Course he had a good long life, no complaints there, whatever age he was, seventy or something. But twenty-three? Malnutrition probably has something to do with it.

Have to pack this existence in. Start looking for a job, a proper job. Just the clothes, I needed the clothes. Maybe if I did do a moonlight. Serve that old bastard right for not helping me out. If he just let me

Ah shite, shite shite shite. My own fault anyway, me to blame. Old John man he wasnt that bad. It was me.

I cut down a side street for a change of luck. That

happened. Lo and behold an amusement arcade, Jesus Christ almighty. It was an old-looking place with a sunken entrance, and cobbles too—not too far from the river. I flipped the two-pence coin. Tails. In I went.

Ah the dog machine. This was that whatdyecallit word—fate! Fate. The two-pence coin was made for it. The Gods are in my favour.

Wondering what dog to back.

Hey! How come I'm the only punter in here? Maybe it's crooked. Never mind, crooked, who gives a fuck if the Gods are in your favour, the red dog, Trap 1, on you go.

Only evens of course but still, if I can do a three timer I'll have six pence, two more and it's a ten-pence silver coin, then on to the slots and the sky's the limit.

They're off running 3.36 and it's the six from two, three, one and four. On the one dog. Round the bottom bend it's three going on from two, four, one, round the final bend it's three going clear of two. On the one dog. Go on my son.

Ah bastard.

Always the same. When you're skint. It's just fucking the worst, the worst.

One pence left.

What a life. I shoved it back in my pocket. I heard a voice calling bingo somewhere in the depth of the arcade. All the senior citizens, lifelong losing bastards man the entire fucking bunch.

I walked over the bridge, stopping about halfway across to gaze upriver. I wonder what it'd be like falling in. Probably wake up in a lovely clean and warm hospital bed with a luscious nurse leaning anxiously over me. Big tits nudging my ears, saying things like Would you like a mug of steaming, piping hot coffee, liberally laced with black rum. Also a cigarette, a decent one, where ye can taste the fucking nicotine?

Well thank you, wouldnt say no.

The sky up above, deep and overcast, murky clouds. Any chink in the armour? A squeak of light. A fucking sunbeam? Come on God, I'm only asking for a couple of quid. I'm not a greedy guy it's just the belly, the belly the belly. Please make that old lady walking in front deaf and blind then let her drop some dough out her purse. I promise to note down her name and address and send it on later.

Jesus Christ the rain, the fucking rain, the bastartin fucking rain. Heavy too and getting heavier. Who cares! I shouted it. Who cares! My feet are soaking already, ha ha ha.

The State of Elixirism

Near the hut where I slept that night there was a brick-built barn. A tap fixed into the wall supplied drinking water. I drank then washed, collected a certain bag of possessions and departed swiftly, hoofing it along a narrow winding road banked by thick bushes and occasional small woods designed that the mansions and castles of superior persons be concealed from the gaze of the yokelled minionry of whom I was one, yea yea yea; three times wit the yea. A bird whistled. I answered the call. My answer went unheeded. Unheeded! Hey Mister Bird, why dont you fuck yourself! I looked to find this culprit with a view to killing it stone dead, and partaking of breakfast, instead discovering a lane. One cannot eat a lane and I was fucking hungry man I was fucking hungry. Pulling out the feathers, one pulls out the feathers. The hunger affects one. Such that pain, more of a discomfort, the stomach kind of—that like—what kind of pain is that? ach well who knows, one walks, though the road be weary. Down this lane and beyond a cluster of white-washed cottages a sudden flash signified a mirror, positioned that drivers might identify danger before exiting the blind-spot driveway. I was blinded a moment and blundered into a ditch

even blundering, what an act! I blundered. So human, so human. I am a human he screamed, prior to choking on his tongue, mistaking it for a slab of ox liver

where I spied a bottle of strong cider. A spectacular but by no means extraordinary turn of events: I once found two bottles of a not-inferior fortified wine.

But strong cider?

Nice.

I twisted open the cork and swigged, swigged and again swigged. Le cidre le cidre 'twas elixiric. I sat on the bank of the ditch. Whew. Man, but what a hit. Really, fuck, wow; the insides exalteth.

Prior to then my state had been somnambulistic, barely considering my life, not as a retrospective concern but as to how good it had become. It had become good. Really. This was incontrovertible, not given that one starves but as an effect of it.

I had to grin, sitting there on the grassy bank, the dampness a reminder. My bum is damp! ergo sum.

This area was devoid of lushgris which is my only name for these God-bestowed long stalks of grass that one tugs individually, and out each comes, the lower ends so so juicy.

I continued along the lane. Soon I found myself returned onto the narrow winding road, pausing now and again for a swig of le stoof. How had that happened? This was magic man, fucking magic. The experience. Yea, and thrice yea.

Yet a gap existed somewhere or other at the back of my mind while also a developing anticipation of finding a place for a genuine sleep, one of lying-down proportions. I refer here, for sociological purposes, to the notion of *phased sleep*. We have singular sleeps, magical sleeps, natural sleeps and honest sleeps, fitful sleeps, and false sleeps. A genuine sleep is one of lying-down proportions, and I stand by that. And when one refers to "finding a place" one, in general, refers to *the* place. There is only one. This is located, perhaps, on the grassy bank of a little fortified stream sited providentially for the weary wayfarer.

A strange land. Once upon a time I was familiar here, a familiar, familiar here and within. I needed a seat, oh God, a seat is equal to, is equal

The hedge at the side of the road had become less big and less thick while the tarred surface of the road softened beneath the strong sun, the smell reminding me of childhood days in cramped city streets. My feet had become hot, hot, very very hot and I had to sit quickly, again by the ditch, unloosening the laces and taking off my boots. Bare feet. I massaged my toes, Oh God in Whose Existence I do so believe. All of this. Existence. In toto. Conveyed by a sigh. Serenity has a place here, finds its niche.

I walked a few paces and entered a bower. Here were trees but sun rays entered. I had by then taken off my T-shirt and brought out the bottle. I sat down on the good earth and swigged the last of le cidre.

Oh.

The sounds of the country, the silences too, and the fragrance. I became aware of one sound, similar to the slow movement of a stream and turning to peer through the near bush I saw its glint a hundred yards off in a gully, the sun on the ripples, mild ripples. I gathered the empty bottle and stuff into the bag, knotted the laces of the boots together round my neck, and walked towards the gully. On the bank of the stream I spread the contents of my bag on the grass, awarding each article its own space. I was pleased and made to do something, whatever it was, maybe just sit down beside them and examine them or something, I dont really know, my stomach seemed to have risen, the internal diaphonous bag, the cider gurgling, bubbles up further, the gullet. Oh dear. Now I lay me down to sleep.

I did indeed, I lay myself down closing my eyes but spun off someplace and quickly reopened them. The spinning resumed. I braved it out, clinging on

The sense of late summer, a peaceful quality, days yet to come. Raising myself up, lying on my front, staring into the water. It was deep in places. Clear brackeny water; pebbles and rocks on the bottom, weeds moving gently in the current. So there was a current; these waters were not stagnant. Obviously I had to go in. There was no question about that. I needed to move within the water, whether to swim or not was irrelevant, I just had to walk in it, stand still in it. I picked a dozen of the juiciest docken leaves and laid them along the bank. I could use them instead of soap because of course I needed to wash, and seeing my feet, my toes in sore need of a wash, not just the feet man I was a smelly bastard, the undersides of my arms—what my granny called "tidemarks," Get rid of these tidemarks son, you will have to, sooner or later, later. Life's tide-marks, marks of the tide, of life itself. Life life life. Yet the undersides of these arms of mine! More than tidemarks. Dirty white streaks. Leftovers from my last job. What had that been? Jesus! What the hell was it? My last job! I had had to leave in a rush the day before yesterday, two days before yesterday, or was it three? Through no fault of my own it might be said, given one's temper can be frayed, frayed and these gaffers, managers and foremen. Farms may be factories, but I aint no fucking chicken.

Who cares.

I drapt the jeans and stepped to the edge, dipped in the right side toes. Freezing cold water. I submerged a foot. This foot, old pal of mine, I submerged it, seeing the hairs on my lower leg rise in protest. Old pal or not this gnarled extremity required the cold water treatment. I forced the foot down onto a flat rock amid the pebbly bottom then stepped in the other. The water rose to that knuckly bone beneath the knee. Cold, yes; freezing? I do not know except there was little feeling in these lower limbs of mine and the feet could have been cut and leaking blood, for all I knew, piranha too, plentiful in the land of Angles. These feet were numb and deadly white in colour. Too cold for comfort this water. I returned to the grassy bank, pulled on the jeans and sat, using the docken leaves on my feet, pressing the sap into them. I stretched out on the grass. I am a vegetable. Sap or blood. The sun had been hidden by a cloud of many layers but the last of these evaporated. I watched the sun revealed. The heat from it was quite amazing. I got an erection immediately in a most natural manner. The vegetable aspect of one's body. I sat up. This was no time for erections. Yet it maintained itself in spite of certain mental efforts. "Think of churches." Who gave such advice? Unless I dreamt it.

Guzzy, is there a word "guzzy"?

When I wakened

Thus had I dozed.

Was the heat greater now? Yes. Past midday too, and the sweat on my body! I slid down to the water's edge and onto my hunkers, resting there. I submerged my hands, my arms, ohhhh breathe in breathe in. I could sluice the water up under my oxters, over my shoulders, onto my chest, I cleansed my face and neck. My eyes closed; my eyes had closed. I was crouched there and motionless I was motionless I must have been motionless, but then gazing at the water, the lady's reflection, my eyes no longer closed. She was sitting on the other side of the stream, close by clumps of ferns, this lady. The bank rose higher here and the line of the stream slanted strangely that almost she lay out of my field of vision and may have assumed I did not see her. A stately and majestic country home or castle was located in the immediate vicinity. 'Twas her abode. 'Twas my conviction, wearing a summer dress of a kind favoured by all, having two little thin straps across the shoulders, Oh my Lady. Those straps may be thin but but for them the dress would collapse onto the ground, falling or crumpling in a heap at her feet and these feet might step out of such a garment. She was sitting with her knees raised, her elbows resting upon them, hands cupping her chin. And I did see her, truly I did and now of course pretending that I had not and again dropped my jeans, dipped both feet into the water until touching the pebbles, then I rose, pushing myself up from the bank. The water was cold and necessarily so, creeping over my knees, but not so cold as before; I stared into the water, concentrating on this, and waded a third of the way across. It was a little deeper now and I might have swam. Instead I returned to my own side and stepped out onto the grass maintaining the pretence that I was alone, leaving my jeans where they were and lying stretched out on my original place halfway up the grass slope, shielding my eyes from the sharp ray of sun. She perhaps would have thought my eyes closed but they were not and I could see her clearly enough, this beautiful beautiful lady, of indeterminate age. My legs had dried but the chopper was rigid and it would not go down and I thought to cover it with my T-shirt, yet seeing her shift position, her legs now outstretched and her hands underneath her thighs. I shifted my own position, laying my arms alongside the length of my body, closing my eyelids. I was waiting, I waited. A rustling movement, as of her rising and entering the stream, lifting her dress clear of the water, carefully stepping her way across, focused on the water alone as though in ignorance of me, then approaching from the stream, passing where my jeans were lying. She lowered herself down to kneel on the grass oh so carefully, lifting her dress that it flopped to cover her legs entirely, her hands lightly on my ankles, rustling the hairs over my knees and upwards to where the hair stopped on my upper thighs and they moved to each other, her hands, meeting together round my chopper, gently, but increasing the pressure until I had to flex strongly to withstand the firmness of her grip. When she released it imprints of her hands would remain on the skin. I stopped flexing. A mild draught, the wafting of her dress; she had risen and was standing, or had moved, kneeling closer to me. I needed to look at her, needed to see her, and if she had arisen her knees would have crisscross marks from the grass. Had she settled back, sitting on her heels? Perhaps I think perhaps, the unzip of her dress, it falling from her onto my feet, and her hands returned to my legs, moving upwards again but where they had come together previously they now parted, off from my body and onto the grass on either side of me, her wrists set firmly against the sides of my chest. She lowered her body until the top of my chopper touched the insides of her thighs, she moving forwards again until her face rested against my cheek, her tongue touching my lips, now her hands propping herself, manoeuvring herself, enclosing me, taking the weight of her body on her hands and moving slowly upwards, and down and now I thrusted and thrusted again but then was able to stop. Neither of us moved for several moments and when eventually we did we did together. I had raised my arms and placed them round her. We were moving together, we were. I marvelled at this. On it went and I knew I was smiling a true and honest smile. There are many types of smile and this was one such, there by the stream, my bag of possessions, thoughts of food.

Pieces of shit do not have the power to speak

Date of arrival: April.

Another dream laid waste.

I had prepared my defence but when the time came they gave me no chance to deliver it. I wasnt allowed to shave and my hair was in an unkempt condition. The Accompanying Officer showed me into court, told me where to stand and the proper way of standing. The Court Official read out the bare facts of the charges so rapidly I had little time to mumble your Honour, Lordship or Worship and wondered what term I was supposed to use hereabouts. Different authorities different formalities. The Court Official's speech consisted of rambling passages that degenerated into confused utterings. Then he added a bit on. I was to be kept in the cell for seven more days, then taken to the port of departure, set onto a boat and returned posthaste to the mainland. A clerk coughed. From local-government coffers a sum was to be settled with the shipping company such that a single fare might be purchased.

I smiled, a reflex action which only antagonized the Accompanying Officer. The fellow gripped my wrist forcibly once they departed the inner area. I allowed it. What else could I have done. I smiled again. I was going to speak, I said, I thought I would have had the chance to speak.

Didnt nobody tell you you're a piece of shit, pieces of shit dont speak.

I nodded. It sounded sensible.

I had to hold on to my jeans at the waistband, they

had taken my belt and my belly had shrunk. Skin and bone. When I lay on my back the skin at the front rested on the skin at the back. The cell entrance was ahead. Now. And I flexed my upper arm in preparation for the push in the back. When it came I went: Aaahhh! to improve the Officer's temper. Useless being a right-wing sadist bastard if naybody notices. He was a heavy lump of a man and could have knocked the stuffing out me. If he had caught me. What they call a big clumsy ox. I was wiry and slippery and could escape from tight corners. I also packed a punch. The Officer maybe inferred as much and gave me a lengthy stare. Just you try it buddy. Such was the guy's thought. Yet Accompanying Officers are also human beings. The doors closed solidly, with a juicy kind of thump.

I stepped back and sat on the edge of the palliasse. Here was reality and yes it was grim. A time for reflection, when fellow beings are excused scrutiny.

Later I felt better.

Too soon for a wank. It was to be used for sedation purposes only. Okay. I pondered the past days. My sorry luck; it had been so bad there was nothing to be done, nothing to be said. Bemoan it, then proceed. Life would continue even though I had been absented from it. But if this palliasse had been available to me a few days ago then I would have been okay. I patted it. You should have been mine, I said, I would've taken care of you, kept you warm in winter.

So I was talking to a bed, so what.

Yet a sigh was warranted. This was to have been paradise. The only thing better than not working was not working in a land of sunny climes. This was such a land, where young women tourists freely gave of themselves to local young males of unmanacled spirit, suntanned and with healthy limbs.

Why do suntans and healthy limbs enter it? The unmanacled spirit one can understand. Outdoor lives! I was thinking of those, where one could become fit and well, a lithe individual; maybe working as a beachguard. Once upon a time I could swim. If I escaped from the island gaol then certainly I might throw himself into the sea and thresh towards the horizon.

But really, I didnay want to be deported. Had the Court Official stated such categorically? Perhaps he meant something else. Ambiguity was a feature in small southern towns. Sure they had found me "lurking" beside the garbage bins down a "back alley." But all alleys are out the back and anyone found in such a byway is said to be "lurking." Come on now tell the truth and state the case fairly: Mr Duncan was sheltering from a gale wind.

I was. That was a hellish gale wind and no mistake. Sure I had the smell of alcohol on my breath. What in God's teeth was wrong with that? I was twenty-one years of age and beyond the age of legitimacy. It was my first day in the place and I had got ashore safely, safely. A celebration had been in order. Such behaviour was normal. What did "normality" mean in this here burg.

No job; okay. Abode there was none; okay. Cash ditto; nothing new in that. And no Verifiable Information as to Previous Whereabouts. So they said. Mr Duncan begged to differ. I did. I offered to verify anything, anything. To no avail. Then too, there also existed, and freely confessed: Bad Tidings from a certain Ship's Restaurant.

Such was the crime, such the criminal.

At 4:30 a.m. they had chanced upon me. My first day in the place. Two glaring flashlights inches from my eyes. Eighteen hours earlier could life have been rosier! Bestriding the upper decks in jaunty fashion bidding fellow passengers G'day.

Envious stares all round. I had been the only person left at the bar with a pint of stout in front of me. That was no sentimental nonsense. Truly the case. A six-hour sail had become a ten-hour battle through some of the worst seas the stewards had witnessed in fifteen years on the run. So they said.

Ah but it suited me. I was trying a new approach to life and so far it was working. It was simple. I had ceased being stand-offish. I was always interested in the lives of other people but in the past had looked on from afar. The idea of opening a conversation with a guy behind the bar would have been unthinkable, even more unthinkable that I would carry it forwards. But I persisted and the barman repaid me by blethering on about all manner of oddities, some boring, some not so boring.

At long last I was becoming a sociable animal. It was bound to aid my job prospects. I bought the guy a couple of black rums, then tried one myself. I sniffed at it firstly. Mm, an okay aroma. But the taste itself made me groo. The barman was relishing his. Black rum was a tradition, a fighting tradition. Besides being an old salt he was a decent guy and chatted away about life in general. He came from a wee island himself and had been raised to a life of easy servitude. He was even content! Tips were good and although a married man of somewhat advanced years, female tourists beckoned occasionally.

It sounded the thing to me. But were there vacancies aboard the boat? I was set to enquire but for some reason the thought of work vanished from my mind. I certainly fancied life as a sailor. On short trips definitely. But if pushed I would hire on for longer sojourns. On ocean-going vessels only. Above all they must be sea-worthy!

These ruminations were at an end when came an announcement. Last orders for the restaurant which soon would be closing.

But man man man I was starving! I had not noticed this until that very moment! This call to knives and forks had been announced for me and me only. There was naybody else left. I bade the barman G'day and followed my nose to midships. I had to hold on to bannisters and walls. The sea was going up and down to heights my fellow travellers found tricky and the floors were slippery with a mixture of vomit and the golden briny. But the God of Empty Bellies urged me on. Shipahoy, I was starving.

The place was empty. A waiter showed me to a table and passed me a sheaf of menu pages. I thanked him, nodded appreciatively at the listed contents then ordered a meal that plundered more than half of my entire life savings. But Gahd sir it was worth every coin. A three-course meal, plus a half carafe of casa rosa. The Starter I had was this: the **Chef Special with Prawns and Mussels and Choice Fruits à la Mer** and it came in a fishblood gravy—how else to describe it—with wee splashes of syrup at the side of the plate and a skinny trail of green peppery stuff. And thick bread to wipe it up; a sweet bread with a cake-like crust that one hesitates to describe as crust at all and yet as tasty a bread as ever succumbed to my advances.

I was not alone after all. Gadzooks. This reached the higher slopes of sentimentality. Two fine-looking elderly ladies were to the side of the room, having a laugh together, both tucking into whatever it was, marzipan jelly and devilled ice cream with marshmallow sauce, chocolate nuts and very thin, mint biscuits, onchontay madames. These ladies were French, à la chic chic

Meanwhile strong men crumbled, their bellies succumbing to the heaving seas. Why oh why did we have the last six pints of stout, they screamed to an uncaring hurricane! Or was it eight pints? Oh for fuck sake, Quick quick quick, was the shout, and which way doth the wild wind blow? Always spew portside. Such I had learned from a venerable sage of the sea.

Between courses I endured a moment's anxiety. Okay now my life had been short. Who could argue with that? Me!

I would have argued. It had been forever! But I had already ordered the grub so no way back. Sink or swim.

For the main dish I ordered another **Chef Special.** And never antagonize a Chef. We all know that. Chefs are unpredictable creatures in diverse ways when off-duty but not in the fucking kitchen.

But no Chef worth his salt ever disliked a trencherman. Any Chef worth his weight in biscuits was above and beyond the call of La cuenta por favor. For any creature such that that creature was a Chef, what occurred on the plate was the sole and overriding issue.

The strict course of action was to finish the plate and wipe it clean, to cry for bread and sook up the gravy. That gave one a head start. Sympathy would be mine. Whereas to order such a meal and dilly-dally with it! A veritable slap on the face. No Chef worthy of the name could endure the insult.

It was true. I knew it for a fact. I had experience of Chefs, having worked in a restaurant on three occasions, howsomever in a cleansing capacity, having failed to traverse the higher rungs of the cookery ladder.

For the Main Course, oh boy: **Halibut Steak in Basic Garlic Sauce, with Chargrilled Tomatoes and Okra.** Chargrilled tomatoes! A girl of a loquacious bent once advised me that along the Chargrilled vegetable route lay a cancerous labyrinthe, that once entered could only advance. What did I care. Plus a melange of thick red onions, red cobweb cabbage and chunky red peppers. Placed alongside this a pewter bowl with a further trio of vegetables: dark-green broccoli, blue-white cauliflower and slender green items that may have been beansprouts, peapods, or a luxury vegetable item rarely seen on workaday dinner plates and whose name seldom registers in the brain of such as oneself, to wit, me. Little wonder the two elderly ladies laughed so loudly. I waved across.

A waiter lingered by the ladies' table for a moment's conversation, poured tea from the pot. I noticed that the fellow's crisp white teacloth dragged from his elbow across the dessert plates. It must have been the roll of the sea for these waiters were top-notch servers, given they operated as gigolos on the side and were wont to exhibit a smug exhaustion. Of course I envied them. Of course I did. I was a personable young fellow. The position of gigolo was not beyond me.

Ah but a most delicious and succulent repast. The waiter now served me **Choice Cuts of Cheese and Rare Stuffed Olives.** One's compliments to the Chef. A brandy to follow would have been injudicious. On second thoughts

No. No second thoughts. Not even the cheese and Stuffed Olives. I moved to a leather seat by a porthole. The shutter had been drawn. I tried to push it up but it was set fast. It would have been too narrow to clamber through. I knew how to clamber through narrow apertures but this would have been impossible, certainly in consideration of the recent repast.

And alack alack alack oh, the waiter was presenting a la cuenta. He was of a kindly demeanour. I smiled and accepted the slip of paper. I folded it twice over without looking, slipping it into my pocket. I toyed with it for many minutes, unable to confront what could only be a disaster. Life had never been easy. Today was no different. I glanced sideways and roundabout.

And the porthole cover remained stationary. By a glazed display cabinet the waiter was reading a folded newspaper. By the upper-deck exit stood his uniformed colleague. I was on guard misooh!

Ach well.

Time certainly passed. Where had the elderly women gone?

I was in a state of extreme dolority, always a time for sore reflection. But what transpired during this time for sore reflection is anyone's guess. Did I faint? I was resting with my head against the side of the wall, on the other side of which raged a hostile sea. Maybe I dozed. I sighed and my breast heaved and my heart was heavy, and oh, all manner of self-castigatory musings were mine. My fuck. I couldnt afford the damn meal what in God's teeth was I to do may the decks open up and the seven seas swallow me oh Lord, for such would have been my fervent prayer had I been inclined towards such a course. Oh Maid de la Mer rescue me.

But no such rescue occurred. Reality had never been more stark. At last the light tap on the shoulder. I sighed and braced myself. It was more of a bad dream than a nightmare.

Both waiters were before me: We are approaching the harbour sir. The doors of this restaurant are closing, they are closed.

I have no money.

You cannot settle the bill sir?

I cannot, no.

They sighed.

I apologize, truthfully. I do not have the money. I over-extended myself. Is there a Catering Manager?

You have no credit card sir?

No.

It must go badly for you.

Is there nothing can be done? Your food was just so good and enticing I mean it was just so so good.

The waiters shook their head. It was apparent that what was happening had not been unforeseen. They had spotted me from the outset. They knew me for a risk. Och well. All to the good. Such was my conclusion.

I shrugged but my brains were going nineteen to the dozen as my grannie used to say. Where was my grannie now, now that I needed that venerable worthy? She would have gathered me unto her vast skirts and hidden me asunder.

The harbour police greet our arrival, said one waiter.

You will be handed over to them, said the other.

May I go to the upper deck until then?

Alas no, it is not permitted.

I nodded. Nothing was to be done. Once more I was afoul of the Fates. I closed my eyes and imagined stepping over bodies to the upper deck and outside, letting the wind blow the sweaty staleness from my clothes, the rain like buckshot, one's head bowed, the scalp spattered.

I again prayed. In an earlier time I prayed regularly to ward off evil and to bring material gain. How come I gave it up? Goodness me.

The storm abated. The small islands would have emerged from the heavy mist and torrential rain.

Soon the ship docked, the passengers disembarked; the two elderly ladies, the dishevelled and recovering stout drinkers, the lithe-legged female tourists.

I alone, I alone.

The waiters sat by the upper-deck exit. This left the lower-deck exit. I might make my way below, a speedy search for lost coins, lost bags and other properties. But this would be futile.

Life was beyond me. It had never been sweet. Adequate luck was all I sought; the occasional discarded, half-eaten jellied pork pie. But ah me, the stuff of dreams. I saw the waiters. One dozed. Had I tried a fly move they would have been instantly alert. Instead I called: Hullo!

They looked across.

I have discovered money! May I now settle the bill in full?

Yes, they said.

The difficulty is that it represents three-quarters of my entire life savings.

Ours also sir, we are a poor people.

On a previous occasion and in a different location I had

landed in a new town at the start of a new life with funds whose extension was negated by one coffee and a cheese and pickle sandwich. I thought to narrate this to the waiters. They would have been interested.

Nothing was to be done. My pockets were not vast. I brought forth the money and concluded the transaction. The waiters nodded me towards the exit.

Lubbers yawned as I stepped down the gangway. Apart from the boatstaff I was last man ashore.

I strolled the nearby streets and alleyways, familiarizing myself with the landmarks. Evening approached. I returned to the promenade and a small coffee stall, but it had closed. I moved to a pub and eavesdropped conversations, sipped long on water, hoping for reports on temporary abodes and immediate job prospects.

Then it was closing time. The barman was upturning chairs onto the tops of tables. The pub doors were open. I had to leave. My bag was at my feet. I lifted it and walked.

Later I settled myself on a bench, and tried to doze. But a hurricane appeared as from nowhere. I returned to the nearby streets and alleyways, seeking a likely place, a place of repose. Enter Officers with Flashlights.

Tomorrow the sun would shine, cooking the tar on the roads, upon which feet might squelch. On the walk to the beach an agreeable suffering. Of course posing along the hot sands, flicking grains of sand onto people's skin, stepping across brown curvy bodies, whither a one may rise and follow, an heiress searching for the simple unmanacled life, the sensual masculine animal to lead her and show her that which exists for the bolder imaginations, and how to take it without disturbing other souls, to spend that fortune wisely, seeking only happiness at a cost other than rippling waves, and so on, into the water. Enter Officers with Flashlights.

Ach well.

One day I would gaze back upon this escapade wistfully. Yes me hearties, this yere were the point my whole life did change.

I sipped at the mug of water. A uniformed fellow had brought me this mug of water. The Gaoler. He looked ages with me and was self-conscious, almost embarrassed. In another life we might have gone to the same school or else been a pair of coconuts on the same tree, if one believed in reincarnation. Some of these beliefs embraced the world of objects; former or future lives might include lower vegetative states. Fanciful but appealing. Coconuts too have a life. They hang beneath a clear sunny sky, sipping their own palm wine, gazing upon a placid sea.

The sex life of coconuts.

My ferry fare back to the effing mainland had been paid by the island authorities. I would have accepted half of that sum roundly and in the palm of my hand. It would have enabled me to go forth on a full stomach to seek work and sustenance. I would have accomplished the mission. Never no more would I have been a burden on the island citizenry.

Honest!

In the name of God's teeth it was surely bad sociological economics to deport me to the effing mainland. In days past such offers were surely afforded the more exotic beggar. And I was of that ilk.

Date of departure: April.

I aimed a kick at the palliasse but did not perform the action. Instead I flopped into the corner that had become my favourite. I once considered joining the regular army as an escape from reality. Now here I was.

Why had the Accompanying Officer not allowed me to shave and get my hair in order?

I belonged to that class of fellow whose existence antagonized a particular kind of older male. The Court had been composed of these Older Males. A "smart appearance" was always of the essence. Thus had the Court Official stared upon me, lips curling, nostrils flaring. He coughed three times before speaking, which denoted a grave conclusion:

Pieces of shit do not have the power to speak.

All aboard!

These and similar musings. I lay on a palliasse in a cell six feet long by six feet wide, or was this too a part of the dream? Would I awaken from this?

In the outside world people enjoyed living. The sun shone. The salty island air, the salty freshwater.

In the town dungeon, a young man of sound limb awaits a ship to points north.

Points north. I stopped talking, for I had been talking, not to an imaginary listener but to myself, hands clasped behind my head. Not a time for reflection. That too had passed.

The grey ceiling. Trails across it. These trails were silvery. Snails climb walls and cross ceilings. A snail with sturdy suction soles. The world be its oyster. No dungeons in snailworld.

You just pull the trigger

When I woke up the sun was already quite strong and it was clammy in the caravan; also it seemed like the midges had started biting. I had to rise. Chas was snoring in his bunk but in the other there was neither sound nor movement amongst the big heap of blankets. I gave up worrying about that a few days earlier. I struck a match and lit a cigarette. Time to get up: I shouted.

Chas moved; he blinked then muttered unintelligibly. I told him it was going to be another scorcher. He nodded. He peered at the big heap of blankets and raised a foot and let it crash down. An arm reached out from the blankets, it groped about the floor for the spectacles beneath the bunk. I picked them up. Then Sammy appeared with his other hand shielding his eyes. I passed him the spectacles and also a cigarette. When he inhaled he went into a coughing paroxysm. Jesus Christ, he managed to gasp.

Never mind, just think of the bacon and eggs, and these boiled tomatoes.

Chas had pulled his jeans out from underneath his bunk and was dressing. He glanced at Sammy: Some smells coming from your side last night.

Ah give us peace.

Chas is right, I said, this farting man, it's fucking ridiculous. I'm complaining to Joe about it.

Ah shut up. Anyhow, when you get to my age it's all you're bloody good for.

Chas grinned. A different story last night—you and that auld wife of yours, the way you were telling it! I could hardly get to sleep for thinking about it. Aye and I'll be saying what ye said next time I see her.

Sammy chuckled. Last time I let yous get me drunk. I'll no have a secret left by the time we get back to Glasgow. He tugged the blankets up over his shoulders. Me and Chas went to the kitchenette for a wash. When we returned Sammy was sitting up and knotting the laces on his boots, ready to leave. Ach, he said, I cant be bothered washing. I'll wait till we get to the canteen.

Clatty auld bastard, I said.

Not at all. It's to do with the natural oils son. That's how yous pair keep getting hit by the midges.

Rubbish, said Chas. Like the boy says, you're a manky auld cunt. Them blankets as well man they're fucking minging.

Why dont ye get a sleeping bag? I said.

Fuck the sleeping bag, said Sammy.

At least get a duvet. These blankets are fucking disgusting.

Sammy chuckled. Listen to the boy!

We parked the van in the place behind the canteen. Nobody was around. It was a Saturday, but even so, the three of us were always first into the canteen each morning. The woman smiled. As she dished out the grub she said, You lot were the worse for wear last night.

Aye, said Chas, what happened to that dance you promised us?

Dance! you couldnt walk never mind dance. You Glesga keelies, you're all the same.

Aw here wait a minute, cried Sammy. Less of that race-relations patter if you dont mind.

It's these teuchters Sammy, I said, they're all the same. Sooner we see a subway the better.

Away with your subways! The woman laughed, piling

the boiled tomatoes and bacon onto my plate. What're you wanting subways for?

I was drooling, not able to speak.

Chas chuckled. Never mind what we're wanting subways for!

Aye hen, grinned Sammy, you can do a lot on a subway!

Is that so! well just dont be trying any of that here. And are you going to the club the night?

Aye, said Chas.

We carried our trays across to the table near the big windows, lifted off the grub. Sammy said, I dont think I will go to the club the night.

Thank Christ for that! I said, slicing a piece of bacon and dipping it into the egg yolk.

Naw son seriously.

Chas winked at me. Dont count on it. He'll be there spoiling the night as per fucking usual.

Naw Chas honest. I'll have to take a look at the car. That bloody chinking sound is beginning to annoy me. Besides which, we're spending too much on the bevy so we are.

Ha ha, I said.

Sammy shook his head, speaking through a mouthful of grub. O Christ this food, it is bloody marvellous.

While he spoke me and Chas were covering our plates automatically. Sammy seldom put in his teeth this early.

I've got to agree with you, said Chas. It is some grub right enough. I've never eaten like this in my puff.

I snorted. I'll never know what yous pair got married for.

Sammy grinned. Will you listen to the boy!

After the second mug of tea we went back to the car to get the working-gear. When Sammy opened the door to the boot the smell of all the stuff hit us. First thing in the morning was always bad. The boilersuits we had had to borrow from the factory stores were stiff and reeking of sweat. Probably they had been left behind years ago by a squad of brickies.

Chas had slapped himself on the wrist suddenly, turned up the palm of his hand to show us the remains of a midge. Look, he said, a bit of fucking dust.

Aye Sammy, I said, we definitely need a tin of cream or something; what d'ye call it—repellent.

I'll see Joe.

O good.

Sammy frowned at me. Chas said nothing.

The chlorine tank we were stripping stood at the rear of the factory buildings, not far from the lochside. Its lining was being renewed. We had to strip out the old stuff to prepare the way. Guys would come in and do the new lining. The tank was about forty feet high and about eighteen feet in diameter. A narrow walkway separated it from a factory outbuilding. On the top of the tank was small outlet through which the scaffolders had passed down their equipment. There was also a small tunnel at the foot which us three had to use. It was quite a tight fit, especially for Sammy. He wasnt fat, he just carried a bit mair weight than Chas. I was quite skinny.

To allow us maximum daylight the scaffolders had erected the interior staging with minimum equipment. Generated light was also necessary. It would have suited us to have had the maximum scaffolding stuff rather than extra daylight. The platforms on which we worked were spaced about eight feet apart. When we finished stripping a section of old lining we had to shift the planks and boards up a level and make it safe to work ourselves. Nobody was doing it for us. It was safe enough, we just had to be careful. The tank was circular and that made it worse. The platforms couldnt cover the entire eighteen feet. Chas had spotted a potential problem in connection with this. It was a bevel in one side. He had pointed it out to us the evening before.

While he went off to switch on the compressor I fiddled around with the air-hoses, giving Sammy a chance to sneak on ahead into the tunnel. Somewhere inside was where he planked the chisels and stuff. He was a bit neurotic about thieving and wouldnt tell us where he stashed them. That was the kind of job it was, ye had to steal the tools ye needed.

It was a fair climb to the section we were on. One of the snags was this continual climbing. The chisels kept on bouncing out the hammer nozzles and it seemed like it was my job to go and get them, and when they fell they clanged their way down to the bottom. Once Chas arrived I adjusted the end of the hammer onto the air-hose, fixed on the chisels then one by one we triggered off.

Half an hour later we stopped. Earlier in the week I got a spark in my right eye. While along at the factory's first-aid I discovered we were not supposed to stay in the chlorine tank any longer than thirty minutes. After that we required a quarter of an hour break in the open air. It was them that said it, not me.

Sammy had gone off to make his morning report by telephone to the depot. Back at the lochside he explained how Joe had been unable to drive up yesterday. They had needed him for an urgent job. But he would definitely arrive sometime today.

Is that all? I said. What I mean is did they no even apologise?

Aye, what would've happened if we were skint! said Chas.

Well we werent skint.

That's no the point but.

I know it's no the bloody point. Sammy sniffed then nudged the spectacles up on his nose a bit. The trouble with you son you're a Commie.

Naw I'm no, I'm a good Protestant.

Sammy snorted. After a moment he said, I could always have seen that whatsisname, Williams, he would've subbed us a few quid.

Aye and that'd be us begging again!

He's right, said Chas. How come we've got to tap everything? They must be sick of the sight of us in this fucking place. Fucking boilersuits and breathing-masks by Christ, midge cream, we're never done.

Aw stop your moaning.

Chas sighed and shook his head.

Heh Sammy, I said, you definitely no going to the club the night?

None of your business.

Chas smiled. Course he's going. Saturday night! Dirty auld bastard, he couldnt survive without sniffing a woman.

Ah well, said Sammy, nothing wrong with sniffing. And I'll tell you something . . .

We know we know—when you get to your age it's all you're fucking good for.

Sammy laughed.

Joe turned up in the afternoon, during one of the breaks out the tank. We were at the shore, skliffing pebbles on the surface of the water. The last time Joe came we had been standing gabbing to one of the storemen, and it was pointless trying to explain about conning the fellow out of a couple of new boilersuits. Joe never heard explanations. His eyes glazed over. That was how it was when we spotted him walking towards us. Sammy made a move as though to meet him. I whispered: I'm going to tell him.

Sammy nodded. Chas said nothing. I called to him: Heh Joe, the first-aid nurse said we were supposed to get a quarter of an hour break after every half hour.

Joe looked at me.

Half hour on, quarter of an hour off. Because of the fumes, I said, the chlorine and that. It's contaminating our inners.

Huh.

Sammy shrugged. That's what she told the boy.

Is that right . . . Joe had a cigarette out, striking a match. He inhaled and chipped the match into the loch.

I've no made it up, I said, that's what she told me.

Joe didnt reply, he had glanced to the side and was peering across the loch where several small boats were sailing north, the gannets flying behind and making their calls. Joe waited a few moments, he sniffed and glanced at his wristwatch, glanced at Sammy. Fancy showing me your bevel? he said.

Aye Joe.

They walked up the slope. Me and Chas waited a bit before following. Then Joe went off alone and Sammy paused for us to catch up with him. He's away to see if whatsisname has arrived yet, that what-d'you-call-him . . .

Williams, said Chas.

Aye. He's supposed to be coming up to see the bevel.

Chas grinned. He didnt like seeing us hanging about.

Well we werent hanging about, I said, we were getting a break from the fucking thingwi, the chlorine.

Sammy had pulled a rag from the pocket and wiped his brow and neck. He wrapped it round his head like a sweatband. Must be hitting the eighties, he grunted. I'll tell you something, we're better off in the fucking tank.

What did Joe say about it? said Chas. Did he say anything?

What about?

The bevel.

Aye. Him and Williams are going to have a look.

Heh Sammy, I said, D'you notice the way he went *your bevel; your bevel*. As if you had put it there.

Ach its just his way.

I bet you he asks that cunt Williams about the quarter of an hour break.

No danger, said Chas.

It wouldnt surprise me if he knew about it in the first place, I said, just forgot to tell us.

Aye, said Chas.

For God sake! Sammy halted; he turned and glared at us.

Well no wonder Sammy, sometimes he treats us like the three fucking stooges.

The boy's right, said Chas. I notice he's no saying nothing about the wages.

They'll be in his bloody car.

I mean it's Friday.

I know it's fucking Friday Chas.

He's scared we're going to nick away for a pint.

Jesus fucking Christ. Sammy shook his head, nudged the spectacles up his nose. He turned and strode on to the tank. We watched him crawl inside the tunnel entrance.

Chas shrugged. We've upset him now.

Ach, no wonder. The quarter an hour isnt even up yet and here we are going back in. Joe's taking the piss out him.

He's no really.

Aye he is. How come he's still climbing scaffolding at his age? He should be permanent down in the depot.

He likes being out on the road. Come on—we better go and show the auld cunt we still love him.

Sammy was pounding away with the hammer. He ignored us while we were preparing our stuff. Finally he switched off the power. About bloody time and all, he said, I thought yous had went for a pint!

How could we! I said. It's your fucking round!

The boy's right! Chas laughed.

Sammy shook his head and turned back to the wall of the tank again, and triggered off. Chas winked at me. We worked on steadily. Then without having to ask I knew we were past the half hour. I saw Chas pause to demist the goggles he wore. He adjusted his breathing-mask and shrugged when I gestured at my wrist. We continued with the hammers. About five minutes later I looked to Sammy but he was battering on. Another five minutes and the signal came from below. Then somebody was climbing the scaffolding—the two of them, Joe and Williams.

We were four stages up. We stopped work when they got there. Sammy showed them the bevel. Me and Chas sat down on the platform. We could hear snatches of their conversation. Williams said something about Monday being a Bank Holiday and Chas chuckled quietly. I fucking knew it, he whispered, we've knocked it off.

What d'you mean?

He whispered: You still fancy having a go at the Ben?

Fucking right I do—climbing it ye mean? Aye man absolutely.

Chas winked.

Heh, heh yous two! Joe was calling. We got up and climbed to the next platform. He and Williams stood beside each other. A couple of yards away Sammy stared at the platform floor. Joe gestured us closer and said, I think we've got it beat. Look ... he pointed at a couple of planks. See with they planks there Chas, one on top of the other: if you and Sammy stand at the bottom end, yer hands on the scaffold tubes, yous will balance no bother and the boy'll be able to go out. It's only a couple of steps, he'll reach it from there. It's just that one bit.

Chas frowned.

Look ... Joe stacked the two planks and pushed them out from the platform, narrowing the gap. See?

Chas was still acting baffled. Joe looked at me and I knew what he meant. Chas and Sammy would stand on the planks to take the weight at the back while I went out on the front bit. Their weight would keep the two planks steady. The scaffolding was there too so they could grip the tubes with their hands. Joe and Williams were watching me. I kidded on I didnt know what they were meaning.

See son ... Joe was waving at the gap between the platform and the side of the tank. If you're on the planks there you'll make it to the wall easy, you'll zap that lining no bother.

Williams spoke to Chas. The thing is with your weight, he said, the two of yous. You and Sammy. Yous make four of the boy. Five!

Williams chuckled and he glanced at me. Know what I mean son, them two big bastards! I'm no calling them fat! But if they stand at the bottom end of the planks they'll no budge an inch! You'll be able to reach in at the wall, easy.

Joe said to Chas: What d'you think?

Williams said to me, Eh son? Think ye could manage?

Eh . . . I looked at Sammy.

It's just that one wee bit. It will save us good time. Williams turned to Sammy: What about yourself Sammy what do you think?

Ah . . . Sammy frowned, shaking his head slowly, and half turned to Joe. I'm no too sure, being honest.

Joe said, The boy's quick but Sammy he's good on his feet.

I think it'll work fine, said Williams. We could use three planks if you want.

O naw naw, three planks will just spread, it's got to be two.

Right, aye.

Joe looked at me, and Chas: What d'you reckon Chas?

Eh . . .

Worth a try but eh? Eh young yin? Joe said to me, What do you think? Could we give it a go?

Eh I dont know, I suppose I mean . . . I glanced at Sammy who was staring at the platform floor.

I've got a suggestion, said Williams. What weight are you son?

I'm no sure.

What weight d'you think I am?

I dont know.

I'm twelve stone two. A good bit heavier than you.

Williams gestured at the two planks, turned to Sammy and Chas: Yous two stand at the back there.

There was a moment's silence.

Seriously, said Williams. Go ahead. I'll stand at the end myself. The two of you to balance me.

Make it the three of us, laughed Joe.

Ah well! Williams chuckled, patting his belly. He said to Sammy, What d'you say?

At least give it a go, said Joe.

It's no the same, I said.

No, I know it's no the same.

Ye see it's the hammer, said Sammy, It's the hammer Mr Williams—once ye trigger it off, the vibrating and that and like how you're putting yer weight for the force.

Aw I know.

Its different from just standing, I said.

Williams smiled at me. He said to Joe, I'll give it a blast with the hammer while I'm out.

Joe nodded.

After a moment I said, It's no the same.

Well we're no saying it's the same.

I just want to see how it works, said Williams.

Joe said to Sammy, What do ye think Sammy? Will we go it a go?

There was a moment's silence. Then Sammy shrugged. No harm in seeing how it works, he said. He sniffed, shifting his specs up his nose; he scratched at the side of his ear. Come on Chas ... He waved me forward too. I hesitated. Sammy said, You too son, you go in the middle. Chas at the back, me at the front.

Joe passed Williams one of the hammer-guns with the chisels already fixed onto the nozzle. Eh Tom, you ever worked one before?

Williams smiled. Dont tell me—you pull the trigger! He took the hammer, checked the chisel was firm in the nozzle, that the end of the air-hose was securely attached to it, then he gave it a short burst, and again. He glanced at the three of us on the planks, then stood at the front end close to the edge of the platform. He called back to us: Okay?

Fine, called Sammy.

Williams manoeuvred his way forward, beyond the edge and out over the gap. He stood steadying himself, Good, he said and brought the hammer up, nudged the chisel in on the lining and triggered it off, the planks spread and we lost our footing, the hammer-gun clattering and Williams yelling but managing to twist and get half onto the edge of the platform, one hand grasping a scaffold tube. His mouth was gaping open and his eyes wide wide.

Sammy and Chas were already to him and clutching his wrists and arms, then me and Joe helping. When he got up onto the platform he sat for a long time, until his breathing approached something more normal. Nobody spoke during it all. His face was really grey. Joe had taken his cigarettes out and passed them round again. It wasnt allowed but we were having one anyway. When he had given Williams a light he said, How you feeling Tom?

Williams nodded. We continued smoking without speaking. Eventually Williams said, Think I could do with a breath of fresh air.

Joe nodded. The four of us climbed down the ladders. Williams was still shaky but he managed it okay. He crawled behind Joe out of the tunnel. Sammy went next then me then Chas.

Outside the tank I saw Joe and Williams walking towards a door at the side of a building. I was going to say something but I didnt. Me and Chas exchanged looks but there wasnt anything to say.

We were down at the lochside when Joe reappeared. He distributed the wages and subsistence money. While we checked the contents against the pay-slips he peered away towards the far coast of the loch. The mountain peaks were distinct. Below the summit of the highest peak a helicopter was hovering. Joe watched it for a time. Good place this, he said.

Full of tourists but, said Sammy. Can hardly get moving for them. Dutch and Germans.

Joe nodded, he lit a cigarette. Pity about that fucking bevel, he said, eh?

Aye, said Sammy.

We'll no get the scaffolders out till Tuesday at the earliest. Probably Wednesday . . .

Aye.

Puts us back.

Sammy nodded. Then he sniffed. Mind you Joe, he said, there's a fair bit of clearing up we can be getting on with. There's piles of that fucking what-d'ye-call-it, that stuff we've stripped.

Joe inhaled on the cigarette. It's a nuisance but.

How's thingwi, whatsisname?

Aw he's fine. A bit shaky.

Sammy nodded.

Heh look at that! Joe was suddenly pointing out to where a motor launch and a water-skier could be seen. Christ sake! he said, look!

We sat watching the water-skier for a long while.

At last Joe glanced at his wristwatch. He turned to us: So where is it the night? the social club?

Nah, said Sammy, fucking van Joe, its acting up again, I'm going have to get underneath it. I think it's the starter motor, I'm no sure.

Joe nodded.

What about yourself?

Aw! The time I get back down the road . . . Joe glanced at his wristwatch. Okay Sammy, he said, mind and phone in as soon as the scaffolders arrive.

Will do.

We watched him walk away. We continued sitting there, just smoking, not talking for a while.

Naval History

I met them in the doorway of a bookshop up the town, just as I was leaving. They were absolutely delighted to see me. Alan and Sheila; I hadnt been in touch with them for years. It was fucking embarrassing. She put her arms round me and gave me a big cuddle and then planted a big kiss on my lips while he stood to the rear, a big beaming smile on his coupon; then he shook my hand. Heh steady on, I said.

Ach but James it's really good to see you.

James? I said. What do ye mean James?

They both laughed at that. Come on into the shop, said Sheila.

I'm just out.

Aye I know you're just out, she said, but come bloody back in. Even just for a minute.

Are you insisting? I said, trying to get my face muscles into a relaxed condition.

You're damn right we're insisting! said Alan, gripping me by the shoulder and aboutturning me.

I'm a small-sized bloke so this kind of thing happens too often for comfort and I shrugged his hand off. He apologised, but smiled as he did so. I fucking hate people doing that, I told him, making a point of brushing my shoulder.

Aye, you've no changed!

Of course I've changed, I said, then I smiled: For a kick-off I'm baldy.

You were baldy the last time we saw you, said Sheila.

Was I?

Aye.

I just looked at her although I found it hard to believe. People have a habit of throwing things at you about your past in such a way that makes it seem like they're making this great statement which unites all our experiences into one while at the same time they dont really give a fuck either way, about the reality, how things truly were, whether you were baldy or had a head like Samson and Delilah. You dont need this kind of thing even when it's genuine and this definitely wasnt genuine. Plus these days I find it difficult getting enthusiastic when I meet old acquaintances. I dont know what it is, I just seem unable to connect properly, I can never smile at the proper places—it's like a permanent condition of being browned off with life. And no wonder either, when you come to think about it, with cunts like this always interfering.

Soon the pair of them had started dragging me round the place. They led me to a display table where they picked up a huge big tome. And landed it on my forearms. I couldnt believe it. It was like an absentminded fit of idiocy. I tried to snatch a glance at the title but they led me off immediately, him propelling me by the shoulder. They started lifting other books from here and there, piling them on top of the first one at a fierce rate with this crazy fucker Alan insisting I dont say a word and each time I tried to he did this stupid fingers-into-the-ears routine with big laughs at his missis, it was like a nightmare, me wondering if I was about to wake up or what. I gaped at him, unable to open my mouth for a couple of seconds. I managed to speak at last. I dont know what you're fucking playing at, I said, but one thing I do know, I dont fucking want them.

Ah come on! he laughed.

What ye talking about come on?

They'll be good for your home study.

My home study?

You need them, said Sheila.

Do I fuck need them what you talking about? Then I managed to spot a couple of their titles and it looked as if they were naval histories. Naval histories! I said, trying to keep my voice down, What you giving me them for? You think I'm a fucking naval historian? I mean look at this! For christ sake! RECOLLECTIONS OF A FIRST LORD OF THE ADMIRALTY. What would I want to read that for! And look at this yin ...

It was MISTER MIDSHIPMAN EASY. In the name of god, I mind my auld man and my big brother reading that when I was about five fucking years of age. And then I almost collapsed. What's this! I said, trying to keep my voice down. It was two more books they were trying to land me with: big glossy efforts. Hollywood movie-star photographs. What the fuck's going on! I said, this is definitely a nightmare. Katharine Hepburn and Humphrey Bogart. What yous up to?

Sheila replied, We're no up to nothing.

Aye yous're bloody up to something alright.

Alan sighed in an exaggeratedly amused way; as if we had always been great mates and he understood me from top to bottom. You're a failed scholar, he said, a failed trades union organiser, plus you're a failed socialist.

Dont be fucking cheeky.

More important, he said, you're skint, and we know you're skint. We bumped into Willie Donnelly yesterday morning and he told us.

Who told you?

Enough of the nonsense, said Sheila. And anyway, if that girl behind the counter knows what ye do for a hobby, she'll give you a good discount.

What d'ye mean what I do for a hobby, what ye talking about now?

Are ye no still writing your wee stories with a working class theme?

My wee stories with a working class theme . . . Do you mean my plays?

I thought it was wee stories.

Well you thought wrong cause it's plays, and it's fucking realism I'm into as well if it makes any difference.

It'll no matter, said Alan with a wink. As long as she knows ye write something plus if you give her a nice smile.

Do you know who you're talking about, I said, you're talking about Sharon! Sharon . . . I glanced quickly across at the counter to see if she had heard. Lovely Sharon! Beautiful lovely Sharon who wears that tight black T-shirt!

Fucking joke man you're crazy, the pair of yous. I stared at him: You must be a headcase, and I'm no kidding ye. That's Sharon you're talking about. A nice smile! What do ye think this is at all a fucking charity shot man this is a fucking classy bookstore and she's a fucking classy woman. Christ! A nice smile! Give her a nice smile! A lovely lassie like that! Look, in the first place I dont want the bloody things. There isnay a second place.

Rubbish, says Sheila, who are ye trying to kid? Then she smiled at Alan: He thinks we dont know!

Alan grinned. And he added, So that's okay then James . . .

Okay? It's not fucking okay. It's not fucking okay at all. Forget that James stuff too. Come on, take these fucking books out my arms and let me go. Christ almighty yous've landed me with at least fifteen here so it's going to cost a bloody small fortune.

Aye but they're a surprise, said Alan, plus you'll like them. I know you'll like them, because you always did.

I always did?

You were aye the same, back when we were weans the gether.

You're actually mixing me up with somebody else I think. Unless you're just trying to annoy me.

He's no trying to annoy you at all, said Sheila, poking

me on the side of the arm, and I had to step forward to balance the books and stop them falling:

Heh watch it, I said, careful.

Well he's no trying to annoy you.

That's a matter of bloody opinion because I think he is. And I dont know either how you wanted to butt in there and poke me Sheila because it's no got fuck all to do with you there, that last sentence, the statement I made to him because if it had been intended for you I would've fucking done it like that, I would've addressed myself like that, to you I mean.

Sheila grinned. You've definitely no changed!

I stared at her. I've totally changed. Totally. I kept on staring at her because one of these funny wee mental things had happened in my nut where the word totally was sounding like it had changed its meaning or something and if I had been working at the typewriter I'd have probably knocked over the fucking tipex bottle—and what was the name of the guy that sang the I Belong to Glasgow song? Because for some reason this is what I wanted to know at that precise moment. Then I was speaking:

Since yous two knew me, I was saying, since yous two knew me . . .

Sheila was nodding, encouraging me to speak on.

I breathed oxygen into my lungs to get myself ordered. Not only have I went totally baldy, I says, I'm divorced. Mary chucked me in for another man.

Mary chucked you in for another man . . . said Sheila in a loud whisper. My God!

Who did she chuck you in for? asked Alan.

After a moment I told him: That eedjit McCulloch.

McCulloch! He laughed out loud then shook his head to put a check on himself. He calmed down and frowned man-to-man. James James James. But that's serious eh? And he winked to destroy any semblance of genuine sympathy.

I dont really know what yc mean, serious. And to be honest with ye, and you as well ... I said to Sheila, I dont know how come yous are calling me James all the time; friends call me—well, I'm no goni tell you what they call me. You know what I'm talking about.

The pair of them looked like they were bewildered. I carried on speaking. Aside from that, being divorced and all the rest of it, I've given up all habits of the flesh; that includes alcohol, cannabis, marijuana, masturbation as well. I'm probably heading towards that strange state Charles Dickens mentions once or twice to get himself out of plotting problems, internal combustion.

Internal combustion? said Sheila.

Aye. He was a novelist but. I'm a playwright. Know what I mean, I'm involved in drama. Drama. Because according to yous pair I'm no, I'm a naval historian or some fucking thing, a compiler of Hollywood movie-star bio-pic photographs—mildly titillatory as well by the looks of these cover designs. But it's the naval histories that are the worst, I've never been interested in them in all my entire puff. And in some ways I should take it as an insult that that's what yous think of me because enormous tomes like this smack of an unhealthy fascination with the trammels of empire building and as you were so ready to point out a minute ago Alan, my concerns have aye been communistic at the very right of it, to put it fucking mildly.

Alan smiled. Ye aye had a good sense of humour as well.

Did I?

Aye.

You could've fooled me.

Well it must've been somebody else then.

Exactly.

Somebody awful like you.

Aye. Maybe the guy that saved up books on naval history for a hobby. And I stared at him so he knew I was not kidding.

Behind him I could see Mr Moir who managed the bookshop gazing along at us. This was all I needed, my credibility destroyed completely. Look, I said, I would be grateful if yous took all these books out my arms and I'll help yous return them to their proper places. Honest, this is like a bad dream.

I leaned closer to them both and whispered, It's my favourite bookshop. I sometimes get reductions ... Aye, you're right, the lassie at the desk does know that I write plays. I think she does honestly like me although I dare say she probably just expects me to die young or something and it's romantic, like what she expects out of literature due to the influence of some totally fucking crazed teacher of English. She waits till Mr Moir goes off somewhere else and then I go up and get my purchases weighed in at maybe thirty-three and a third off.

Jammy bastard! whispered Alan. I knew that was how it'd be. You were exactly the same when you worked on the buses, that wee bird you were shagging over in Gartcraig Garage, mind?

I gaped at him.

I hate that word, Sheila was saying with her eyes closed, it's really ugly.

I looked at her. Come on, my fucking arms are falling off. Get these fucking books off or else I'll have sprained wrists—my tendons have been inflamed for years, fucking tenosynovitis.

Having sex with I meant to say ... said Alan to Sheila, Sorry love ... then he winked at me.

Everybody knew! said Sheila, smiling. When yous waited in the office for the last staff bus and then never sat the gether, and then yous aye got off two stops separate as if we didnay know yous were going to run into a close as soon as our backs were turned and the bus was out of sight!

Randy buggers! winked Alan.

And then Sheila started that laugh she did—she was

famous for it—a hoo a hoo a hoo, a hoo hoo hoo; that was the way she laughed, it would have drove you fucking potty.

Yous two are crazed eedjits, I said, that wee so-called bird you're blethering about me shagging was Mary, the woman herself, her that walked out on me for this dirty evil bastard that she walked out on me for and I'm not a guy to go over the top, if you ever knew me at all you must at least credit me with that. And if her brothers get me I'm a dead man.

Her brothers . . . ?

Her brothers, aye.

Ye talking about McCulloch? said Alan.

What? I'm talking about Mary, my Mary, my fucking ex-wife—scabby bastard. Her team of brothers, I said, they've been after me for fucking weeks.

Aw her brothers . . . Alan nodded, then frowned for a moment: Did they used to play for Brigton Garage?

Back in the bygone days, aye.

Dont start talking football, muttered Sheila.

Alan was watching me. If it's the same ones I think it is then you're in trouble.

Thanks.

Naw but I mean it, fucking bruisers they are, bad news.

Bad news, I know they're bad news, they're evil bastards, that's what I'm saying. Christ almighty. And if I didnay know I was so fucking paranoiac I would think yous were here plying me with these enormous big tomes just to weigh me down, because ye know her brothers are outside waiting to waylay me, hiding up a fucking close or something, and I'll no be able to run.

That's no funny, said Sheila.

I stared at the two of them. I could easily convince myself this was precisely what was happening. Here they were helping Mary's brothers. It was a set-up. They were here to do me in. Bastards, I might have fucking known. Fate at last.

And I want to buy these books for you as well . . . Sheila was saying, honestly James I mean it, as a present for old times' sake. Especially if you and Mary are divorced. That's a sin. When did it happen?

I studied her without saying a word. There was something up here and my memory was trying to warn me.

Eh?

I waited before giving her an answer. Five month ago . . .

Five month ago! She shook her head. That's hard to believe.

I kept on studying her.

Hard to believe . . . she murmured, glancing at her man.

Mind you, I says, I would've thought you'd have knew already, being as how yous two were supposed to be so fucking close and all that Sheila, friends I'm talking about, you and Mary, confidantes and all that if I recollect certain parties we attended in a mutual capacity. And I'm talking about you as well Alan unless you've fucking spuriously forgot.

Listen, he said, and I'm being honest, if these headers are waiting outside then you'll need all the help you can get. And I do mean handers James handers. Alright? That's all I'm saying.

What?

You've got a hander, I'll hander ye.

Thanks but no thanks.

Dont be daft.

I fight my own fucking battles.

My Alan's a good fighter, said Sheila and she gave me a funny look.

I know he is. I'm just saying I fight my own battles, that's all.

Sheila's nose wrinkled: Well you aye did do didnt ye.

What's that supposed to mean? I said. But I knew fine well the one thing it did mean; Sheila didnay like me and probably never had liked me. She probably thought I had been a bad influence on Mary, because aye, the more I came to think about it, these two had definitely been close—whisper whisper whisper! Thick as fucking thieves was a better way of describing it.

Sheila was talking. And then she stopped talking, right in the middle of the sentence. As if maybe Alan had gave her a signal. I tried to think what it was she had said but I couldnt. The next thing Alan says: Come on and we'll get you some more books James, especially now if this wife of mine's going to be doing the buying. Ye know what like she is with money!

Naw, I said, no way, leave me alone, I want nothing to do with this.

The pair of them stared at me.

Cut it out, I says, whispering, and I glanced from them to the cashier's desk and then to the exit, wondering if I could make a quick dash for freedom, because there was definitely something no right about this. But there was Mr Moir watching me with a funny look on his countenance so I had to speak just to be seen to be acting naturally. I'm finished with all that personal stuff. I says to Sheila, trying to give her a smile but failing: I'm finished with it, women, yous just do my fucking nut in, I just cannay work yous out at all.

Heh steady on, says Alan.

Steady on nothing, I says.

You're a bad-tempered so-and-so, muttered Sheila, no wonder Mary left you for Tommy McCulloch.

Ha ha ha, I said. And Sheila gave me a such a look I thought for a minute she was going to wallop me one so I stepped back. Right that's enough, I said, that's just bloody fucking enough! I turned and strode straight along to the cashier's desk—I had just seen Mr Moir go into the back of the shop which meant I had a moment's breathing space. I gave Sharon a quick smile to let her know I needed urgent assistance.

What's up Jimmy? she whispered.

A pair of crackpots out of my past, wanting to dump this huge pile of books onto me—here, help me get them onto the table eh? Naval histories, look, unbafuckinglievable!

But Sharon stopped in her tracks. They had come up from behind me and I felt this hand clamp down on my shoulder like to aboutturn me again and I jerked out from under it and turned to face them: Any more from yous two and I'll call the polis!

We are the polis, says Sheila.

What?

You heard, says Alan.

What?

And we could do you for breach if we wanted, but lucky for you we're off duty and we cannay be bothered.

And he was looking straight at me, contempt written all over his face. And here it was all now fitting in. Folk like you give us a pain in the neck, he was saying, we try to do you a favour for old time's sake and look what happens.

That's right, went on Sheila, because you used to be married to my pal when we all shared the same uniform. Whereas the truth is you were aye a bad-tempered wee bastard—you and your bloody union.

Is he giving you any trouble officer? said a voice—Mr Moir it was, coming out from the back shop.

You could say that.

We've had our eye on him for a while, he says, is that right Sharon?

Sharon kept her head lowered and muttered something that wasnt intelligible to me and her face went red because she was involved in dishonest company.

Is that right Sharon? says Moir again with an insinuating voice.

Dont be feart of him hen, said Sheila indicating me.

I'm not feart of him.

He's just a wee bully.

He always was, said Alan, even when we were weans the gether in the Boys Brigade—until he got done for shoplifting.

Well that's a lie for a start, I said, because not only have I never got done for shoplifting, I was never even a bloody protestant and you've got to be a bloody protestant to get into them, else they turn ye down, they dont let you over the door. And I gave a quick smile to Sharon, letting her see I knew she was trying to be on my side and if she wasnt allowed to because of the situation then it was fine, it was fine, and I wouldnt think any the less of her. My da brought me up a good socialist, I said.

Sharon gave me a quick smile back and I knew I had figured her out correctly; she was a great lassie and would always stand by me.

That's the truth, I told her, we used to sing the Red Flag morning noon and night. Our house was full of books. Piles and piles of them, economic histories, political biographies, the lot.

Rubbish, said Alan.

Rubbish! What do you mean rubbish! I'm fucking telling ye the way it was.

Less of the language, replied Sheila.

Well you're bloody upsetting me. I dont know what the hell's going on, unless these crazed eedjit brothers of my ex-wife have fucking bribed you to find me.

Your mouth needs soapy water, said Alan.

Put the books down on the counter, cried Mr Moir.

With great pleasure, I says, with very great pleasure. But I didnt; I whispered to Sharon instead: This is so bad, I says, it's just so bad. I want you to be my witness to what's happening. I was in this shop minding my own business—I wasnay even inside it I was outside it!—and then this pair waylaid me.

Waylaid ye, says Alan, who the hell waylaid ye?

You did, the two of yous.

Did we hell.

Well what's this then? I said, pointing at the pile of books. What did you pile me up with them for except to slow me down or something?

Instead of replying the two of them shook their heads, and Alan gave a weary smile at both Sharon and Mr Moir. What I find so upsetting, he said, is that me and him used to be mates.

Once upon a time, I added. Like all good fairy tales it came to an abrupt end.

What do you know about fairy tales, said Sheila, these wee stories you write are all cheap thrills and sex.

That's no true, I said to Sharon, she's just lying.

You calling my wife a liar? said Alan.

The facts speak for themself.

The facts speak for themselves! That's a good yin. What do you know about facts?

More than you.

Ha ha.

Aye I know ha ha, I says.

That's because you're a joke, replied Alan and it made his wife burst out laughing. He winked at her.

Some man you are, I said.

I know, a man and a half.

You make me want to boke, I said, but I was playing for time, looking to find a way out of what was going on. Sharon was gazing at me. I've always loved you Sharon was what I thought but couldnt get it verbalised, probably because if I had I would have compromised her and I didnt want to do that. She was a brilliant lassie. Then a thought: if I flipped the books up into the air there was a chance I could make it to the door. But they were watching me carefully for just such a move—especially Sheila; it seemed like she was the brains behind the squad. When I knew her she was dangerous as well; in fact it occurred to me that she had always been out to get me, right from the kick-off back in the old days. A crazy idea was beginning to dawn on me: maybe she had fancied me and it had turned to hatred, maybe because I had fell for Mary she had set out to get me, and she had started by poisoning my marriage. And if that was the case then this whole business was just hair-raising. I looked at Sharon. She was the one voice of reason. Yet there standing next to her was Moir, the guy that ran the fucking place. What a smug bastard he was. I had always thought that. Even the way he scanned the books I bought whenever I was unlucky enough to get served by him, it was like he was casting judgments. I stole another glance at Sharon, if I could somehow get her to realise what I was going to try, if somehow she could realise what it was and could maybe create a diversion. That tight black T-shirt too, she always wore it and it was like she had forgot to stick a bra on first thing every morning the way her nipples poked out it was hard to even think what you were buying sometimes, she just rang up the till, gave you the receipt and waited for the dough, it was just too much, too much:

You come with us, muttered Sheila, taking me by the shoulder, and I had to go with them, my forearms cramped under the weight.

The Block

The body landed at my feet. A short man with stumpy legs. He was staring up at me but though so wide open those eyes were seeing things from which I was excluded, not only excluded from but irrelevant to; things to which I was nonexistent. He had no knowledge of me, had never had occasion to be aware of me. He did not see me although I was staring at him through his eyeballs. I was possibly seeking some sort of reflection, of a thing that was there to the inside. What the hell was he seeing with his eyelids so widely parted. He was seeing nothing. Blood issued from his mouth. He was dead. A dead man on the pavement beneath me—with stumpy legs; a short man with a longish body. I felt his pulse: there was no pulse. I wasnt feeling his pulse at all. I was grasping the wrist of a short man. No longer a wrist. I was grasping an extension, the extension to the left of a block of matter. This block of matter was a man's body moments earlier. Unless he had been dead on leaving the window upstairs, in which case a block of matter landed at my feet and I could scarcely even be referred to in connection with "it," with a block of matter describable as "it"—never mind being nonexistent of, or to. And two policemen had arrived. O Jesus, said one, is he dead?

I was looking at them. The other policeman had knelt to examine the block and was saying: No pulse. Dead. No doubt about it poor bastard. What happened? And looking at me, addressing me, the policeman was addressing me.

I said: A block of matter landed at my feet.

What was that?

The block of matter, it was a man's body previous to impact unless of course he was out the game prior to that, in which case, in which case a block of matter landed at my feet.

What happened?

This, I said and gestured at the block. This; it was suddenly by my feet. I stared into the objects that had formerly been eyes before doing as you did, I grasped the left extension there to . . . see.

What?

The pulse. You were saying there was no pulse, but in a sense—well, right enough I suppose you were quite correct to say there was no pulse. I had grasped what I took to be a wrist to find I was grasping the left extension of a block of matter. Just before you arrived. I found that what was a man's body was in fact a block and . . . I frowned. The missing connection, it is what happens. It is this.

Do you live around here? said the policeman.

What, aye, yes. Along the road a bit.

Did you see him falling?

An impossibility. That is uh . . .

He was here when you got here?

No. He may have been. He might well have been alive, it I mean. No—he . . . unless of course the . . . I had taken it for granted that it landed when I arrived but it might possibly . . . no, definitely not. I heard the thump. The impact. Of the impact.

Jesus Christ.

The other policeman glanced at him and then at me: What's your name?

McLeish, Michael. I live along the road a bit.

Where exactly?

Number 3.

And where might you be going at this time of the morning?

Work, I'm going to work. I'm a milk man.

Do you have any i.d.?

Pardon?

Give me your phone.

I dont have one.

The other policeman was rifling through the garments covering the block. And he brought out a wallet and peered into its contents. Robert McKillop, he said, I think his name is Robert McKillop. I better go up to his house Geordie, you stay here with … He indicated me in a vaguely surreptitious manner.

I'm going to my work, I said.

Whereabouts?

Partick.

The milk depot?

Aye, yes.

I know it well. What did you say your name was?

McLeish, Michael.

Fine. You're better just to wait here a minute.

The policeman named Geordie leaned against the tenement wall while his mate walked into the close. When he had reappeared he said, Mrs McKillop's upset—I'll stay with her meantime Geordie, you better report right away.

What about this yin here? I mean we know where he works and that.

Aye … The other one nodded at me: On your way. He gestured along the road, the direction I should take. You'll be hearing from us shortly, he said.

At the milk depot I was involved in the stacking of crates of milk onto my lorry. The milk containers were made of glass. They were bottles. One of the crates fell. Broken glass and milk sloshing about on the floor. The gaffer swore at me. You ya useless bastard. Get your lorry loaded and get out of my sight.

I wiped my hands and handed in my notice. Right now, I said, I'm leaving right now.

What d'you mean right now you're leaving! Get that fucking wagon loaded and get on your way.

No, I'm not here now. I'm no longer . . . I cannot be said to be here as a driver of milk lorries anymore. I've handed in my notice and wiped my hands of the whole carry on. Morning.

I walked to the exit. The gaffer coming after me.

McArra the checkerman who always was singing had stopped his singing to be gazing at us from behind a row of crates. I could see the cavity between his lips. The gaffer's hand had grasped my elbow. I looked at it. He withdrew it. Listen McLeish, he was saying. You've got a job to do. A week's notice you have to give. Dont think you can just say you're leaving and then walk out the fucking door.

I am not here now. I am presently walking out the fucking door.

Stop when I'm talking to you!

No. A block of matter landed at my feet an hour ago. I have to be elsewhere. I have to be going now to be elsewhere. Good morning.

Fuck you then. Aye, and dont ever show your face back in this depot again. McArra you're a witness to this! he's walking off the job.

Cheerio McArra. I called: I am, to be going.

Cheerio McLeish, said McArra the checkerman.

Outside in the street I had to stop. This was not an ordinary kind of carry on. I had to lean against the wall. I closed my eyelids but it was worse. Spinning into a hundred miles of a distance, this speck. Speck. This big cavity I was inside of and also enclosing and when the eyelids had opened something had been presupposed by something. Thank Christ for that, I said, for that, the something.

Are you alright son?

Me . . . I . . . I was . . . I glanced to the side and there was this middle-aged woman standing in a dark-coloured raincoat, in a pair of white shoes; a striped headscarf wrapped about her head. And a big pair of glasses, spectacles. She was squinting at me. Dizzy, I said to her, a bit dizzy Mrs—I'm no a drunk man or anything.

O I didnt think you were son I didnt think you were, else I wouldnt've stopped. I'm out for my messages.

I looked at her. I said: Too early for messages, no shops open for another couple of hours.

Aye son. But I cant do without a drop of milk in my tea and there was none left when I looked in the cupboard, so here I am. I sometimes get a carton of milk or sometimes a bottle straight from the milk depot if I'm up early.

First thing this morning you could've called me a milk man, I said while easing myself up from the wall. I was a deliverer of bottles.

O aye.

I nodded.

Will you manage alright now?

Aye, thanks, cheerio Mrs.

Cheerio son.

I was in my room. A tremendous thumping. I was lying face down on the bed. The thumping was happening to the door. McLeish. McLeish. Michael McLeish! A voice calling the name of me from outside of my room. And this tremendous thumping for the door and calling me by name McLeish! Jesus God.

Right you are, I shouted. And I pulled the pillow out from under my chin and pulled it down on the top of the back of my head. I closed my eyelids. The thumping stopped. I got up after seconds and opened the door.

We went to the milk depot, said one policeman, but you had left by then.

The second policeman was looking at my eyes. I shut the lids on him. I opened my mouth and said something to which neither answered. I repeated it but still no reply. They were not hearing me. I did not want to stare.

I told your gaffer what happened earlier on, said one policeman. He was worried about you. He said to tell you to give him a call and things would be okay. No wonder you were upset. I told him that. He said anyone would be. Can we come in?

Can we come in? the other policeman said.

Aye.

Can we come in a minute Michael? said the policeman.

I opened the door wider and returned to bed. They were standing at the foot of it with their hats in their hands. They looked roundabout. There were the two chairs. There are the chairs, I said.

Then they were lighting cigarettes. A smoke, asked one. Want a smoke?

Aye. I'm not getting things out properly.

Do you want one Michael?

I'm just not getting out it all the way. The block as well . . . it wasnt really the block.

The body.

The other handed me an already burning cigarette. Then I had it in my mouth. I was smoking. Fine as the smoke was entering my insides. The manner in which smoke enters an empty milk bottle and curls round the inner walls almost making this kind of shinnying noise while it is doing the curling. Any bottle. Empty bottles. The waves, the clouds, how they swirl and curl. The other policeman was saying: Nice place this. You've got some good pictures on the wall. I like that one there with the big circles. Is it an original?

Aye, yes. I painted it. I painted it in paint, the ordinary paint. Dulux I mean—that emulsion stuff.

Christ that's really good. I didnt know you were a painter.

It is good right enough, the other policeman said. He peered at it, his forehead strained in effort, seeing the paint and its substance, how the mass exists and attracts or not. The policeman could see this.

I held out my hand to him. Fingers. I used my pinkies; right and left for the adjacents. You know that way of touching the emulsion. Dip in the pinkies. Curl at the joints as though beckoning. That was what I was doing with the … and the milk bottle, the milk bottle too I suppose.

But dont let it get you down, the policeman said. We had a word with your boss and he said you were to get in touch with him and it would be okay, about the job and everything else about it, about what has happened, there are no reports, not from him.

Broken bottles cannot be repaired.

Yes, the other policeman said. The fact is we need to go to the station. Our serjeant wants to hear how it happened with Mr McKillop this morning. How you saw it yourself Michael, how you witnessed it Michael. We can get a refreshment down there, tea or coffee. Okay? Just shove on your clothes and we'll get going.

In the back seat of the patrol car one of them said: I'm not kidding but that painting of yours Michael, it is really good. Are the rest of them yours as well?

Aye, yes. I was doing painting. I was painting a lot sometimes, before I started this job—unemployed although employed, as I was, in the painting.

The policeman was looking at me, between my eyes; onto the bridge of my nose. I closed the eyelids: reddish grey. I could guess what would be going on. The whole of it. The description. A block of matter wasnt it. It would be no good for them—the serjeant, the details of it, the thump of impact. What I was doing and the rest of it. Jesus God. I was painting a lot sometimes, I said to him.

What's up?

Nothing. I'm just not getting the things, a hold ... sploshing about.

It had to upset you Michael dont worry about that. A body landing like that.

Not just that, the block. Not just the block. Ach. I stopped and was shaking my head. The words werent coming. Nothing at all to come and why the words were never. They cannot come by themselves. They can come by themselves. Without, not without. The anything. They can do it but only with it, the anything. What is the anything; that something. A particular set of things maybe.

The policeman smiled.

Open the window a bit, the other policeman said. Give him a breath of fresh air. Gets hell of a stuffy in here. And refreshments when we get there.

A wee room inside the station I was walked into. A policeman and a serjeant following. I was to sit at a table with the serjeant to be facing me. And he saying: I just want you to tell me what it was happened earlier on. In your own words Mr McLeish, in your own words.

A block of matter, it was at my feet. I was ... I glanced at the serjeant to add, I couldnt be said to be there in a sense. A thump of impact and the block of matter.

A block of matter, he replied after a moment. Yes I know what you're meaning about that. Mr McKillop was dead and so you didnt see him that way; you just saw him as a kind of shape—is that right, is that what you're meaning?

I was walking and the thump, the block.

You were walking to work?

Aye, yes.

And the next thing, wham? the body lands at your feet?

No. In a sense though you ... no, though; I was walking, thump, the block of matter. And yet—he was a short man, stumpy legs, longish body. And less then—less than, immediately a block of matter. Eyes. The objects that had been eyes. Not had been eyes at all. They were never eyes. Never ever had been eyes for the block. McKillop's eyes those objects had been part of. Part of the eyes. And I looked into them and they were not eyes. Just bits—bits of the block. There are no reflections, there is nothing.

Look son I'm sorry, I know you're . . . The serjeant was glancing at the policeman. And his eyes!

Quizzical, I said.

Quizzical!

Aye, yes.

He was looking at me then I was looking out at him. He began looking at the policeman. Without words, both talking. I said, It doesnt matter anyhow.

What doesnt matter?

Nothing, the anything.

The serjeant stood up. I'll be back in a minute. He went out and came back in again carrying three cartons of tea and a folder under his arm. Tea Mr McLeish, he said.

I grasped the carton of tea.

So, out walking at the crack of dawn and wham, a block called McKillop lands at your feet.

That'll do, I said.

What'll do?

The serjeant was staring at my nose. I could have put an index finger inside. He was speaking to me. It's okay son we're not thinking you were doing anything apart from going to your work. A bit early right enough but that's when milk men go about. Mrs McKillop told us her end and you're fine.

Serjeant?

What?

Nothing.

After a moment he nodded: Away you go home. Your record isnt the cleanest and it's our job to know all about that and all about you too, a man who goes his own way. I can see you've changed. For the better. Geordie tells me you've a steady job nowadays driving the milk lorries and you've a good hobby into the bargain so—you're fine. And I dont think we'll need to see you again. But if we do I'll send somebody round. Number 3 it is eh? Aye, right you are. The serjeant stood up again and said to the policeman: Let him finish his tea.

Okay serj.

Fine. Cheerio then son, he said to me.

The City Slicker and The Barmaid

I came to someplace a few miles south of the Welsh border and with luck managed to rent a tent on a farm. Not a real campsite. I was the one mug living in the place and could only stay on condition I completed certain set tasks such as painting barn walls and driving tractors full of rubbish. Whenever the farmer was away on business I had to guide his ramshackle lorry into the village.

I also received cash for these tasks.

The tent was pitched in a grassy bit of ground next to a cobbled courtyard covered in country manure equals shite, hay and mud. Dirty mud as opposed to healthy stuff. The grass was long in the surrounding field. In the barn nearest the tent big rats jumped about getting fat on the hay and feed stored there. I discovered paw marks on the grease in my frying pan. This proves the rats found a way into my tent though the farmer refused to believe me. He thought I was a moaner. During the night I liked to sit at the top end of the mattress with a bottle in my hand waiting for a wee animal to creep in. Then too the hedge surrounding the field was full of beetles and all manner of flying insects. When I lit my candle they broke in through rips in the canvas, perched from the roof till I fell asleep then came zooming down on me, eating my blood and knocking their knees in my hair. I was always wakening in the middle of the night scratching and clawing at my scalp and eyebrows; also the lobes of my ears, how come the lobes of my ears?

The actual farm animals themselves did not worry me. Although after sundown on my way home from the village pub a pack of cows paced alongside me, sniffing. There were all these lanes to walk down and usually I took a shortcut through a couple of fields. These cows came wastling along at my back without a sound bar the shshsh of their smelly tails. I walked slowly, kidding on it was okay, but it wasnt and I felt like dashing headlong to the tent, but then these guyropes and metal spike things I kept tripping over and twice I fell right on top of the tent. Plus too my boots, all spattered and saturated with dew and whatever else, what a mess. I took them off at the entrance, seated on the so-called groundsheet with the doorflap open. And all the insects flew in from the hedges. The floor inside the tent was always covered in clumps of grass, dung too at times, the colour of baked seaweed. Earwigs crawled the walls searching for ears to crawl in, then the ants, ants were everywhere. I closed my eyes at night thinking "spiders, thank christ for spiders."

No sleeping bag. Terrible itchy exarmy blankets to go with the mattress, hired from the farmer's wife and deducted from my wage at source. Of course my feet stuck out at the bottom and I can never sleep wearing socks, even if I had any.

The farmhands were continually cracking jokes in Oi Bee accents at my expense. I would laugh, or stare. Other times I replied in aggressive accents of my own which got me nowhere since they pretended not to understand what I was saying. Because I drove the lorry I was accorded a certain respect. In the local den of a pub I was known as Jock the Driver. The previous driver was an Irishman who worked seven years on this farm till one Saturday night he went out for a pish round the back of the bar. It was the last they ever saw of him. A man to admire.

The guys working beside me were yesmen to the core. Carried tales about each other to the farmer and even to me if the farmer was off on business. They spent entire days gossiping. I never spoke to them unless I had to. The tightest bunch of bastards I have ever met. Never shared their grub or their mugs of tea. Or their cash if you were skint. And they never offered you a cigarette. Then if you bought them a drink they thought you were off your rocker and also resented it because they were obliged to buy you one back and never did, so that was them marked as miserable in their own estimation, not because they thought it but because you did, or so they thought. But they thought wrong. I could not have cared less. I just did it to flummox them. In their opinion city folk were either thieves or simpletons. An amazing shower of crackpots the lot of them.

The barmaid in this local pub was a daughter of the village. I think she must have hated me because I represented outside youth—otherwise how come. Apart from myself there were no other single men of her age in the dump. She was chaste I think unless the Irishman ever got there which I doubt. I never fancied her in the first place. A bit tubby. Just if I had not tried I thought the regulars might have felt insulted—the barmaid was not good enough etcetera for a city slicker like me. The night I made the attempt was awful. It reminds me of B feature imitation Barbara Stanwyck films.

Once or twice the manager used to bolt the doors and allow a few regulars to stay behind after closing time. Probably he done it more than that but never when I was there. This time he must have forgotten about me till there I was coming back from the cludgie round the back of the bar to find the shutters drawn, I was locked in. I had been away for ages right enough. That country nighttime comes down like a blanket and I could not find the damn trough thing, plus you had to be careful with the ditches. I saw the manager looking daggers at me but too late now and he had to serve me a pint. It was that local splosh stuff I was drinking. A couple of the same later, and with the local constable in the middle of his own second or third I for some reason threw an arm about the barmaid's waist for which I was dealt an almighty clout on the jaw. What a fist she had on her. I was so amazed I tried to land her one back but missed and fell across the table where the constable was sitting, knocking the drink over his uniform trousers. I was ejected.

Long after midnight, maybe as late as two in the morning, I came back to apologise if anyone was still about, and also to collect the carry-out I had planked in one of the ditches round the back. I had been wandering about retching for ages because of that country wine they had been feeding me. Powerful stuff. Inside the pub the lights had been dimmed but I knew they were still there. I could hear music coming faintly from the lounge. I crept round the side of the building then up on my toes and peering in through the corner of the frosted glass I spied the barmaid there giving it a go as the stripper. Yes. Doing a strip show on top of the lounge bar watched by the copper, the manager and one or two regulars, including an unhealthy old guy called Albert Jenkinson who worked alongside me on the farm. And all silent while they watched. Not a smile amongst them. Even the drink was forgotten. Just the quick drag on the smoke.

I lost my temper at first then felt better, then again lost my temper and had to resist caving in the window and telling them to stick the countryside up their jacksie.

No one noticed me. I did not stay very long. Her body was far too dumpy for a stripper and her underwear was a bit old-fashioned. Her father worked as a gardener in the local nursery and rarely went into the pub.

Once I got my wages the following week, and it was safe, I got off my mark and took the tent with me.

Are you drinking sir?

They had been seeking me for ages but being a devious old guy I managed to give them the slip on quite a few occasions. They found me in the Bureau of Labour. I was in there performing my song & dance routine to music from the first world war. At first I seemed not to notice them standing in the doorway then when I did I acted as though totally uninterested and my bravado had to be respected, not for its own sake so much as the effect it had on my pursuers. I turned my back on them and performed to those queuing to sign the register. Behind the counter the clerks looked slightly irritated although a couple of the younger brigade were smiling at my antics. But their smiles didnt linger, they continued working as though I wasnt there. I didnt bother at all, just carried on with the performance. Somehow an impression had been gained that no matter how erratically I might behave the clerks would never have me ejected. No doubt the reaction would have been different had I become violent, or even explicitly abusive. Then suddenly, towards the end of a song, I lost concentration for a moment and appeared in danger of failing to perceive the course—but then I grinned briefly and continued the game. It was strange to behold. Nearby there were four youths sitting on a bench and they were stamping their feet and cheering and then one of them had flicked a burning cigarette end in my direction. I was dancing so nimbly that I scarcely seemed to interrupt myself while bending to uplift it; I nipped off the burning ash, sticking the remainder of it in an interior pocket of my greatcoat. Then I glanced swiftly at the doorway, whirled to face the counter; onwards I jigged across the floor, wagging my right forefinger at two young girls queuing at Enquiries. I proceeded to address the chorus at them, the girls smiling their embarrassment, laughing lightly that they had no money, nor even a cigarette to spare. Yet still I persisted at them and the girls now having to avert their faces from me while I with the beaming smile, cutting my capers as though the doorway had never existed. And thank you sir, I was crying to a smallish fellow who had rolled me a cigarette, thank you sir. This distracting me from the girls and back again I faced the counter; but my sly glance to the door was unmistakeable and I held the rolled cigarette aloft in my left hand, blatantly displaying it for their benefit. And I laughed at no one especially and again cried thank you sir, thank you sir, with both arms aloft now and waggling my hands round and round in preparation for the launch into my final chorus, but just at this point I made good my escape, and it wasnt till much later that again they found me. I was in a stretch of waste ground near the river. I stared at them when they approached, but the stare only expressed the vaguest curiosity. My head lolled sideways, knocking the unbuttoned epaulette askew. They came forward and prodded my shoulder until my eyelids parted and my groan became a groan of recognition. Thank you sir I muttered thank you sir, and them, stepping back the way as though alarmed. But they werent alarmed, they were angry. And judging by the manner in which my gaze dropped to the ground I was trying to avoid witnessing it. And then they began talking to me in a language that was foreign. At length they stopped. I withdrew a half-smoked cigarette from an interior pocket and held it to my mouth until being given a light. I inhaled only once on it, before placing it carefully on the ground; then I picked it up and stubbed it out, smiling in a very sleakit way. I glanced at them and said are you drinking sir? For a moment there was silence. When they began shouting at me there was an odd sense in which it seemed to have lasted a while but only now become audible. But to none of it did I react. I was not smiling, I sat there as though in deep concentration. Eventually there was silence again, and they stared at me with open contempt. It was obvious I was now getting irritated. I looked at them and glared, my eyes twitching at the corners as though I was about to say something but I didnt say anything, I just shook my head and grunted sarcastically; it was being made plain that I couldnt care less. If there was a point for them it was now.

Zuzzed

A load of potatoes was stacked and waiting for me first thing that morning. I got right into it. The farmer's boy brought the jug of tea and once he had gone I sat down to roll a smoke. It was empty, the tin, just a bit of dust it contained. I jumped back at the work. Later he returned for the jug and though he would've seen I hadnt touched it he said nothing. I steamed into the weighing and packing, not stopping at all although when the lorry arrived in from the fields there was still plenty of the original left. The farmer helped the Frenchmen lug it into my area while I continued. They finished. The farmer stood watching me work for a time. Yes, he said, we're getting a fair crop scotti.

I nodded as I carried across another tub of spuds to the weighing machine. I didnt notice him leave. I might have heard the lorry revving or something, gears maybe—the driver was hopeless.

Each tub or barrel of potatoes weighed out 28lbs so it wasnt too bad except if the farmer was about which meant it could only be 28lbs and nothing more or less. It was the constant bending fucked me. The shoulders get it, and the belly muscles. And the heat was terrific—the sweat I mean, I dont know how hot it was in the barn though outside maybe seventy to eighty degrees. I was working stripped to the waist. Clouds of dust all the time, streaks of sweat, the tidemarks everywhere. When dinner time came I wasnt hungry anyway. A bottle of cider would've went down fine right enough but apart from that nothing, nothing at all bar the smoke, of course, tobacco would've been ideal. Not so good being without it, there was just dust in the tin.

The Frenchmen were lugging in the next load. Only French worked the fields, some women with them and—when one of the men needed a slash for christ sake he just carried on never mind the women being there or not, a couple of girls amongst them but no, it never bothered them at all, just got on with it. Maybe that's healthy, who knows. Though the women never helped with the lugging off the lorry, they usually—christ knows, maybe off for a piss for god sake.

Warm out scotti! The farmer was there. I hadnt seen him. I was swinging a sack down from the pile and getting it across to the empty tubs in a movement. He stepped to the side just in time. Fair crop, he was saying.

I had dumped an empty next to the machine and was rolling in the spuds and while I topped it to the 28 mark I said: Can you loan me a nicker?

What was that scotti?

A nicker. Can you loan me a nicker?—a pound I mean, eh?

I knew he was looking at me but I continued with the work. A moment later he said, Yes, I told you about that, these Frenchmen, wily set of buggers, you have to watch it with these dominoes.

What—aye, yes, aye, can you loan me it then? take it off the wages and that.

He lit his pipe and exhaled, Dare say so scotti yes.

Fine.

Well then, he said. And while I was swinging across another sack he wound up by adding, Back to the field I suppose.

Moments later the lorry was revving. I couldnt believe it. By the time I ran out into the sun I saw it turning out onto the main drag, all the Frenchmen and women sitting on the back of it, laughing and joking quietly. A couple of them gave me a brief wave. I shook my head. A hen or a cock or something came walking across out of a fence thing. I looked at it. I went back into the barn. When the boy came with the afternoon jug I asked him if his old man had left anything for me. He stared at me. A message son, I said, did your old man leave a message for me?

No.

He was supposed to—a pound note it was. Maybe he left it with your mother eh? Away and ask her.

He wont have.

Ask and see.

But he wont have.

Christ sake son will you go and do what I'm saying.

He came back in five minutes, shaking his head. He probably had walked about the place and not bothered even seeing her. He stood watching me for a bit then said, When're you taking the tea scotti?

Eh . . . does she smoke son, your mother?

No.

Christ.

She wants to finish the washing up. The jug.

What. I stopped the weighing and turned and the fucking barrel fell, the spuds all rolling about the fucking floor. The boy stepped back out the road. It's okay son, it's okay, just take the thing away.

The next load was the last for me although the French would be picking until 8 p.m. Their morning began at 5 a.m. I wouldnt've worked hours like that. The farmer had asked me a couple of days back. Are you interested in a bit of overtime for fuck sake! 5 till 8. Why in the name of christ did they do it! The dough of course. By the time I had cleared and swept the area and shot off home and got back the following morning another load of fucking sacks would be stacked there ready and waiting.

The farmer was hovering around again. He went off

and I heard him calling over a couple of Frenchmen to give me a hand with the travail. I got the time on one of their watches. I stopped work. I looked at the farmer. Well scotti, he said, taking the pipe out of his pocket. A good day's work eh? See you in the morning then.

I couldnt believe my ears. I stared at him. He was patting the tobacco down and when he noticed me he added, Alright?

My hands were trembling. I clasped them, rubbed them on the sweat rags I wore round my waist.

Something wrong then?

Something wrong! What d'you mean something wrong! My christ that's a fucking good yin right enough, a miserable bastarn nicker as well you'd think it was the crown fucking jewels or something.

He went tugging on the stem of his pipe. I grabbed my T-shirt and walked out the place. I heard him start and exclaim: The pound. Scotti! The pound. Sorry.

He was digging into his hip pocket for that big thick wallet and the Frenchmen standing smiling but curious as well. Forgot all about it, said the farmer, coming towards me while unwrapping a single.

Sorry. Sorry by christ, that is a good yin, a beauty. I continued on and out of the yard and kept on until about halfway between the farm and the turnoff, heading up towards the site where the tent was pitched. Then I stopped and sat at the side of the track. I sat on the turf, my feet on the caked mud in the ditch. I had forgotten to parcel a few spuds for my tea. Also the tin but it only had dust in it anyway. I had also forgotten a piece of string for my jeans. I was meaning to buy a belt, I kept forgetting and the threads at the cuffs of the jeans were dragging when I walked. The string would do meantime then I could get the belt. I got up, stiff at the knees. I strode along swinging my arms straight and on beyond the shortcut between hedges farther on up to the front of the field where the tent was and left wheeling across the place, a few holiday-makers were wandering about with cooking utensils.

I was lying on top of the groundsheet, cool, the breathing coming short, in semi gasps maybe. I relaxed. Slowing down, slowing down, allowing the shoulders and the belly and the knees, letting them all get down, relaxing, the limbs and everything just slackly, calm, counting to ten and beyond, deep breathing exercises now, begin, and out in out in out in hold it there and the pulse rate lessens the heart pumps properly slowly does it slowly does it now yes and that fresh air is swirling down in these shadowy regions cleaning the lungs so now you can smoke and be okay and live to a ripe old age without having to halt every few yards to catch your breath, yes, simply continue and.

The sacks were piled high next morning. The lorry long gone to the fields. My mouth was sticky. I opened the tin and sniffed the dust. The boy had poked his head in and disappeared as soon as he saw me. Away to tell his mother probably. Fuck the pair of them. Later the crashing of gears and the lorry coming in. The Frenchmen with the load. I was getting a few looks. Fuck them as well. Then the farmer. Looking as unamazed as he could. Fuck you too. I laid down the barrel I was filling and went over. A nicker, I said, that's all I'm asking, till payday, just deduct it.

Of course scotti . . . He was taking out the pipe.

I mean just now, you know, it's just now I need it.

He nodded and got the wallet out, passed me a single.

Great. Fine. I nodded, I'm just going.

He looked at me.

The wee shop in the village just, I'll only be a minute . . . I grabbed the T-shirt and flew o'er hill and dale.

By the grassy verge beneath the veranda of the local general store with the morning sun on my shoulders, the tin lying open at one side and the cider bottle uncorked on the other, and the cows lowing in the adjacent meadow, and the smoke rolled and being lighted and sucking in that first drag, keeping the thrapple shut to trap it there; with no bout of coughing, not a solitary splutter, the slight zuzz in the head. Instead of exhaling in the ordinary way I widened my lips and opened the throat without blowing so that the smoke just drifted right out and back in through my nostrils. Dizziness now but the head was clear though the belly not so good, and a shudder, fine. Then the cider, like wine it tasted and not too pleasant, just exact, and ready now, the second drag.

Time had passed. The lorry. It came into view, chugging along, the farmer at the wheel. I gestured at him with the bottle and the smoke, but as a greeting only. He returned it cheerily. The French on the back, the women there. I waved. Bon, I shouted. Once it had passed from view I swallowed the remainder of the cider and got up to return the bottle. I walked back to the farm, the tea would soon be coming.

Renee

I had landed in a position of some authority offering scope for advancement. A storekeeper. I kept records of food for the stores of food I had authority of. The Foodstore was a fairly large smallroom. I had no assistants. Those in superior positions held little or no authority over me. I was belonging to the few able to match figures on paper with objects on shelves and was left alone to get on with it.

Members of the kitchenstaff came to obtain grub and it was down to me to check they were due this grub. If so I marked it all in a wee notebook I kept hidden in a concealed spot. The chap I succeeded was at that moment serving a bit of time as an effect of his failure to conceal said notebook. He left the fucker lying around for any mug to find. And eventually someone pulled a stroke with cases of strong drink, and this predecessor of mine wound up taking the blame.

The kitchenstaff consisted of females most of whom were Portuguese but though I found them really desirable they seemed to regard Scotchmen with disfavour. And the rest of the British for that matter. They spoke very little English. I could manage La Muchacha Hermosa in their own language but it got me nowhere. Alongside them worked a pair of girls from somewhere on the southeastern tip of England, one in particular I was disposed towards. The other was not bad. I had to carry on the chat with both however because generally speaking this always transpires in such circumstances viz when you are on your tod and have nobody to help out in 4somes. Obviously I had no desire to escort both on a night out. But neither did I wish to ask one lest the other was hurt. What a mug! Never mind. It could have gone on for ages but for the intervention of the Portuguese. At long last they successfully conveyed to me that a certain girl from the southeastern tip of England wouldnt take it amiss if I was to dive in with the head down. Joan was her name; she seemed surprised when I asked her out but she was pleased. We walked down to the local pictures after work. The Odeon. People considered it a dump but I didnt; it showed two full-length feature films while the flash joints up west were charging a fortune for the privilege of seeing one.

My relations with the other girl declined palpably which was a bit of a pity because I quite liked her. She began visiting the Foodstore only when absolutely necessary. Then soon after this Joan was becoming irritated all the time. To some extent I couldnt blame her. My financial situation was hopeless and the very ideas of equality and going dutch were anathema to her. The upshot was the Odeon three weeks running. She hated it. That last conversation was totally ridiculous, me standing about humming and hawing and trying to assume a woebegone countenance. She said nothing but her face inflamed, she was quite passionate in some ways. The bloody Odeon again, she muttered and set off marching down the Gray's Inn Road.

I strode after her. But not too quickly because I was having to figure out a speech. By the time I had counted through the last of my coins and paid for the two tickets she was through in the foyer at the end of the sweeties queue. She paid a fortune for chocolate but the thought of assisting me with the tickets never crossed her mind. And neither did the thought of walking off and leaving me. Anything was better than spending the night indoors back at the female hostel where she stayed with her pal.

I waited for her to stick the sweeties and so on into her handbag then paused as she stepped past me and into the hall, where I handed the tickets to the aged usherette who was also from Scotland and occasionally gave me a cheery smile.

It was supposed to be hazardous for single women alone in the Odeon but to me that was extremely doubtful, perhaps if they'd had a half bottle of rum sticking out their coat pockets. I never saw any bother. Just sometimes it was less than straightforward distinguishing the soundtrack from the racket caused by a few dozen snoring dossers. By the time we reached the seats the speech was forgotten about and we settled down to watch the movie. Later I slipped my arm about her shoulders and that was that, and we nestled in for a cuddle. On the road home afterwards we continued on past the local pub, straight to the female hostel. We stood in at the entrance out from the worst of the wind. There was no chance of her smuggling me inside. The place was very strict about that. Men were not wanted at all costs. She had hinted once or twice about my getting her into my own quarters. But it was not possible. In fact—well, the rumour circulating amongst the kitchenstaff at that precise moment concerned myself; they were saying I used the Foodstore as a sort of home-from-home to the extent that I actually slept in it. It was the main joke and I helped it along, telling them I was having a coloured television installed, plus a four-poster bed and a small portable bar, the usual sort of nonsense. The truth of the matter is that I was sleeping in the place; but nobody knew for sure and none had the authority to enter the Foodstore unless I was with them, this last being a new condition of the post because of the plight of my predecessor. Two keys only existed: one was held by myself while the other was kept in the office of the security staff. That was in case of emergencies. But I reckoned that with me being there on the premises most of the time there would be very little scope for "emergencies." I had overheard a couple of those in superior positions refer to the plight of my predecessor as an "emergency." The idea of becoming one myself was not appealing. But as long as the Foodstore remained under my control I had grounds for optimism; for the first time in a long while I was beginning to feel confident about the future. Even so, just occasionally, I could suddenly become inveighed by a sense of panic and if outside of the Foodstore I had to rush straight back to ensure everything was okay, that I hadnt forgotten to lock the bloody door. That Saturday night I started getting fidgety with Joan.

It was getting on for midnight according to her watch and I had visions of folk stealing in and filling swagbags full of grub and strong drink. And also there was an underlying suspicion that all was not well between Joan and myself, a sort of coldness, even a slight impatience. Eventually I asked her if anything was up but she said there wasnt then told me she had been invited to a good party the following night and would it be okay if she went. Of course it was okay. I quite fancied going myself. Good parties are uncommon. Especially in London. Things have a habit of going badly. I told Joan that but she said it would probably be alright, it was taking place in the home of the big brother of a former boyfriend. That sounds great, I said.

What d'you mean Jock? she said.

Nothing.

Joan was good at kidding on she didnt notice things, my sarcasm was one of them. And five minutes later I was striding back down the road and sneaking in past the security office and down the long dark corridors to the Foodstore.

All of the next day I didnt see her at all but she sent a note via one of the Portuguese women to say she would meet me at the lounge door of the local pub at 8 that evening. It was after 9 when she arrived and I was into my third pint. She apologized. She was looking really great as well and there was a perfume she had on that was something special.

Then too the material of her dress; I touched the side of her arm and there seemed to be a kind of heat radiated from it. Or else the Guinness was stronger than usual. And I kept having to stop myself from touching the nape of her neck. I noticed the landlord of the pub glancing at me in a surreptitious fashion as if fearing I might do something that would embarrass us all.

Joan kept looking at her watch until I swallowed down the last of the beer and collected my tobacco tin and matches. It was cold and blowy, and nobody was about. Nor were there any buses in view. It was as well to start walking. Joan wasnt too pleased; each time a taxi passed she made a show of looking to see if it was for hire. Eventually we reached Chancery Lane tube station.

As it transpired the party was not too bad at all, plenty of food and stuff. Joan's pal was there too but she seemed to be ignoring us. I lost sight of her amid the people who were bustling about dancing and the rest of it. Joan as well, eventually I lost sight of her. I went into a wee side room next to the kitchen, opened a can of beer and sat on a dining chair. A fellow came in who was involved with another of the girls from the hostel; he supported Charlton Athletic and we spoke about football for a time, then women. His girlfriend was older than him and it was causing problems with her parents or her roommates or something. His voice grated on me and it was as if he was just kidding on he was a Londoner. He kept on yapping. I began to wonder if maybe it was a plot of some sort to detain me.

Shortly before midnight a girl told me to go along to the end bedroom on the first floor. Joan was there. She nodded me inside but bypassed me, shutting the door behind me; and there was her pal, Renee was her name, she was sitting on the edge of the bed crying her eyes out. I took my tin out to roll a smoke then put it away again. She knew I was there. I stepped across and touched her shoulder. Okay? I said.

She shook the hand off. She had stopped crying but was trembling a little. I rolled a smoke now and offered her it but she didnt smoke. She dried her nose with a tissue. I laid my hand on her arm and asked if she was feeling any better. When she didnt answer I said: Will I tell Joan to come in?

No, she replied. She sniffed and dried her nose again. I stood smoking while she continued to sit there staring at the floor.

Do you want me to leave? I said.

Yes.

Joan had gone. Downstairs in the main dancing room I found her doing a slow one with this monkey dressed in a cravat and strange trousers. Over she came, she was frowning. Jock, she said, how's Renee? is she alright?

I think so. What was up with her?

She paused a moment then shrugged briefly, glanced away from me. Look Jock, she said, I better finish the dance with David.

Oh good. Ask him if he's selling that cravat.

It wouldnt suit you, she muttered, and off she went. A loud dancing record started and other people got up onto the floor. I returned to the wee side room. The Charlton Athletic supporter was sitting on the floor with another guy; they both watched me enter. That was enough. Cheerio, I said.

It was time to get back to the Foodstore. I went into the kitchen first though and lifted a handful of cocktail sausages, wrapped them in a napkin and stuck them into my pocket and also as well a half bottle of gin. Out in the hall I bumped into a couple at the foot of the stairs. I asked them if Renee was still in the end bedroom but they didnt seem to understand what I said.

Closing the front door after me I waited a moment in the porch, then I opened the gin and swigged a mouthful. It was really fucking horrible and didnt even taste like gin.

I set off walking. Along the street and round from Basset Road I saw Renee away about fifty yards off, standing at an empty taxi rank. A man approached her and looked as if he was trying to chat her up. She stood stiffly, gazing directly to the front. He stepped towards her and she said something to him. Hey Renee! I shouted. Hey . . . I trotted along the road and the man walked smartly off in the opposite direction.

Renee was frowning, and she looked at me. He thought I was a prostitute, she said, he asked me how much I charged . . . She turned and stared after him but he had vanished.

Dont worry, I said, that kind of thing happens all the time. London. You waiting for a taxi?

Yes. She stepped back the way and continued speaking without looking at me. I shouldnt've come. I had a headache most of the day. I just shouldnt've come. I wasnt going to. I changed my mind at the last minute.

It was rubbish anyway, I said. Looked as if it was going to be good at the start and then it wasnt.

She nodded. Where's Joan?

Joan? I shrugged. I pressed the lid off the tobacco tin but put it back on and brought out the gin instead. She didnt want any of it. She rubbed her forehead. If you've got a sore head, I said, this night air'll clear it. Eh, come on we'll walk for a bit.

She continued to stand there.

It's quite a nice night.

Jock, I just want to go home.

I know, but just eh well a lot of queeries hang about here you know—we'll probably pick up a taxi quite soon. Eh? hey! I brought out the cocktail sausages, unwrapped the napkin, passed her a couple. Then we carried on, eating as we walked. I began telling her about some sort of nonsense connected to the Foodstore to which she made no comment though she was quite interested. Then she started talking about her life, just general stuff to do with her family back home in this southeastern tip of England which is apparently very green. Joan was her best pal and they had come up from there together. This was their first job and they were supposed to be sticking it out till something better turned up. Meantime they were supposed to be saving for this great flat they planned on acquiring. Has it got all mod cons? I said.

Pardon?

I shook my head but when she saw me smiling she started smiling as well. And she added, Sometimes you're funny Jock.

I am not always sure about women, about what exactly is going on with them. This was just such an occasion. But I knew it was okay to put my arm round her shoulders. She continued talking about the hostel then about the kitchen and the Portuguese women whom she liked working beside because they were always having a laugh. And then I knew about the blunder I had committed; it was Renee I was supposed to have asked out back at the beginning, not Joan. It was basic and simple and everything was explained. I was glad she wasnt looking straight at my face.

A taxi trundled past. We were walking quite the thing though and scarcely noticed till it was out of earshot. Beyond Marble Arch the wind had died and it was not a bad night considering it was still only March. We had the full length of Oxford Street ahead of us but it was fine, and the shop windows were there to be looked into. I took Renee's hand and she smiled as if she had just remembered something funny; it had nothing to do with me.

When we arrived at the hostel she didnt want to go in. We moved into the space to the side of the entrance and started kissing immediately. And the way her eyes had closed as she turned her face to meet me, a harmony. I asked if it was definitely out of the question to smuggle me inside.

Honestly Jock.

Are you sure?

There's just no way.

I was breathing her perfume, the point behind her ear. She had her coat open and my jacket was open, our arms round each other's waist. I had been hard since stepping into the space, and Renee was not backing away from it. We continued kissing. She definitely did not want to go in and up to her room, and it was because of Joan. She'll be there in the morning, said Renee, and I wont bear to look at her. Not now.

That was that. I opened my tin and rolled a cigarette. She was waiting for me to make things happen. Eventually I said, Listen Renee, the trouble with the place I stay in, it's eight bloody beds to a room and that I mean you cant even get leaving a suitcase because somebody'll knock it. No kidding.

She pulled away to look at me properly. I brought out the gin, offered her a swig, took one myself when she declined. There was an all-night snackbar across at the Square and I asked if she fancied a cup of coffee. She shrugged. The two of us came out onto the pavement, walked for a couple of minutes together without speaking. Then we had our arms round each other again and we walked that way that the bodies link, the thighs fast together, the feet keeping pace and so on. At last I said, Right: how would you like to find out where I really stay?

I didnt look at her. But when she made no answer I did, and I could see she was trying not to smile. What's up? I asked.

Oh Jock!

What?

She shook her head, lips tightly shut; but not able to stop smiling now.

I dont stay in the Foodstore if that's what you're thinking.

Yes you do.

What?

You do Jock.

Naw I dont.

Oh well then I'm looking forward to meeting your landlord! And she laughed aloud.

I chipped away the cigarette and had another swig of gin, gestured with it to her but she shook her head. You're wrong, I said.

Am I!

Well you're no, but you are.

Oh, I see. Renee shook her head: All the kitchenstaff know!

They dont.

Jock, they do.

They fucking dont! I'll tell you something, it was me started the rumour in the first place.

You?

Aye, of course.

But the Portuguese women all laugh about it Jock.

Aye okay, but it's like a double bluff; when it comes right down to it they dont really believe it.

Joan does.

Joan . . .

It was her that told me.

Oh christ. I took out my tin and rolled another fag immediately. Look, I said, Renee I mean the only reason I do is because of the thieving that goes on in there. You cant turn your back. Christ, you know what like it is!

She didnt answer.

As far as I'm concerned I'm only going to stay there till I make sure I'm no going to get fucking set up—cause that's what they're trying to fucking do, and I'm no kidding.

There's no need to swear about it.

Sorry.

Anyhow, you dont have to worry.

What?

About who knows; it's only the kitchenstaff, and they wont say anything.

How do you know?

They wont.

What a life!

Jock, dont worry.

I wonder how the hell they found out.

Renee chuckled. Maybe you were snoring!

She seemed to take it for granted I could smuggle the two of us inside with the greatest of ease, and showed not the slightest interest in how it was to be accomplished. I led her round into the narrow, enclosed alley at the back of the building and told her to wait at a special spot. She smiled and kissed my nose. Renee, I said, you're actually crazy, do you know that?

Not as crazy as you. She raised her eyebrows.

It was never easy getting inside the building at night and that was another reason why I didnt go out very often. The security man on nightshift was from Yorkshire and me and him got on quite well together. Usually the way I managed things was to chap the window of his office and go in for a cup of tea and a chat. He assumed I was just stopping off on my road home and when I said goodnight he paid no further attention, never for one moment even dreaming I would be sneaking back beneath the window and along the corridor to the rear staircase. Tonight he kept me yapping for more than twenty minutes. I left him seated at his desk, twiddling the tuner of his transistor radio; he spent most of the night trying for a clear sound on the BBC World Service.

She stepped forwards from the shadows when I appeared at the window. We were both shivering with nervousness and it made it the more awkward when she clambered up and over the sill. I snibbed the window afterwards. That was the sort of thing Yorky would have discovered routinely. We went quickly along and down to the basement, and along to where the Foodstore was situated beyond the kitchen and coldrooms. Once inside I locked the door and stood there with my eyes shut and breathing very harshly.

Alright? she said.

Aye.

She smiled, still shivering. Can you put on a light?

No, too risky. Sometimes I use a candle. I crossed the narrow floor and opened the shutters; the light from the globes at either end of the alley was barely sufficient to see each other by. I opened them more fully.

God, she said, it cant be very nice staying here.

Well, it's only temporary remember ... I brought out the rags and sacking from the teachests, fixed us a place to sit down comfortably. It was always a warm place too. She unbuttoned her coat. I opened the half bottle and this time she took a small mouthful of the gin. We leaned our backs against the wall and sighed simultaneously, and grinned at each other. This is actually crazy, I said.

She chuckled.

Perishable items? I said.

Pardon?

I've got milk stout and diabetic lager and butter and cheese and stale rolls, plus honey and some cakes from yesterday morning. Interested?

No thanks.

More gin?

She shook her head in a significant way and we smiled at each other again, before moving closely in together.

The daylight through the window. I blinked my eyes open. My right arm seemed to be not there any longer, Renee was lying on it, facing into the wall. I was hard. I turned onto my side and moved to rub against her; soon she was awake.

When eventually I was on top and moving to enter her she stared in horror beyond my head, and then she screamed. Through the window and across the alley up in the ground-floor window a crowd of female faces, all gesticulating and laughing. The Portuguese women. I grabbed at the sacking to try and cover the two of us. Renee had her head to the side, shielding her face in below my chest. Oh Jock, she was crying. Oh Jock.

Dont worry, dont worry.

How long've they been watching!

It's alright, dont worry.

Oh Jock, oh Jock . . .

Dont worry.

Shut the shutters, please.

I did as she asked without putting on my clothes first. I quite enjoyed the exhibitionist experience of it. Renee dressed without speaking. I tried to talk her into coming down to King's Cross for a coffee so we could discuss things but she shook her head and mumbled a negative. She was absolutely depressed. I put my hands on her shoulders and gazed into her eyes, hoping we would manage to exchange a smile but there was nothing coming from her. It had just turned 7 a.m. I'm going to go home, she said. She lifted her bag and waited for me to unlock the door, and she left saying, Bye Jock.

Aye, and the more I thought about it I knew it was time for me to leave as well. This was a warning. I gathered the chattels and filled a plastic bag with perishables. I got my all-important notebook from its concealed spot, just in case of future emergencies, and left, leaving the key in the lock.

The Glenchecked Effort

This jacket had a glencheck pattern and one back centre vent, two side pockets and one out breast welt, two inside pockets and one in-tick. It was made to fit a 42" chest and the arms of a 6'4" gentleman. The buttons, two down the front and one on each cuff, were of dimpled leather. Inside the in-tick were ticket stubs and four spent matches. The inside pocket to the right contained a spotless handkerchief of the colour white, having parallel lines along the border. The left outside pocket held eighteen pence in two-pence pieces. It was a warm jacket. Handwoven in Harris read the label. It hung on a hook from where I lifted it neatly and stepped quickly outside and off. Though hanging loosely upon me it was a fine specimen and would have done much to protect me during the coming harsh winter. It should be stated that previous garments have afforded a more elegant finish but never before had I felt more pleasure than when surveying that person of mine while clad in the glenchecked effort.

I positioned myself to one corner of a rather quiet square to the right-hand side of Piccadilly looking south i.e. southwest. Two males and two females approached, all four of whom were of the Occidental delineation; each pair of eyes was concealed behind medium-sized spectacles with darkened shades. Can you spare a bloke a quid? I asked.

Pardon?

Proffering my right hand in halting fashion I shrugged my shoulders, saying: A quid, can you spare a bloke a quid?

They were foreign. They conferred in their own language. At intervals I was obliged to glance to the ground when a gaze was directed towards me. I shuffled my feet. Then suddenly a handful of coins was produced and projected towards me. Many thanks, I said, many thanks. I clicked my heels, inclining my head. And off they went. Upon depositing the money into the left outside pocket I lowered myself to the pavement; folding my arms I sat on my heels and thus rested for several minutes. A discarded cigarette then appeared in close proximation to my shoes. Instantly I had collected it. I sucked the smoke deep into my lungs, managing to obtain a further three puffs before finally I was forced to chip it away towards the kerb. I reknotted my shoelaces and rose to the favoured standing position.

An elderly couple had entered my line of vision, the progress of each being considerably abetted by the instance of two fine Malacca canes. With a brief nod of appreciation I stepped hesitantly forwards. Can you spare a bloke a quid? I quoth.

With nary a sideways glance they hobbled past me, their canes striking the pavement in most forcible manner.

You sir, I cried to a youngish man, can you spare a bloke a quid?

What . . .

Across the road I spied two uniformed fellows observing me with studied concentration. Slowly I turned and in a movement, was strolling to the corner, round which I hastened onwards. The skies were appearing to clouden. Yet my immediate prospects I continued to view with great optimism. Choosing a stance athwart a grassy verge I addressed successive pedestrians but to no avail. A middle-aged couple had paused nearby, viewing my plight with apparent concern. Madam, quoth I, can . . .

You're a bloody disgrace, she said, that's what you are; giving us a showing up in front of the English.

I'm really most dreadfully sorry missis, I gave as my answer, I have been disabled.

That's no excuse for scrounging! She turned to her companion: Have you ever seen the like?

Missis, said I, I've a wife and two weans and I can assure you, having flitted down here in search of the new life I had the bad misfortune to fall off a roof.

I dont believe you, she said. And would you look at the state of that jacket he's wearing! He's lifted it from somewhere.

I have not.

Maybe he's genuine, hazarded her companion.

Ha ha.

I am missis, I really am.

Oh you are are you!

About to retort I inadvertently sneezed. I tugged the handkerchief from my pocket: out popped a membership card to the British Museum. You see, I said as I swabbed at my nostrils, here's my membership card to the British Museum; since my fall I've been embarking on a series of evening classes with a view to securing a light post.

I think he's genuine, the man remarked and withdrawing a fifty-pence coin from a trouser pocket he handed it to me.

You're too soft, muttered the woman.

Now you're not letting me down? asked the man firmly.

Definitely not mister. Thanks a lot. I can assure you …

Not letting you down! cried the woman. Hh!

Come on Doreen, muttered the man then taking her by the arm, they continued on towards the very heart of the City. But I continued northwards. Soon I was entering the hallowed portals of our splendid literary museum. Moving briskly I proceeded beyond the lines of uniformed worthies at a pace I deemed seemly. Finding a more secluded room I occupied a chair at a table and settled for an indeterminate period. At length a bearded fellow who had been staring intently at the bibliographical pages of an handsomely bound volume rose quietly and walked off. On the chair adjacent to his own lay an anorak, a plastic container and a camera. Moments later I was strolling from the room, the camera safely secured in my inside left pocket. Entering a lavatory I continued to stroll, and passed into a vacant cubicle wherein I would remain for a lengthy interval. To occupy myself I examined each pocket and the gap between Harris Tweed and nylon lining, hoping against hope that I might discover other articles of monetary value.

It was not to be. Yet during my time in the cubicle no solitary voice of an excited nature had pierced my repose. There was much for which to be thankful. I counted to three, pulled the plug and promptly unsnibbed the cubicle door. With practiced eye I glanced to the washbasins before stepping forwards. I washed my hands. In the mirror I surveyed the glenchecked effort with undisguised satisfaction. Just then, as I prepared to dry my hands, an object attracted my attention. It was a knapsack, and the area deserted. In a movement I had turned and was strolling for the exit, uplifting the knapsack without checking stride and out through the doorway, allowing the door to swing backwards.

Various uniformed personnel. I considered their respective positions and demeanour then was moving briskly, stepping into the magnificent surroundings of the vast entrance hall, and downwards onto the paved pathway to the iron gates, mingling with diverse citizenry.

My getaway had been achieved with absurd ease. I was elated. You lucky bastard, I thought, you've knocked it off again!

The clouds were forming in puffs of the purest white. Surely a sign! Quickening my pace I crossed the Square, marching resolutely to a small grass park some two furlongs distant. While making my way to the rearmost bench my attention was drawn to a tearful urchin whose ball was ensconced on top of a thorny bush. I reached for it and gave it an almighty boot. The ball travelled high in the air. I patted the little fellow on the head and off he scampered in pursuit.

When seated on the bench I sat for a time before examining the contents of the knapsack. But at last the moment had arrived; with a brief glance to the sky I tugged at the zip, and could list the following articles:

(i) One pair socks of the colour navy blue
(ii) One comb, plastic
(iii) One towel
(iv) One pair swimming trunks of the colours maroon & white
(v) One polythene bag containing:
  a] cheese sandwich
  a] lettuce & tomato sandwich
  a] slice of Madeira cake.

I smiled to myself and, withdrawing the camera from my inside left pocket, deposited it at the bottom of the knapsack. As I rose from the bench I chanced to glance at "God's fair heaven," and was reminded of these few lines of the lyricist:

Tell me—What is the meaning of man,
Whence hath he come, whither doth go

Slinging the knapsack over my shoulders with a mischievous grin I walked onwards.

Where I was

At least I am elsewhere. A wind like the soundtrack of a North Pole documentary rages underneath. I have absconded from my former abode leaving neither note nor arrears. I left arrears, I left no cash to discharge them. No explanations of any kind. Simply: I am somewhere else. No persons who knew me then or in fact at any time know of my whereabouts. Season: Midwinter. Equipage: to be listed. But boots as opposed to other things I may have worn previously. And also a leather pouch instead of my old tobacco tin. Jesus, and also a piece of cloth resembling a tartan scarf.

There are no lights. I am resting having walked many miles. I am well wrapped up; brown paper secured round my chest by means of the scarf crossed and tucked inside my trousers, a couple of safety pins are in there somewhere too. My health has got to remain fine otherwise my condition will deteriorate. At present I do not even have a runny nose. I stopped here because of the view. No other reason, none, nothing. I look down between mainland and island. Both masses ending in sheer drops, glowering at each other, but neither quite so high as where I am though maybe they are. Miles separate us. How many, I would be guessing. Rain pours. Sky very grey. The truth is I cannot tell what colour the sky is. May not even be there for all I know. And I reckon it must be past 10 o'clock. A car passed some time ago. A Ford it was but a big one. Expensive model.

Below, the tide reaches up to the head of the loch. No islets visible. My boots are not leaking. I laid out six quid on them. In the glen at the head of the loch are houses; I see lights there, and also opposite where I am a big house can be seen—white during daylight I imagine. It looks far from safe. Surrounded by tall, bent trees. A cabin cruiser tethered to a narrow jetty. Apart from all this nothing of moment.

Back a distance sheep were nibbling weeds. I saw them from thirty yards and knew what they were immediately.

I left the room in Glasgow recently and got here before the Ford car. There is something good about it all I cannot explain away. Not only the exhilarating gale blowing the dirty scalp clean. Nor the renunciation of all debts relating to the past while. Maybe it is as simple.

From here the road twists and falls to a village where there has to be a pub. As pubs go it shall be averagely not bad. I wont stop. The place will be closed anyway. This afternoon I slept in a public convenience. Clean, rarely used by the smell of it. I should have invested in a tent. Not at all—a good thick waterproof sleeping bag would have been sufficient. I am spending money as I go but have a deal of the stuff, enough to be without worries for some time. If I chance upon a rowing boat tied near the shore I may steal it and visit the island across the way. Unlikely. I could probably swim it. The gap is deceptive but perhaps no more than two miles. Drowning. At one time it would have presented no problem. Never mind.

I enjoy this walking. Amble and race, set off at a trot, and once I ran pell-mell for quite a stretch—until a tractor saw me. Taking baby steps and giant steps, assume odd postures and if a car passes I shriek with laughter. Sing all songs. My jaw aches. My ears ache. Maybe the wind clogs them up.

Noises in my head. Sounding like a lunatic. But my nose remains dry. Impending bronchitis, maybe. Next time I waken with a bone-dry throat I shall know for sure. When I become immune to the wind everything will be fine. Immune to the wind.

Well stocked up on tobacco, always carrying cheese and whisky in case of emergencies; fever and that. The notion of buying a pipe. I have no room for useless piles of tobacco. I handrolled pipe tobacco in the past. Terrible stuff.

From Arivruach the road curves steeply through a glen owned by someone whose name escapes me. Stiff climb. Tired my knees in particular. For the eventual relief of walking with straight legs I firstly walked with bent ones, at the knees. Black specks in front or slightly above my eyes. The blood cannot be as good as the best. But the wind, I heard it all the time. Loud racket never dying. I thought of climbing a mountain. The real problem is rain. Whenever it falls I am affected. Soaks in knocking my hearing out. I am unable to look up for any length of time. It is damaging my boots and perhaps my coat. If my hair is plastered down over my brow in too irritating a manner water will drip down my sleeve when I push it up. Terrible sensation. The vehicles splash me. The face red raw; my nose must be purple, the constant drip drip from either nostril. Beads hang onto my eyebrows, cling at my eyelashes, falling from my chin down my neck—from the hair at my back down my neck it streams down my spinal cord, gets rubbed and rubbed by my trouser waistband into the skin at the small of my back. And no respite for my hands inside the coat pockets. The sleeves of this coat are far too wide so only my flesh actually enters each pocket, the wet cloth irritating my wrists, and tiny pools of water gathering within the nylon material. The rain spoils the walk but it brightens. Always brightens eventually. Then I see water on the leaves of bushes and I can skite the branch of a tree to see beads drop. The road dries in patches, swiftly, sometimes I can sit on such a spot though not for long of course.

In the future I hope to sleep during the day, regularly. Apparently some people do sleep on their feet the bastards. And I try striding with my eyes shut once I have noted the direction.

I enjoy night. Not dusk so much because I know pubs do business; possibly it gets easier once the days lengthen. I shall sleep all day perhaps. With this constant exercise four hours' kip wont be enough. And I shall be swimming when the water heats. Eating does not worry me yet. My money will run out. My best sleep so far was had in a hostel closed for the winter. Very simple to enter. No food but plenty of firewood which burned fine. I spread all my clothes on the backs of chairs in front of it. And washed both pairs of socks. And had a complete bodywash which might not have been a good idea since two or three layers of old skin went down the drain. This explains why I am freezing. Unfortunately I appear to be really particular about clean feet thus socks although I do not bother about underwear, seldom have any. Up until the wash I was wearing each pair on alternate days and both when sleeping. They had a stale, damp smell. My feet were never wholly dry. Small particles stuck to the toejoints, the soles. I had to see all this during the socks-changing process. In future I may steel myself if warmer feet can be guaranteed. And may even take to wearing both pairs daily, in other words keep them on at all times. Christ I wont be surprised if I catch the flu. I have acted very foolishly. No wonder tramps wash rarely. Yet what happens when the summer comes and I want a swim.

I considered staying in the hostel indefinitely. I could also have erected a sign for other wayfarers explaining how easy it was to break and enter, but did not. The reason reflects badly on me.

This day was bitter. Never warm inside the coat. That fucking wind went through me. Tried everything from walking sideways to hiding behind trees. All I could finally do was stride along punching my boots hard down on the road with my shoulders rigid, hunched up. This induced prolonged shivering but was the best I could manage. Every part of me cold, sick cold. Now and then I stopped for a swig of the stuff.

When the road closed onto the water again I cut off through the marsh and down to the edge of the loch or maybe it was the sea. There was land far out. An island? Amazing silence. Nothing but the waves breaking, lapping in over the pebbles. Where I was the wind was forgotten. Almost warm. I took off the coat and used it as a cushion on a dry rock a little way back. No fishing boats. I saw only small birds, landbirds, the country equivalent to sparrows I suppose. My mind got into a certain state. The usual blankness. A trance or something like it. Time obviously passed. Clear, a clarity. I finished my whisky and chain-smoked. Staying put. No wish to walk the shore in search of a better position. The rain came later. Fine drizzle, spotting the water. I watched on for a bit then had to put the coat across my shoulders and shelter beneath the trees. But I remained for quite a while and might have pitched a tent there.

Onwards to Tor a'Chreamha

The phone was in her hand and she was reading a text, I think, I didnt ask. Then she started texting and stopped. She smiled. What at? I dont know. It was her Granny I was thinking about, this wee cottage she had someplace on one of the islands, although her people came from a village west of the coast. I didnt know a "west of the coast" existed except by boat or a wet-suit but I was wrong. Here we were in a hostel, sitting the gether in the cold kitchen, over a late morning mug of instant coffee which tasted like a five-star bunch of beans, enjoying this long weekend we were snatching. I say "enjoying." I could never tell with her.

We had nay dough and this was a break from the city. We needed the break. I worked in a shit job in a shit part of town. I liked her job better. Hers was what ye might call a vocation. I wanted out of mine. I needed out. I needed away altogether, so a long weekend. Oh jees, I sighed at the very thought. There was stuff we had to work out, for one thing. Even if we just dropped in at yer Granny's, I said, surely that would be okay? Although we could drive up to the tip of the mainland and take a ferry from eh . . . I stopped because she was grinning. What? I said.

What?

Why are ye laughing?

She frowned a moment. There's a bridge, she said.

A bridge?

A bridge, to the island where yer Granny lives? Jees, I didnay know that.

Are ye being sarcastic?

Yes, but thanks for yer attention.

In fact I had forgotten. Why call it an island if it isnt an island? Ah but the land mass is separate. Yes, I remembered, so that was why. I nodded. She also nodded, laying her phone on her lap, a most pleasant location if ever there was. Why are ye smiling? she asked.

Me? Ha ha. I took her hand and kissed it. My lady, I said.

What was it you meant?

Well it wasnay that. I know that song Over the Sea to Skye and I know there's a bridge there. What's that wee village again? I'm talking about yer Granny's island. The good place for curries?

Tor a'Chreamha. But the car wont make it that far.

Och away.

It wont.

Of course it will, I said, and if it falls apart it falls apart. We can always push it.

It's hilly, ye cannay push a car up hills. Ye shouldnt have bought it.

Cars arent my strong point.

It's falling to bits. It is, it's falling to bits. Ye didnt have to buy it. I'm not being critical.

When I bought it it wasnay falling to bits. And I did have to buy it. I didnt realize it was on its last wheels.

Ye didnt need to buy it.

Of course I did. Well—what else, at that money?

Ye could have waited. My brother would have come and advised us.

Ha ha.

Ye always jump in.

No I dont.

Of course ye do. It was a bad buy, ye should have waited.

I was about to continue but why bother. I nodded, because what else, what else. She was waiting for me to speak but it was just to jump down my throat. I had a book and I looked down at it. She was still waiting. If I didnt say something she would go away. We can aye take a bus, I said.

Mm.

Why not?

We cant just drop in.

Uch come on.

No, not without advance notice.

Could ye not phone a neighbour?

She gazed at me with a certain look on her face. That is an aggravated form of skepticism if ever seen one, I said. And I laughed, and so did she. Eventually I said, Seriously. What's wrong with phoning a neighbour?

Phoning a neighbour! She grinned.

It's yer Granny for god sake! Surely grannies get a bit of leeway?

Elidh didnt smile, she sipped her tea. The folk thereabouts attend these fundamentalist churches where it is better to jump off a cliff than not go. Unless ye arent married and living in sin, with ordinary expectation of weans born out of wedlock, given we had stopped precautionary procedures and she had missed her period but was giving it another couple of days. If the locals got a whiff of that it was a Wicker Man scenario, burning bushes and here comes the antichrist. I made a joke about garlic and the undead but it didnay go down well. Weans out of wedlock sounded good to me but I think she was having difficulty.

Weans out of Wedlock.

There was something nice about that, a kind of solidarity. A great title for a movie. I imagined this amazing club, a secret community, the WOOW, what an acronym! Better still Weans from Wedlock. Ssh, we are the Weans from Wedlock. WFW, not as good as WOOW, here come the ghosts.

Truly but in these tight little communities nonconformity is despised. If the truth came out about me and her, the entire family would be wiped out! It was like the Mafia, you mess with me and I shall kill you and your mother and father and wife and children's children, children of your children's children, tadpoles, kittens and wet-nose puppies

Surely not?

Who knows. I had read these stories by Diego Ramsbottom. It sounded a bit like that. If it was a movie it would be one of these auld Talkie Pictures channel on cable starring guys like Spencer Tracy and Marlon Brando, Robert Mitchum. Members of the Jury, let not the prisoner's callow youth stop you from recognising the truth, open your hearts and let it in. Verily saith the Lord who is our Redeemer.

But why did the truth need to come out anyway? Who cares? I would just have lied. But that is me. The girlfriend tells the truth. I dont. "Telling the truth" is a personality trait, in my opinion. People have it. Some people. I never had it myself. In my family it was a jesting Pilate scenario, as my old man used to say, and left it to us to find the reference. He was an aggressive atheist, old-school antiparliamentarian. My maw described him as that.

So what.

Nothing—just me and her, we went wur own way, we preferred to get on with life. My position was about truth, it got in the way of life—getting on with life. My old man was a character. He brought us up to be irreverent wee shites. Ignore the truth he cried and we all struck out for the deep end. Go for expediency, and we all reached for the handrail.

I'm looking forward to meeting yer Granny, I said, I would swim the wide seas o'er, that beautiful song, in Carrickfergus.

Dont make jokes and please dont say anything about churches and God if we do go, and dont mention Ireland.

Hurreh! I said, is that us going? Seriously? I touched her wrist. Are we going?

She didnt answer, not in words. She smiled in that internalized way she had. It meant I was not involved. She had heard me but it was as though I was a voice on the radio. One doesnay go about having conversations with voices on the radio. I was to hear and note what she said, and let it go, let it rest, say nothing further. My lady would make the decision. It was my duty to accede, I think, to go along with the decision, whatever it was. I had never been in this kind of relationship where people make decisions, and other people follow them through.

Wait a minute! Of course I had. That was a definition of labour relations. It's called giving orders, taking orders. So there we have it my Learned lord, the case is rested.

I liked how it worked but at the same time, well, ye were careful, tread warily etcetera. Too many jokes spoil the broth. The way she looked at me sometimes. I had to remind her that I was not an example of maleness, I was one. I wasnay some sort of generic form of living entity, I was me, an actual guy. I was about to speak when she said: I know you stopped being an atheist at the age of four, but it gets boring after a while.

Beg pardon. I never said a word. And if I had it was nothing to do with that, honestly, I was on another planet.

Ye say it all the time.

Say what all the time? Say what all the time? The existence of Supernatural Agency is neither here nor there.

Ssh. She lifted her phone again and checked for texts, murmuring to me at the same time: I was lapsed for years then I became whatever I am now. But I dont go boring everybody.

But Elidh I was not talking about that.

Ssh.

Anyway, I said, telling and boring are different.

Not with you.

Pardon?

Ssh. She began the murmur again: Because you dont know yerself what ye are, ye can hardly tell other people.

Not true.

She glanced up at me, smiling.

O dear, I said.

What?

I feel like sex.

Ssh.

But I do.

She looked sideways, and behind her. Ssh, she said again.

She enjoyed it too, sometimes, I think. The very thought was arousing. What would she do . . . !

She was looking at me now alright.

Nothing, I said.

Nothing what?

Just nothing.

You can be a right fool at times.

Me?

Ye do talk nonsense.

Nonsense? I had to stand up and fix myself, I walked to the kitchen sink. Funny how hostel kitchens have the same smell, where e'er ye go in the entire wide world.

She yawned, her attention had returned to the phone.

I went Ohhh and I stretched as mightily as possible, without falling ower backwards, hoping my arousal was as noticeable as it was, or should have been, unmistakeable.

She was watching me; a certain look on her face. I pretended not to notice. I walked to the big fridge and flung open the door. Sorry, I said.

This puzzled her, which made me laugh. She did make me laugh; she came out with things. That stretch I did, it had no significance, I said.

Excuse me?

Just if ye noticed, I said, it was just a stretch and not intended as anything else.

She was bemused. The mighty nude stretching was in vain, she hadnt noticed a thing and didnt know what I was talking about.

Fancy going to bed? I said.

We cant go to bed.

Yes we can.

People are around. That French group. It's 11 o'clock in the morning.

So we cant go to bed?

Ssh.

Why cant we get wur own place? We dont need to get married.

She didnt answer. She seemed to have lost interest. I thought she was smiling, and she was smiling but it wasnay to do with me. We dont need to get married, I said.

She was still smiling.

Does yer Granny make ye smile? I said.

Her phone rang.

Dont answer it!

It's my sister, she said, even before checking the caller.

I could hear her sister's voice, quack quack quack. She didnt trust me. I dont know if she liked me. She might have, but pretended not to, or seemed to. She was difficult. I found her so anyway. The girlfriend was straight but her sister wasnt. Not with me anyway. That is why I say she didnt trust me. But then I heard her say Tor a'Chreamha. They were talking Gaelic, that was what they done. I loved it but I wish to hell I knew it too. We were going to Tor a'Chreamha. Hurreh. To see her Granny. Hurreh.

I reached for her hand and held it. My lady, I whispered.

She smiled into the phone. I heard her sister's voice saying something like green tea. I think that is what it was, green tea.

Extra Cup

I was to wait in the waiting room, somebody would come to collect me. To pass the time I thumbed through the stack of industrial magazines, eventually dozing off until the door banged open. It was a clerk, clutching a sheaf of fulscapaper, he frowned and told me to follow him; he led me out the gatehouse, through the massive carpark and into a side entrance, along a corridor between offices then out, and across waste ground into another building where I followed him along the side of a vast machineroom into a long tunnel and out through rubber swing doors, onto more waste ground but now with rail tracks crossing here and there, and into another building via a short tunnel leading sharply down then up a concrete incline at the top of which we entered an ancient hoist with crisscross iron gates to go clanking downwards to a subfloor where the clerk questioned a youth on the whereabouts of a Mr Lambtron, but received only a shrug in reply; on we went along a corridor, a deep thumping sound coming to the right of us and men occasionally appearing out of doorways and entering others, pushing all manner of trolleys, bogeys and barrows, and we followed one of them outside and across more waste ground, bypassing one building and into another where we found Mr Lambton sitting on an upturned crate behind a big machine. He saw us but continued chatting to a dungareed man perched on a sort of balcony near the top of the machine, a rag covering his head he looked to be greasing the moving parts which were of course stationary at present. Then Mr Lambton ground out the cigarette he had been smoking and turned to say: What's up with you Eric? Something worrying you is there?

It's the new sweeperup, George.

New sweeperup?

The clerk sighed.

Mr Lambton laughed and winked up at the man on the machine then he glanced at me and nodded, and the clerk strode off. After a moment he continued chatting to the man on the machine. The man on the machine nodded now and again but never spoke. Eventually Mr Lambton said to me, You know the lay-out of this Block?

No.

I'll show you then eh! He smiled and got up from the crate; he yawned and stretched, and sighed before setting off. Every so often he would pause and indicate a machine, maybe telling me what it did in relation to a different machine. He led me outside and we walked round the building and he showed me the railway tracks and pointed out other buildings, occasionally denoting them by number. He knew a great many people and stopped to talk fairly often. Soon a bell was ringing. And I realised we were back where we had started, behind the big machine. Mr Lambton chuckled when he noticed me noticing this and he walked on. He opened a door and I followed him through rows and rows of wall-to-ceiling racks. We came upon a dozen men sitting either on upturned boxes or sacking on the floor; it was teabreak. An elderly man was pouring from a big urn. Mr Lambton called: Extra cup Bert.

Bert didnt answer.

Cup, extra cup—new man Bert, new man.

Bert glanced along at Mr Lambton and grumbled unintelligibly, continued pouring tea then passed the cups out one by one to the nearest seated men who then passed them along to the others.

Alright? called Mr Lambton. And when he received no

reply he grinned at me, raised his eyebrows and walked back the way we had come.

The elderly man didnt give me out a cup of tea but he glanced at me as though I should understand there were no extra ones to be had. Soon the bell was ringing and the men rising and leaving. Bert didnt move; he was sitting near the urn, still munching a sandwich, gazing at the foot of the racks facing him. I got up and walked along and poured myself the last of the tea into one of the assorted cups left by the men. Bert noticed and grumbled.

Did you want it? I said.

He didnt reply; he reached for a newspaper left by the men and unfolded it, brought a spectacle case out from the top pocket of his dungarees, and began reading. Then he looked up: Sweeperup are you? You're supposed to help me you know. Dont suppose he told you that though eh! Did he?

Aye, he said you'd tell me the score.

Hh! Bert shook his head and returned his attention to the newspaper. A few minutes later he put the spectacles back in the case and snapped it shut, put away the newspaper and got onto his feet. He began collecting in the empty cups and the discarded sandwich wrappings. I helped him. There was a brush leaning against a rack; I brushed the floor.

Leave that, he said. He waved me to come with him. We walked through the rows of racks in a direction different to the one used by the men to exit, and arrived at a small door which had two sections, the bottom and top halves being separate. Bert unsnibbed the bottom half and opened it very quietly, he peered out to the left and to the right, then motioned me to follow him across the corridor and into another room; once inside he cut off to the corner and I followed him there, and up a short flight of stairs. When he looked at me I saw the corner of his mouth twitching, then he frowned and opened a door. It was a tiny room with lockers and a long bench. He sighed and withdrew another newspaper from a pocket inside his dungarees and sat down, and took out his spectacle case; flapping the newspaper open he sighed again, began reading. About twenty minutes passed. He got up and walked to the wall to his left and moved a calendar; there was a peephole, he looked through it. Then we went all the way back again and he collected two brushes, giving me one. Come on, he said. He led me around the building for a time then as we turned a corner the clerk appeared from along a corridor. He came striding towards us, gesticulating at me. You've to come to the office, he cried, Mrs Willmott wants a word.

I turned to Bert but he wasnt there. And the clerk was striding off down the corridor. I went quickly after him, out through the rubber doors and across the waste ground, and so on eventually into a building which seemed to consist solely of offices, and I followed him into one with Mrs Willmott's name on the door. She was a young woman, sitting at a wide desk. The clerk closed the door behind me and she glanced upwards, but continued studying a sheet of fulscapaper then reached to a filing cabinet to take out another one, and after a bit she said, New sweeperup . . . Do you have your things? your card and so forth.

No, sorry.

You dont?

No, sorry.

O for heaven sake.

I'm really sorry. I laid them out on the table last night all set for this morning but then I forgot to lift them because I was late and having to rush for the bus, it's because I'm

Well you must bring them tomorrow you know there is no excuse; if you dont you'll simply be obliged to return home for them.

Fine, I'll make sure, definitely. What I'll do, I'll stick them right into my pocket as I get home.

A buzzer sounded. The door opened and in came the

clerk, and he carried straight on out again so that I was to follow him. On this occasion he left me at the ancient hoist. I returned to the building where he had led me earlier. The machines were being run-down. Sure enough it was dinner-break. In the washroom the men were washing their hands and their wrists and crumpling the used paper towels into an empty crate. I walked along the corridor and into the room with the wall-to-ceiling racks, just as the bell started ringing. Bert was spreading out the cups on the upturned crate he used as a table. The men began arriving and taking their seats, opening their parcels of sandwiches and laying their newspapers out on their laps. Bert indicated a cup lying a little apart from the rest; it was for me. There was an old newspaper in the empty crate they used for rubbish. I sat reading this for a while. My belly began rumbling and the man sitting next to me loudly flourished his newspaper while turning the next page. Is there a canteen? I said.

He frowned. A man farther along from him called: Canteen? course there's a canteen. Eh Reg! he called to another man. The canteen now where is that? Group 3?

Group 2, 6 Block.

On the other side of me Bert snorted and he leaned over to spit into the empty crate. Some of the men watched him. The one named Reg frowned. Yeah, he said, Group 2, 6 Block.

There was a short silence. Bert gazed at the rack opposite where he sat, and he said: Group 5 it is, if it's the canteen you're talking about.

Bert's right, nodded another man, it's got to be nearer 5 than 3.

Got to be nearer 5 than 3 . . . Reg stared at him. What d'you mean it's got to be nearer, why the bleeding hell's it got to be nearer?

It was Bert replied. Cause when they bleeding changed it Reg that's why.

Reg shook his head.

You sure? said somebody but Bert didnt answer. He was munching a sandwich. He stopped at the crusts and tossed them into the rubbish crate, he glanced along at Reg and sighed. Then someone else began discussing the old canteen in relation to the new one and another joined in by relating this to why the new canteen had had to be built from scratch more or less, instead of just simply refurbishing the old one. A man got up and strolled along the row, pausing to read slips of paper sticking out from the articles stored on the racks. Bert nudged me and gestured at a newspaper lying on the floor and I handed it to him. Most of the other men were now leaving, as though going a walk down the corridor to pass the time. When the bell did ring I lifted the brush to begin sweeping the place but I was finding a great deal of dust lying on the articles along the bottom racks and so I got an old rag and used it to give them a wipe down first. Bert looked in without saying anything, and went away again. Mr Lambton appeared later and he chatted with me for a bit on general matters to do with the building we were in, finally telling me to continue sweeping in the machineroom. I nodded. Once he had gone I carried on dusting the articles at the foot of the racks for a while, before leaving. I took the brush with me. Going along the corridor I caught a glimpse of Bert through in the machineroom, brushing between two big machines. He waved me in. I nodded and continued along the corridor and straight out, across the waste ground and into the next building, and so on until eventually I was in the one with the offices.

It's not the job for me, I said to Mrs Willmott.

I see. She nodded. You havent given it much of a chance.

I just eh—well, I think it's best to make the decision now rather than hang on hoping I'll get used to it.

She shook her head. I wont attempt to dissuade you Mr aaaa . . . She reached for the sheet of fulscapaper from the filing cabinet and paused; she glanced at me: You didnt bring your things this morning?

No, I left them—remember? I was to bring them tomorrow morning.

Mm . . . She closed the drawer and shifted on her chair. She looked at me, before studying the sheet of fulscapaper, and lifting a pen. Is this your address? she said while settling to begin copying it down on another sheet.

Yes but I'll be leaving it.

O.

If you were going to send me anything.

Well, she shrugged, the money.

Could you not just give me it the now?

Mm.

I'll probably be leaving tonight, or early tomorrow morning, so . . .

She clicked her tongue on her top teeth then sighed, picked up the receiver of her internal telephone and asked a Miss Arnold to come in please. When Miss Arnold arrived she got up from her chair and they both went out into the corridor, shutting the door behind them.

About ten minutes passed. There were calendars and framed certificates on the wall.

Mrs Willmott returned alone, she laid a day's wages on her desk and put forwards a receipt for me to sign. I did so, lifted the money and slid it into my left front trouser pocket. She sniffed and went to the door, opened it for me. Thanks, I said, taking the brush from where I had parked it against the wall.

I had to return to the building where I had been working to collect my jerkin. Bert wasnt about. I laid the brush near to the upturned crate he used for the rubbish then I left immediately.

Old Holborn

He was pounding away on the guitar and mouthorgan as if it was 1968. A sad sight during this overcast morning in central December. I had been coming along the pavement, caught a glimpse of something just off the kerb—silver paper, poking out from under a half brick. Then this music. Dear god. He paused to take a tobacco pouch out from his jacket pocket. I called to him: Bad time of year for this game eh? this weather! fucking murder.

He didnt say anything, he spread the tobacco along the rice paper.

Carols, I said, it's carols you should be giving them. This time of year man that's what they're fucking looking for, carols.

Could be right Jock, he said.

Jesus christ the accent! What a relief hearing a London voice man where you from?

London's right.

Well well well, London eh! Heh what's that? I sniffed. Old Holborn a mile . . .

Yeh Jock.

That distinctive aroma; that sweetness. That's what I think about—ye could fucking eat it man, know what I'm saying.

He licked the gummed edge while I spoke and handed me the pouch while bringing out a box of matches.

I rolled one quickly. I said, How long ye been here?

Half an hour.

I nodded. He handed me the box of matches. When I

inhaled I went into a fit of coughing, it ended in a bout of the sneezes. Always the same. I gave my nose a wipe. That first drag man, never changes eh. Nectar but. Bad for ye as well, so they say. Hh! Makes ye think right enough.

He was looking along the road, not listening, though maybe he was. An old tobacco tin was lying to the side by his feet, where the dough was collected. I nudged it with the toe of my left shoe. Who knows how much, hardly anything. Christ sake, I said, half an hour too!

Yeh, he said, bleeding hopeless Jock. He began to footer with the musical instruments and then launched into a dirge of some kind. I listened to him. Nay wonder he was skint. Not a bad guitarist but the song he sang was rotten. And he couldnay sing very good either. The pedestrians marched past. I didnay blame them. I reached down and lifted the tobacco tin. He looked at me.

It's alright man. I shrugged. I'll do yer collecting.

He didnt answer, continued the singing. A middle-aged man with a rolled-up brolly approaching. Here we go, I moved in, holding the tin out. Couple of bob for the singer jimmy couple of bob for the singer! Eh? I stood in front of him, holding the tin beneath his chin and into it he dropped a ten-pence piece. Easy business. Next along came a man and woman. Heh, I said, the singer, what about the singer? Eh missis? a couple of bob for the singer?

The purse snapped open and she dropped in some copper stuff while he chipped in with another ten-pence piece. The next miserable bastard carried on marching, his ears purpling when I shouted after him. In this game ye can get so ye want to strangle some cunt. It's best not taking it personally. Savage glares and leave it at that. Once or twice I was having to catch myself up from chasing some of them. While yer man there continued with the singing. I was shaking the tin. Young boys and lassies were the best. They thought it a good laugh, maybe because of the voice, the guid

Scotch tongue and aw that. But they usually came across with the dough and the coins were rattling in the healthy manner.

Then the guy stopped. The singing had been deteriorating anyway. He brought out the pouch, rolled himself a smoke in this slow way, just slow slow taking his time, then he sniffed and looked at me. Can you sing Jock? he said, in that London voice.

Naw no me man I'm no up on that country and western stuff.

Folkrock, he said, frowning. I dont sing that country crap.

Del Shannon I'm into, stuff like that.

Del Shannon ... he nodded.

I always forget the bastarn words but. That's my problem. I've been singing that Runaway for years man, know what I'm saying.

He was squinting across the road. The building there was a Post Office. It had a big clock in the window. He started strumming the guitar in an absentminded way then looked at the collecting tin. I cleared my throat. I put it down on the ground, and right away I began with the singing. He stopped immediately, stopped the strumming. Fucking hell! he muttered.

It's a hard one to sing, I said, then the words too. I usually just remember them if some other cunt's singing it. What about that other one, that Kelly, what about Kelly, Kelly and I? D'you know that Kelly at all?

He scratched at his ear, glanced at the tobacco tin on the ground, then up and down the street, before shifting the glance into my direction, but without really looking at me, as if he wasnay including me although here I was. What about Dylan, he said, you got to know some Dylan?

Dylan, aw aye, Dylan, that's like Bob Dylan ...

He was looking at me now.

Course, I said, Dylan. I shrugged.

Right then Jock. He waved his hand at me. You go ahead with that. He twanged the guitar strings. And I'll pick it out...

I nodded. He was watching a well-dressed woman walk by. He glanced at me again. Alright?

Aye, fine. I began straight in on that one the Hard Rain Is Gonna Faw-aw-all but I tailed off before entering the second verse. I tried to keep it going by repeating the bit with the Twelve Misty Mountains. He kept on with the strumming but without hardly blowing the mouthorgan. Fucking hopeless. No point. People were just walking past too. I stopped the singing. Look, I said, we were doing good with me just collecting. Know what I mean? Better off sticking to that. You do the singing, I'll hold the tin. At least we'll get a fucking wage out it man know what I'm saying!

He shook his head.

How no?

He shrugged, started picking away on the individual guitar strings and it was making a tune. It sounded okay.

You just do that, I said.

No good Jock, they dont want to know.

Well at least give it a try man I mean if you're

He said: How much I got in the tin?

I looked at him.

Eh? Much have I got?

I dont know, a few quid. Heh, fancy a coffee or something, a sandwich?

Just had me breakfast Jock.

Breakfast!

Yeh.

Hh.

He turned away and gave a sharp rasp on the mouthorgan and launched into another dirge. I watched him for one second and then I said to him: I'll tell you something, I've no eaten for days. Days! A tin of fucking sardines man! And you talk about breakfast! Breakfast by fuck.

He nodded, still involved in that music, whatever it was. I grabbed the tin up from the pavement and rattled it. He stopped playing. He shook his head at me. I laid the tin back on the ground. He continued playing. What's up? I said.

He didnt reply.

Heh man what's up?

He paused an instant: Leave it out Jock.

Leave what fucking out, you'd still have thirty fucking pence if it wasnt for me.

Yeh, he said, yeh, that's the fucking problem mate too heavy, ten more minutes of you and the man would be here sticking me for extortion.

What?

Yeh.

What did you say?

You heard.

I nodded. Right, I said, well I'll tell you something for nothing man I'm due a couple of bob here. I reached to nudge the tobacco tin with my left toe again. Then I bent quickly and lifted it.

Take two pound, he said.

Naw, I said, one's plenty.

Take the bleeding two for christ sake.

Okay then okay. I'm really starving but honest. Heh, listen, you want me to buy ye something? Do ye need anything? More tobacco like, whatever. If you want something . . . I'll go and get it for ye.

Nah Jock.

Bottle of water maybe?

He shook his head. I stood there. He adjusted the guitar on his shoulders and continued with the music, some kind of thing.

Okay, I said, okay. Ta. I'll be back shortly.

On he went with the singing. I didnay go back of course, doubtful if he would have been there anyway.

The Chase

The first thing to do is walk slowly and dont look either way, you keep the hands in the pockets, the jerkin pockets, the shoulders hunched a little. Folk watch you. The police are there as well. It's nasty. There is a thing not good to the mind. But you have to keep going. It is a vice, and the way of all vices, that compulsion. It isnt even of interest. The heads dont turn. They notice though. They notice. They just dont hardly bother because it is so expected. That predictability. Yes, okay, which is a relief. If the predictability did not exist the thing would become the more burdensome, the more destructive to your mind. Not your mind, your soul. Minds are just too uninteresting. But souls. Souls are interesting: they are of interest. Note the irony. Souls are of interest. If you live in an atmosphere that is religious then they are not of interest, but our atmosphere is irreligious, not to say sacrilegious, so, the existence of souls. My own soul

Well now, the unfinished thought, the pregnancy of it. We dont know. That is to say, we are unable to tell. But, the duty to the thought: my own soul is, not to beat about the bush, lacking in effervescence. What do we mean by that. We mean that my soul is in a state. The state is one of trauma, though trauma is too harsh. My soul is the soul of a depressive, manic perhaps, even maniacal. A hundred years ago the notion of manic depression was not in play. I banged my eye. I put up my hand to my face, to maybe rub my brow I cannot remember, but my finger went into my eye! It damn well nips and water streams from it. There is a heatwave too. It is 3 a.m. I was not able to sleep because of the heat. My partner's body was sweating. Each time we closed we stuck, or I stuck. My partner seemed not to stick. It was me who stuck and had to dislodge myself and I could almost hear the sound of it, the slight smacking noise. A car starts up below. A neighbour is mysterious. I hear the car start on other mornings also

The stickiness of my partner's body. I went to the wardrobe and got some clothes on. Three a.m. and I needed to get out. I felt like I was sweating severely. I filled the washbasin in the bathroom with cold water and then dunked in my noggin and let the cold water drip down my neck and down the hairs on my chest so that it was slightly uncomfortable underneath the shirt I wore, but it was worth it to get a feeling of freshness. Besides, I like the night, the depth of it—except that at this time of year it only lasts for something like two hours say, half midnight to about 2:45, and after that you've got the navy blue/charcoal grey tinting the sky.

It was nice being out, I felt that for my soul. I am fond of my partner but it does my soul the world of good to escape, to escape into the air, the still of the dark part of the night. Solitary motor cars. Where I live a couple of shops open right into the late night so it's good, especially good having a place to walk to, you can just stroll as slowly as you like, and if the police stop you you've got the ready made excuse. But if you have a vice, a compulsion—even just walking the street, if that's your compulsion—then they stare at you. They are not at all certain. You look so normal and natural an individual, so normal and natural, that they cannot gauge you, what it is, the police, they cannot think that thing about you. Therefore what happens next is always tinged not by despair but the utmost nervewracking excitement. I know the district you see and in knowing the district it is a fantasy of mine that the police are trying to capture me. I am standing giving answers to certain questions and they look one to the other, suspicious of me, I see it in their very face, their gestures, the way they stand ready to grab me if I so much as make a move. But that split second prior to them reaching out to get me I sprint suddenly sideways and through a close, down the steps and out by the dunny there or else into the dunny except I hate the idea of being trapped there and them entering with their torches, flashing on my face. I sprint instead beyond the dunny and across the wall, leaping down into the next backcourt and out through the gapsite down Brown Street and to the waterfront, down the steps and rushing headlong, but quiet, controlling my harsh breathing, the moonlight over the ripples of the Clyde, the tremendous elation of that, and maybe hearing the harsh-sounding breaths of the chasing policemen, the slap of their boots on the tarmac, the concrete paving. This is my area and there is the old tunnel too and there is bound to be some old forgotten side entrance I can slip through, clattering down and down and down, my knees almost caving with the force of my movement. God.

A Hunter

I returned home shortly after closing time with a minor carry-out: two cans of stout. One would have hoped for more but it was not to be. Where had one's money gone! One might as well have bayed at la luna. The room was cold and bleak, as always it was, and I shuddered as I stooped to light the gas-fire. Not an enjoyable evening. The pub had been jampacked. I only stayed through a combination of laziness and utter boredom. But if not there then where else, where else would I have been?

And how long must it go on! Oh my God! I chuckled at that one. It was amusing. The entire experience! Of course that red-haired girl had stared at me. She stared over the top of her partner's right shoulder. Of that there is no question. A fellow of bourgeois proportions! And that for a lengthy period too, she did, the girl of the flaming red hair. How come! I did not trust that stare. I assumed someone was standing behind me; one of those guys that appear in adverts for weightlifting apparatuses. The thought struck me that the landlord was paying this girl a retainer to ensnare young and old males into staying in the lousy place, and buying his lousy beer. Whoever would drink in a place like that for pleasure if choices were to be had, yea or nay questions, matters for the taking or hesitatory manouevres, and so on, these choices to make, as if one held such a chance in the first place, my chance being less than evens at all times, all times, perennially so, such was my life. My 2/1 is somebody else's even money. Then of course the partner, he of the bourgeois proportions, a burly fucker, one of these straight down bodies from shoulders to ankles. I would have whacked him except I'm not a whacker, not by trade, not by inclination. To make matters worse I was overcome by a bout of the hiccups. Hiccups are tricky in social settings. I tried to pretend I was engaged in a breathing experiment but at the end it became all messy and I drew attention to myself such that the landlord himself became involved. I could see he was hoping for a way to turf me out the place. I suspect he was the father of she of the flaming red hair whom I looked for, having noticed her absence. I lifted my copy of the Racing Life, rolled it up and stuffed it in my pocket, glad to leave, glad not to have made an utter fool of myself. Supernatural entities were taking care of me, after all, I strolled home, over hill and up hill, down dales we go, in that jolly state we sometimes enjoy where conversations with oneself have us laughing aloud. I was happy! This was a happy time. God knows how come such was the case but that it was, or had so become, for that fleeting moment of which we are all capable.

I had three cigarettes in my pocket. They were to last me to Xmas. After that I was finished. Never again, never never. I would face up to one after a coffee.

Hell of a bad habit smoking. Causes cancer, bronchitis and several other diseases of the lungs, heart and throat.

At home—or "at room" as one might put it—I sprawled on the comfy old armchair, kicked off the sandals and leaned to switch on the kettle. I had the beginnings of a headache or something of that nature. A dearth of H_2O.

Maybe I should have followed the red-haired girl. But where did she go! And what about her partner, the power-guy, was he with her!

Of course he was with her, bourgeois bastard. How come they have all the luck. Because they've got all the fucking money.

My life takes the biscuit, but only on occasion. Sometimes I enter darkened states of mind. By now I had a cigarette burning. Drink too of course, another bad habit, I'm surrounded by the fuckers, stuck in the middle of what is bad for one, for two for three. Liver trouble. Plus the bladder. And alcoholism. And what about the gut the gut the gut, if women ever were to countenance a fellow such as oneself. Talking about if ye bevy too much and the beer goes sloshing around inside yer belly and when ye lean, one can hear the gurgle, a swollen sea of it. Not to talk about gambling, these negative qualities, if women are ever, ever ever. I refuse to talk of horse-racing. Good God Almighty! Some women would rather be married to an alcoholic than a gambler. So they say but who can trust such a weighty statement. The nerves get it, supposedly. Watch a gambler's hands, how they keep twitching all the time and not just when he makes a bet but all the damn time, putting the fork to the mouth one stabs the damn chin. Hear his heart thump boompity-boomp as they race well inside the final furlong, go on go on go on. Fuckt again. An alky sometimes will tell you he is trapped, no way out, but a gambler! A gambler says he does not gamble. He denies the fact, the fact! the veritable fact, verifiable, losing everything.

I thought I heard somebody snoring! But it was not that, it was the roaring of the water's arrival at boiling point, at boiling point, the kettle, the veritable kettle was boiling! I reached down to switch it off. Who was it turned it on in the first place! Ha ha. I picked up a can of stout from the brown paper carrier bag. I only had the two. Which one did my hand settle upon, right or left? They were both the same, same insides—stout. But one was to the left and one was to the right, thus the same but not identical, suffering from the identical twin syndrome and I was excluded the middle, these two tins so to hell with the coffee, I dumped it.

I had the taste.

Pity none of the lads had been in earlier. Maybe we would have chipped in for a good-sized load of the old booze, made a bit of a night of it, invited a couple of women back. Would they have come? One goes down on the knee, ah come on, laughs are rare in these old times. We would have had a laugh.

Laughs are sorely missing in my life. If ever somebody was to ask that was the answer to the laugh-quandary, the quandary of the laugh. The sexes go together, bit of a laugh, bit of a song and a dance and so on, here and there the bits and pieces of eight, nine and ten, tens the field—I bet a 10/1 winner four years ago. Two furlongs out and I knew I was on a winner, the jockey perched on the nag's shoodirs, nary a muscle moving, silent as a liberal judge, a judge of the liberality, icy cool and making the decision, letting down the rein as they enter the final 100 yards and on we go on we go on we go, thank you very much. I peeled the stopper from the top of the can and took a long slug. Sour! Stout I was guzzling. Sour stout!

Sometimes the old stout could taste sour. I should have bought some lager instead. No sir, not lager, too bloody gassy. And even worse for the liver, so they say, these bedtime doctors or what ye call them, barrackroom doctors.

I rose and went through to the lavatory. As I began urinating one knee buckled and I lurched forward or sideways managing to support myself, clutching onto the downup pipe leading to and fro the cistern, gripping it, whhohh and my foot, I pissed over my foot, enclosed by a sock, my sock. It felt warm and wonderfully pleasant. Steam arose. On the return trip to the armchair I lit a cigarette jees the last, the last, I noticed the other one lying there. I smiled up at the ceiling. Life was a barrel of mysteries. Then scratching, a scratching. A loud loud kind of—scratching. What is this scratching? *The mouse!* Oh God no. I thought it had gone. Had I not killed the little being? Surely I had! I did. That bastard is dead. I killed it, I battered it to death with a rolled-up Racing Life. Surely!

Definitely scratching, a scratching. Under the bed in the recess. Must have been two of them. Good God. My eyes closed. I lay back on the armchair.

Once more the scratching, once more it began. It drives us mad, we are mad, mouses and mice, we have mouses and mice. God, to be deaf.

I stayed motionless, opening my eyes slowly, very slowly, now reaching to place the beer tin on the mantelpiece, rising from the armchair, and grinning at the thought, oh yes, oh yes, with malevolence aforethought, oh yes. This bastard shall join his comrade. The Racing Life! The call to arms. Conscripted once again. I rolled it up, dropped down to my knees on the floor and blinked into the shadows beneath the bed. A strange harsh taste hit the roof of my mouth. I gulped. I bounded back into the chair and stretched my feet out onto the coffee table.

My heart was jumping about I was going mad, I was, going mad it was just like millions, millions. The place was full of them. I bent down, tucking my trouser bottoms into my socks so the little fuckers could not climb the insides and up my legs. I knelt down on the floor. It was hypnotic. Baby mice scuttling and leapfrogging around the wall and far ends of the bed, rolling about in the oose and the dust and my flesh crawled and my scalp itched, itched. The blood thundering through my heart, flooding into my temples. Were the hebee jebees upon me. Maybe the shaking pink elephants would attack next. But not on what I had drunk, six pints or whatever it was, plus half a can of stout, or had I swallowed them both, and did I not have a rum, a rum?

I was back on the armchair, raised my legs and sat on them. I was needing a smoke. I noticed one already smouldering there on the ashtray. Another lay beside it with quite a lot to be smoked. Had I seen that one before? Whose was it? Yet another one oh dear God, a stubbed-out one, unsmoked, it too lying there. I broke it in two, into two halves and sniffed the loose strands of tobacco, smoking the one I was smoking, yea peacefully, peacefully, moving my head nearer the edge of the chair, and I glanced across, and watched a host of tiny mices cavort in circles roundabout the front side of the bed and I was counting them, and they kept interrupting it, and how many did I reach—eight, nine, and began again—recount demanded. I stopped again. Ten? A dozen? How many? How many in a litter? Where there is life. Is that the answer? I ran a hand through my hair, a clammy hand and a clammy head and hair that was damp, dampened and the scalp oily, oily, now itchy.

I lowered my feet to the floor, returned to the lavatory and filled the wash-hand basin with water. I dunked in my head, and again, ice-cold water, down my neck it went and oh oh so much the better so much the better. Much much better. Muchly muchly.

I stared at my face in the mirror. Quite a steely-looking guy. I wouldnay have liked to face myself.

Cometh the hour hath cometh. So to battle. To battle. Onwards! The glorious struggle!

Back at the kitchen recess I studied the floor beneath the bed, considered the armchair and surrounding space, jumped immediately onto the bed and lay crosswise, head over the side, peering under and the stench! the stench! My head was crawling, damp hair and all it was crawling and these little being bastards appeared to be playing hide-and-seek. I crawled to the corner where most of the action was in progress. I could make out their shapes in the shadows here quite easily. One seemed to be crawling up the leg of the bed, and other, and another, their backs to the wall for support. The leader had arrived on the top of the duvet, right beside me, its wee fucking eyes glinting and it darting roundabout and here it was coming to get me, it was coming to get me it was coming oh God Almighty

I sat up, cross-legged, my right hand clutching the newspaper and now coldly, icy-calm, I waited, as patiently as ever, as in a dream, seeing to the edge of the bed, the line of demarcation, I had drawn it with the tip of my tongue on the roof of my mouth and there it was, cross it if you dare, dont you dare you little fucker, if you cross that you cross me.

I thought I heard the topmost crawler fall back but did not look to see, just in case, just in case—perhaps they were crawling up the leg of the bed opposite, the ones behind me oh Jesus I could feel their presence, it was more than the sense of it, this was bodily right behind my back, I felt them, felt them there. And it was just so, man, madness it was all of everything ye did not understand of this world where it all was, every being, and relaxed, I was relaxed, my mouth gaping open as the tension and the strain eased from my limbs and body overall, over it all, breathing in, breathing out, my head swivelling to see and saw nothing, I saw nothing.

I shifted to see down beyond the bed and saw a mouse go hurtling across the floor towards the cooker and the pantry, then another and another. As if I had food. Ha ha ha, nothing there anyway, nothing nothing nothing.

God, oh God. The shape under the inner layer of the duvet moving steadily athwart athwart, ever onwards bum bum bum bum bum bum bum bum ever onwards it came. I stared for about four seconds then screamed and just screamed, screaming at them I went flying off the bed, bolted into the lobby slamming the door shut behind me. I leaned against the lavatory wall gasping and spluttering, my head still wet and now the saliva dripping down my chin. This was the end of it, whatever ye call it, this was it, this was like—oh man, this was me, I wasnay anybody else, it was just me forever and ever, this was it and the state into which I was reduced, them wee being bastards, little mice fuckers reducing me to a lump of lard.

My newspaper? The trusty Racing Life? I must have dropped it in the rush. I looked about the place and in this looking saw that container of blue paraffin oh man and I grabbed it up and of course I was smiling, oh yeah, you fucking kidding I was smiling, smiling, opening the room door oh so gently clicking it ajar and sprinkling it slowly then more quickly the paraffin over towards the floor at the bed, the cigarette-lighter out from my pocket, setting alight the newspaper and waiting and then throwing it in and the carpet, the paraffin, the flames and everything now everything and closing that door and then and then into the lavatory, locking myself into the lavatory. The firemen found me there after breaking the door in. I stood dangling one foot in the pan and and was plunging each one in alternately pushing the button and emptying the cistern every so often and it was marvelous how it all worked and the H_2O saviour of life was there and me too, and I punched my chest when they told me that everything in the room was destroyed, destroyed.

An interview thought to be final

He reached to clinch the deal with me, grasping my hand quickly. I was surprised to have arrived at this stage. How had it happened? He was very serious and looking at me as if I was the equal of him. You have sought-after qualities, he said. I mean it. Qualities I value, that we value, as employers.

I smiled but it was not a proper smile. Anyone who knew me would have known the truth. Oh but his was a strange hand. It reminded me of something. What? A grappling iron? What is a grappling iron? Had my hand not been at the end of my arm he would have batted it away. It hung there at the end of my wrist, waiting to be overwhelmed. I was ashamed. Maybe it was a loss of concentration. My opening question had been relevant, concerning as it did, the interview itself. When does it begin, this interview? Even without his response I knew the answer. This interview had begun when I entered the building.

He hit a keyboard button to knock the computer out of sleep. A few final questions, he said, and frowned.

Excuse me, I said. I had been fidgeting and he noticed. In truth I was in a reverie. I was visualising myself upon entry to the building, cameras trained on the entrance. What a gauntlet! Those reception people. Unimaginable lives. What are their duties other than to distinguish suspect parties, inauthentic beings? The unworthy!

I wrapped my hands together and was suddenly in pain. He could see it in me and worried that I might die in his office. He relaxed when I relaxed. It was more anguish than pain but to save time I apologized. I have chest-aches,

I said, and smiled in man-to-man fashion. That is how they happen. Sudden sparks. They take me unaware. Can we change the subject?

He smiled. Tell me briefly what happened?

I was put out of business by the capitalist.

Ah. You have the details for me?

Contained in the stick, I said.

Give it here.

I passed it to him. He inserted it into its port with immediate effect, studied the screen for a moment, then exited the programme at once, dismissing completely my suitcase folder. Are ye not going to open it? I asked.

Later. You have dealt with it. I knew you would. I say later, it neednt happen at all but tomorrow morning if you want.

I should have remained silent but could not stop myself speaking: I spent a great deal of time on it.

In itself praiseworthy, he said. Have you done this kind of work in the past?

Not at all.

He smiled.

Is that amusing?

I find it so. May I enquire about your wife?

Of course. But she isnt my wife.

He nodded. But is she aware of your plans?

We are not married and have no plans in that direction.

Is she aware of this?

I was not going to answer this question. This was beyond the interview business. This is not a question I can answer and I'm surprised that you raise such a matter.

Do you intend advising her that you have applied for this position?

. . .

Do you intend advising her that you have applied for this position?

. . .

Have you two had a fall-out?

Pardon?

Have you two had a fall-out?

Is this relevant?

Relevance is a retrospective judgment, he said and he was chuckling while he spoke. What of your wider family circle? he asked. No family feuds?

I stared at him. He was staring at me. No family feuds? he asked.

Not at all, I said. Not at all. I wondered whether to repeat it a third time when he failed to respond but I noticed his attention was distracted by an on-screen message. He smiled and resumed. I beg your pardon. I've been in this business a long time, as you may have guessed.

Families are personal business.

Indeed. But we ourselves are family affiliated. The end-line is that if your application is successful we shall find out anyway. If you were not to work here then we shall remain strangers and whatever is recorded during this interview is guaranteed future nonexistence.

What do ye mean?

I mean that it's destroyed immediately.

Do you mean deleted with immediate effect.

He smiled. I'll do it myself if you prefer.

Well ... I paused, then I shrugged. I had understood what he was saying, and what was intended and was very aware of the difference. But there appeared to be a presupposition of some sort bound in with his statement and here I played for time.

He smiled knowingly. I found this exasperating. Excuse me, I said, but I've not agreed to take the position yet.

Oh.

Not that I know about.

Is there a chance you wont accept our offer should we choose to make one?

I shall think about it.

Mm.

What's wrong with that?

Nothing.

That's the normal thing surely?

What you mean is the beginning.

Do you mean my beginning?

He nodded but it was an ambiguous nod and I was unsure what to take from it. Some see different beginnings, he said, for example, your arrival through the main door entrance. The fact of your arrival indicates you had applied for the position and were sent for by us. It suggests further an acceptance of the terms and conditions.

I groaned.

Are you alright?

I patted my chest. I needed a breath and snatched one while he waited for my explanation. How little we value human life. I waited another moment or two. He watched me. Can you talk now? he asked.

Yes, I said, but such ambiguity, your ambiguity. I find it difficult. I would greatly appreciate if you could uh

What?

I had tensed and was in danger of being overcome.

If I could what? he said.

Go more easily.

Ah. He smiled.

I came here on the assumption that if offered the position I would consider acceptance. And so on and so forth. I stopped and clenched shut my eyes. I concentrated on the rhythms of my soul, my body, whatever the nature of my being meant, if it meant anything, in situations like this, reduced to a frazzle, a speck of dust, sometimes like nothing at all, no reproductive organs, above all, a worker-ant, scurrying around the kitchen floor, the stonework and weeds.

I could not know in advance the precise nature of what I would do, I said.

Not at all. Not at all.

Otherwise, otherwise ... I patted my chest, shook my head slightly

There is no need to apologize, he said. He shrugged. I am surprised by your response. It suggests a lack of faith. If we are to pave the way for your coming you must allow us the chance to be thorough.

Of course.

Included here, and I refer specifically, let me say, to this interview

After a moment he stared at me. I was waiting. I thought he still had to finish the sentence. Now I realized that he too was waiting. The two of us were waiting. He must have asked me another question, or else left a statement hanging in such a way that I was expected to answer it, without having to be asked.

Time is our necessity, he said. If you insist upon sharing this equally then it renders a curtailment on my capacity to arrive at a proper judgment. If I cannot be thorough I am of no value.

I understand that.

There will be no point making contact half an hour before you expect to start.

I would not do that.

It would be foolish.

I would not do that.

Dependency is a new experience for you?

I regard it as bad practice.

He studied me.

You owned a business then gave up?

It was not a proper business. I brought it to an end. It was a proper decision. I owned nothing and gave up nothing. I am not sure what is meant by dependency.

He nodded.

Once upon a time it was a human quality.

Yes.

Nowadays germane qualities are ironed out, abstracted, spirited away. Stolen.

You would say stolen?

Ironed out, abstracted.

And, you would say, stolen?

Perhaps I would, yes.

Qualitative judgments are useful, he said. What will you do now?

I shall sleep on any offer?

And in the meantime?

I shall weigh all pertinent factors, consider matters, then come to you with my decision

He waited. Eventually he nodded. I refuse to apply pressure, he said, but I do have other interviews, some of which are more complicated than this. You must know that sleeping on any offer will occasion an additional stage in the process. Such stages are needless yet require completion, and completion entails decision-making. We should come to an understanding in the here and now, and this we may shake upon, if you have no objections.

This was the point he proffered his hand. The deal was accomplished in a spirit of informality. Not as friends meeting. Of course not. Sentimentality rarely arises in interview-settings. I knew there was no going back.

The interview had ended and I made to leave. He smiled politely. Some of us have been fighting for years, he said, closing the door behind me.

Lost in the Preamble

Strange affairs can happen to people and I am no exception. All my life I have been fearful of an assortment of phenomena. In the morning I would be fearful to get out of bed, of what might befall me in the afternoon. Yet, simultaneously, I would be fearful not to get out of bed, of what might befall me if I remained beneath the blankets. Others share in these curiously personal deliberations. Stories and articles abound by individuals whose lives have moved in singular routes, in quite the most unique of circumstances. Typically there comes a day when a decisive factor arises, one that may—and often does—change a person's life. This might be heralded by a loud crashing at one's door and one may wonder what could it be. Many a time I have been roused from bed in like situations, in a state of excited delirium, derived chiefly from one's own experience, a shadow of the bygone glory days, the halcyon days when as a student I attended a certain college in a city it is perhaps wiser to leave anonymous. Such was my preference. My examination results at high school had been rather more than satisfactory, thus I was awarded a bursary. My parents—Richard and Elizabeth—were sorry that I had to leave the family home in order to make my way in the world but were realists and quickly acceded to necessity. They offered to "top up" any financial shortfall out of their relatively meagre income for, indeed, both parents worked long hard hours in elemental drudgery, often cold, often hungry. At midterm break I would visit them. My father was a miner and had been ill for several months with a severe lung problem that appeared to have begun from a chest infection, following the onset of a somewhat severe cold. My mother's own health was unexceptional and besides her full-time occupation in the boxmakers' factory she tended the needs of my father and other members of our poor but extended family. She earned a further crust or two performing menial, domestic work for a local businessman whose position on the ladder of success had been accounted dubious by those of his personal acquaintance. My mother, God bless her, had little time of her own in which to resolve the 101 daily chores that crop up in ordinary family life and, I believe, had once a pastime as a young girl. Providence had then dealt a further blow, settling upon her a debilitating ageing condition from which her own mother—my grandmother—also suffered. My grandmother was known to have been a girl of great fortitude, forever excluded from the running, jumping and chasing games practised by her friends. It was her misfortune to have married a man who was, by all accounts, a miscreant; a fellow whose improprieties were deemed more grounded in what gave rise to his notoriety, in the words of one who had made his acquaintance. He was her first husband. Her second husband was my grandfather, who had fled to this country by the northeastern reaches of the Baltic Sea, in search of his maternal uncle whose passion for song was matched only by that for the solitary delights of scholastic pleasures which had forced him to concede his dreams of becoming a singer, following the wondrous example of his renowned aunt, Amelia Vov Narzikopff, whose husband had familial connections to the younger sister of Pablo Pouleyna who, towards the end days of his time as conductor of the illustrious Taliminian chorus, led the masterly rendition of the Duke Erakzonin masterpieces, which provided the basis of entry moved previously by the Dowager-Countess Stankleheldt, ill-starred friend of the legendary Anna Ricouer, then a member of the secretive debators club of Reuven whose adherence to the rigors of the Bael scholasticism had occasioned tremors in the souls of the worthy, unable to escape the intellectual stranglehold imposed by her own grandmother, having the good fortune to know personally the hidden appetites of the older Ricouer family. Fortune had rescued the younger sisters when the elderly rapscallion died—whether peacefully or no remains shrouded in mystery—in the back room of the Cheim Lanscombe, a local hostelry of dubious origins whose tenant was an illegitimate third son of a distant relative of the first Duke, whose personal acquaintance with the legendary Anna had led to the demise of the late Duke's second cousin and bosom companion, a ruddy-complexioned young fellow of an irritable disposition, deemed to have been brought about by the emotional torment suffered through a youthful regard for Samantha Nicneil, she of the cheekbones, a progressive headteacher and foremost athlete of her generation but whose career had been shortened dramatically, having lost her right leg in a tragedy in the aftermath of a local field-event, having been

Yellow in Red Tulips

Last year a 36-year-old guy dropped dead after a game of football. Gus, a lorrydriver. He carried a bit of weight but not that much although he probably shouldnay have been playing football. It was his day off. He was a good guy, married with two kids. Probably his wife blamed herself. She shouldnt have let him play; she should have found a way, made him take the kids someplace; chores about the house. The guys playing with him too, they would have wondered. All sorts of stuff happens during a game. Ye go up for a high ball, somebody shoves ye in the back and ye land on yer neck or else crack heads with ye. Ye go in too hard on a tackle. Ye have a fight, lose yer temper, all these different things. If he hadnay done a certain thing the person would still be here. Then what if it was you, if it was you put in the tackle? If it wasnay for you such and such might have happened, or not happened. If only I had done this instead of that. So ye start blaming yerself. People do that too. But there is nothing you could have done. You had nothing to do with it. Somebody dies they die. Stop getting in on the act. It is self-indulgent selfish crap. There is nothing you can do and nothing you can say. You arenay the centre of the universe. Life is life and on ye go. That is what happens. There isnay any centre. Human beings are microscopic nonentities crawling about a minor planet because that is what this is and the sooner we admit the fact the better it will be for mankind. My Mother had passed and here I was. I didnay like saying "passed" either. She died. Mum died. Why cant we just say it, just say it. She died, she had been ill, I didnay come and see her. I meant to come home and didnt manage, not until afterwards. I had been trying. I am not blaming myself. Nay point in that. Things are never straightforward.

Ye sit around wallowing. What was and what might have been. She would love to have seen me before it happened but she didnay. It was nobody's fault. It was me that was the loser. I was working in England and had been for a while. Now I was home. Here I was.

I felt like going for a walk but apart from a couple of shops there was nothing to see except houses—houses houses and houses. A housing scheme, that is what it was. The place I was brought up. Same old street. Some of the gardens were different but really, it was all just the same. Out the back window the same old backgreen and the clothes lines there and women still hung out their washing although something about it was different. It wasnay the same at all. What was it? The people! The people made it different.

It is always obvious. These stupit things man they always have straightforward answers.

Funny how ye forget. That was it at the funeral, then afterwards, people talking about Mum and Dad and stuff ye couldnt remember. I couldnt anyway. My sisters and Mum's own family, old Uncle Alex and his kids, all these people and old friends, church people too, they were talking and it was all fine, and it was just me, what was I? apart from the fucking prodigal son!

Ye forget people still go to church. One old lady had come up from Ballantrae or someplace, an old Covenanter, ye could imagine her voice booming out a psalm when she saw the troops arriving. Mum died too young; that was what they said, just like Dad, ashes to ashes.

My sister Linda was coming round later to collect some of Mum's stuff. She asked about bringing me in something to eat. It made me smile. People care about ye. They look after ye. Even when they need looking after themself. What had I ever done?

I turned off the television. I hardly watched it anyway, especially in the morning which was especially awful—it was only the Scottish voices made it interesting. Ye never heard them anywhere else. Did it matter? No really.

What am I going to do with my life but that was the question, that was the real question. I seemed to ask it every day. I thought about phoning the girlfriend. She was at her work but that wouldnay matter, I could still talk to her. I just wasnt going to. The problem was that if I did phone her it was like I was committing myself in some totally final way as if she was in this life up here the same as the other life down there. Was she? Maybe she was. I hadnay thought of that until now. I thought they were separate. Was she the one! Maybe she was! Which made me smile. That was aye Mum's question:

Yes but Derek is she the one?

How the hell did I know, I didnt know. Mothers ask these questions. I was her baby boy. Baby of the family. Baby baby, aye contrary.

O christ what was I doing what was I doing my life was just everywhere, up in the air, whatever was going on, I dont know, I just did not know. Poor old Mum.

My eyelids had been shut, clenched, clenched shut. I relaxed myself, forcing it. I fixed a cushion at the end of the sofa and I lay down and curled up.

It was true but I was the baby of the family. Plus I was her only boy. I had three big sisters. Three sisters.

It was a hard time for her, Dad dying. Ten years without him. That was hard. He was her life partner.

Life partner? What is that, life partner? What does it mean? People say these things and ye dont know what they mean.

It was hard for her and it was hard for us all. I was still

sixteen. That is a horrible time for yer dad to die for christ sake, that is hard man and it was hard. Everything is just fucking shite man that is how it is.

I was the baby. The big baby, the babbling baby, the big fucking wean of the family man that was me.

Good old Mum, that was her. It takes ye a while to admit it. Mum had gone now. It was good Linda was coming. She was practical. She was the eldest, she just got on and did things, whatever.

Times of change, this time of change. There were these things in my life. They were not events, not as such: just things. They were things, just things that happened, they happened to people. My old man dying, me doing the stupid thing at Art School and now my mother. I was 28 which is quite old. Not making a good job of my life. I wished I was but I wasnt. No wonder I was getting tearful, I kept getting tearful, no wonder. It was alright, I didnt, I was just

I wasnay sleeping, I just was not sleeping. It was being here in the house, the family house, I was not comfortable. Ghosts and echoes, and dreams, growing up. What like was it growing up? How did I manage it! How did I survive!

Christ. I got up from the armchair. I went over to the mirror and looked into it, stared into it. There was the pad and the pencil, I started sketching. I had a bit of a sore head. Nor were my sockets red rimmed.

Tears from a tap. There are the tears there are the eyes. I was not wiping them. Seeing my face in the mirror. Grief. There was nothing to convince myself about. I was not telling lies and I was not exaggerating. Grief was grief. I sketched quickly. A different type of face. Sometimes that is what it is; ye see the face and it's different.

I needed a shave. There was nothing wrong with my eyes, I just was tired, tired.

If I had phoned more often. I could have phoned. I could have kept more in touch. I should have kept more in touch. Ye get out the habit. That's all. There was nothing to reproach myself about. It was not my fault. It wasnay anybody's fault. She just died. She was ill. The family knew, we were prepared. My sisters told me and that was that. So it wasnay a shock. That side of it was fine, there wasnay any grumbles there, not as such—whatever that means, as such? Ye say these things, as such, as fucking such—such what? Death, what is death? Adult experiences, we get them, being adults, even death, the first

Shut up. Just . . . shut up.

What is a mirror? We stare into it. What is it that happens?

My eye sockets were not red rimmed.

I would handle it. I couldnay have brought Audrey. She didnt fit. I looked about and didnt see her. Nothing, not of hers, of her.

Mum was gone and I was gone. My sisters were great. Each one was a mother. I had nieces and nephews. I was the uncle from England. Everybody had uncles in England, I was one of them.

My life was easy compared to everybody. I was fine and ready and okay about whatever was next, something was next, what was it? Life is step by step by step. I used to be an atheist. I was now a believer. I had become convinced, convinced. I didnt have an answer except for that, convinced, I knew. It was not deep-down but everywhere, scratch the surface or bury down, and there it was. So that's that. Mum was there in the universe—here in the universe, where I was, and where we all were.

But what was I going to do next?

Audrey wanted kids and so did I. I did, whatever that was, kids. Having kids. What does it mean! I dont know what it means. This is the baby I was the baby, babies know nothing and that is what I knew, nothing. Now Mum had gone what was there was naybody, except me! So I was the one. I could just head off someplace else altogether. I liked Plymouth but the idea of it now, I wasnay sure if I wanted to go back. I had left stuff in the flat but most of it was junk, the stuff I had, it was junk, pure fucking junk. That was me. Ye look in the mirror. Miaow miaow. Mum's cat. Linda wondered if I wanted it. Are ye serious? No, not really, Linda smiled. But I think she was serious.

Anyway, that cat was a nightmare. Mum was the only one could have loved it. Fucking scabby bastard, straight out of a Walt Disney horror movie but with the strut of the King of Jungle.

Ah Mum. Mum Mum. A weeish sort of woman with a surprised look on her face. No wonder, no bloody wonder.

I wiped at the wetness round my eyes with the knuckles of my right hand. Macho tears a-falling; ye want to punch yerself for the indignity.

The word is inexorable. Fate is inexorable. The universe. Nothing is central. God is outside. The rest of everything is inside. Two worlds, the world of the universe and the world of the thing that surrounds it. In the being of God, that was that.

I needed to eat. All this wallowing. I should have let Linda fix it for me. She had offered. I scoffed. Eight years since I had been out in the big bad world, eight years on my own. Strange how women think we're feckless fucking idiots. I checked the fridge. One reasonable-sized lump of cheese. I would eat it later.

I returned among the memories, not just the photographs, I rooted about cupboards and drawers. I did this as a boy. I was sneaky. I liked the smells. Mothballs I suppose, that kind of—how do ye draw a smell? A lot of my early stuff was here. It was weird. Schizophrenia type H: Under the beds. Never mind the gold and bullion, I used to hide myself under the bed, and come out all oose and dust, the sisters shrieking at me, kidding on I was a ghost from the underworld.

There were all these memories. They were everywhere. Mum had kept a whole stack of stuff. Although it came from other folk it was all hers. Although it wasnt. She had all these things but she didnt really "keep them," not as such. They were just there, waiting for somebody. I was the ideal person. When I saw the photos it was her I was seeing, because it was her had kept them but gradually too I saw Dad was here. Not just Mum but Dad, poor old Dad. These things had the old man himself, that was the presence, almost the smell of him. Not just photos but mementoes and if I went to the bottom drawer in the big wardrobe I would find his Royal Marine cap and belt. Stuff from places of war, of imperial splendour and medals and death and crushing rebellions. He wasnay even old christ almighty a total tragedy but there ye are, life is full of them. The surprised look on Mum's face, that was what I remembered. The world did things to ye. It was the world to blame. The world did it.

I kept finding these things. An armband with my badges from the Boys Brigade, the BB—or the BB's as Mrs Cassidy used to call it, the auld next door neighbour. The BB's. Some lassies at school said it as well, the BB's. They did it to annoy us. Quite right.

More photographs, ones of me at Primary School. The class all sitting together, arms folded. Poor wee bastards. The different smiles. The world lies ahead.

Fear.

But what had I done?

That's the problem with memories, nostalgia, sentimentality, ye end up on a downer because of yer own life, yer own shortcomings, yer own load of shite.

Seeing the faces. Probably half of them were still here in the scheme, never having gone anywhere, except for a faraway park or the fucking seaside. Three of mine lay propped against the back wall in the lobby press. Glazed efforts. I knew they would be here. They were amazing!

How did I manage it! How did I paint these things! The Great White Hope of the family. And nay wonder, seriously, they were decent efforts: two still lifes and a landscape. I painted the three of them in my second year at Secondary School—Mrs Campbell, she was a good teacher. Come away Mister Hannah. She addressed the boys as Mister and the lasses as Miss, like ye were adults. They were part of the portfolio. They were bloody good as well. Mum praised me. Dad too, who was secretly proud according to Mum. Dad never said anything, not out loud. He spoke into himself—so other people couldnt hear him! Logical, it made sense to me.

The landscape especially I liked, I found it—stimulating is the wrong word, and the wrong experience. Nothing like stimulating. It was exciting and fresh and stuff was just, growing, alive, life, trickles of what's the word, like the liquid, the liquid in plants, a plant's idea of blood man the life-force, that was what it was, that was damn landscapes. What is the opposite of lifeblood? A fucking landscape. I had an argument with somebody at Art School. This is a Still Life Mister Hannah, it is what we call a Still Life, it is a group of fruit in a bowl. Fuck you and your group of fruit in a bowl. Ever looked at the inside of a fucking apple ya fucking idiot. How does a good apple become a bad apple?

There is no such thing as a still life. That is an absolute contradiction.

I was exaggerating. Guilty of exaggeration. Okay fruit in a bowl but what happens if a vibration occurs, some heavy bastard jumps on the floor?

The three pictures were fine, fine. I couldnay deny it even if I wanted to and why would I want to, why would I want to? Why would I deny something like that?

Why do people do that? Because they have failed. The pictures showed promise, and so on.

See it the other way round: how could objects of such pleasure to my family be unfine? Primitive art, the work of a youthful member of the working classes, rather naive dont you know, but elements of a conscionable being. Is that even a word, conscionable?

The landscape was the view from my bedroom window. I had the wee one at the front of the house which looked out on the street. By the time I was ten only one of my sisters was still at home. Linda was married and Marilyn was away working down the Ayrshire coast and living in digs.

I did the scene from my bedroom window many many times, and at different ages. It was a good view with a wooden fence in particular, a garden fence. It had all these pointed stakes, all different sizes, all individuated. The neighbour it belonged to had painted the top bits red and the bottom bits white with one thick blue line through the middle, to let people know he was a Royalist Loyalist, poor bastard; God Save the Queen, Defender of the Faith. Political buffoonery.

What do we do with it! Parcel it up and send it to Whitehall. The fence was still looking good, and fresh, always always that freshness, the sharp-cut hedges. Mr Johnstone was the man. Him and dad were in the church bowling club or something. He was one of these guys that hated a ball landing in their garden: boys playing football in the street was his worst nightmare. Out he charged. Away yez go away yez go. What was he doing now? Died of heart failure? Probably he was alive and kicking. Crabbit auld bastards like that, they usually lived to a hundred. He would have been near enough 80, more than ten years older than Dad. If Dad had been alive he would have been 67.

But it was nice seeing the three pictures, seeing what I was up to at 13, 14. Maybe the present was a hiccup, maybe I would recapture that boyish vibrancy. Hope remained! I wasnay a waster after all! My life would change! This was a turning point! My destiny, my destiny! The Lord of all the Artists, I bow to you.

A noise at the front door. It was Linda. By this time I was back in the living room, back sitting on the carpet. I shouted to her but stayed rummaging through another shoebox collection of photographs. I was chortling when she came in. She knelt down beside me to see what I was chortling about, and was chortling before seeing the image. You were married when I was at Primary School, I said. Ye were an auld woman. My pals thought ye were my maw!

The cheek of them! said Linda.

Well it was true in a way. Mum and Dad were older. I was an afterthought.

Dont say that.

I chuckled. It was true but. There was nothing more obvious. I found it cheery. Mum and Dad were still having sex. It didnt stop at the age of forty! That was definitely cheery.

Sad as well as cheery. Only because life is sad. Sometimes I never felt there in the family, other times like an only child. It was weird how it shifted. One minute the most loved, then the least. It was never the same all the time. That was it with the talking after the funeral. Too many stories about Mum were early and concerned the three girls growing up the gether. Dad was there and everybody was together—except I wasnay there! So much had happened either before I was born or when I was too wee to have any say in the matter. Elizabeth and Marilyn were my other two sisters. Linda the eldest, Marilyn second, Elizabeth third. Linda was looking at a photograph showing me on Dad's shoulders. I could only have been two at the time. He liked you, she said.

Well I hope so, I said.

Dad's shirt open at the neck but smart-looking in a way that seemed ancient. I was wearing a strange white hat which had a familiarity about it.

I was looking at his Royal Marine cap and stuff before ye came.

You should take it.

Oh no.

Liz and Marilyn wouldnt mind.

I smiled. I've got nowhere to put it.

She shook her head at me. Her attention was now on one of Mum and Dad together, strolling a promenade. It looked liked Kirn. Mum smallish and carrying a bit of weight. That smile on her face. I knew that smile. And the coat she was wearing, I knew that as well. How come she carried that bit of weight? She never seemed to eat. Funny. That whole world, whatever it was, totally gone now, vanished forever. I had my left arm round Linda's shoulders.

It's nice you're doing that, she said.

You're my sister. And ye're wearing perfume!

It is Kirn, she said, I recognize where Mum and Dad are. Ye know the wee tenement building across the road from the harbour? There was a connection there with Granny. She knew somebody who owned a wee room and kitchen there. We had it two or three times. Usually for a week during the schoolholidays. I think this was the time Liz fell off the bike and skint her knee. We never heard the last of it. You wont remember.

I do.

She was always a moaning-faced wee besom.

She still is, I said.

Linda laughed suddenly. Oh goodness me, remember the drive! Up the Rest and be Thankful and then that turn-off and everybody was sick, oh God! I dont know how we all got in the car! Dad must have stuffed us in.

Me too?

Oh you were just wee—we passed ye about.

Thanks very much.

Dad didnay think we would make it, we would all be out pushing. It was a nightmare.

Linda was studying the photograph. I lifted another—the pad and the pencil were somewhere—it was Mum and the girls. Dad must have taken it. It was an early one and I wasnt there. It was a smasher. Something great was captured. Dad must have waited. Maybe he didnt. Maybe it was just there. Ye get it in families. Ye can. Not all families but most. Just something. I shut my eyes. What ye should do is drip yer tears into a cup and then dip in yer pen, the nib. Who said that? Some book I read; who was the artist—cannay remember.

Linda had laid down the photograph.

Dad liked playing games, I said. I was in my teens and he was still looking to kick a ball about in the park, he was still just ... he was just there. That was his place and ... I shook my head. You all were away I mean it was just really us, me and Mum, and with Dad, when he died, so I mean ...

Linda waited for me to say more.

I was the only one left, I said.

What do ye mean?

Nothing, just ...

Derek, it was bad for everybody.

I know it was bad for everybody. I'm only saying how it was me, him and Mum, the three of us, that's all I mean.

He was a grandfather.

I know that.

My two were his grandkids. They were his grandkids. We saw him all the time. He loved playing with them and they loved playing with him. I'm talking about *your* niece and *your* nephew.

Well I'm not here.

Linda nodded. Her head was lowered when she spoke, gazing at the photograph and she spoke quietly. Mum never recovered, she said, she went downhill.

I know. I was here.

Ye were, yes, for a while.

Four years.

Was it?

Yes, four years.

What age were ye when ye went away?

I was twenty.

Linda was watching me now. I stepped to the armchair across from her. She got up from the carpet, and sat down on the sofa. I smiled but she didnt smile in reply. I knew what was coming. Linda, I said, I couldnt have stayed home. Mum was fine, she was doing everything herself and she was fine.

Not right away she wasnt.

I didnt say she was.

Yes she was fine at first but only at the very first then she wasnt. She was forgetful and she couldnt do anything.

But she was trying to!

Yes but she wasnt managing.

But later on she was. Surely that's what it is, grief, it hits ye hard but then ye get through it. That's life surely. Mum was getting through it, she was getting on with life.

Aw Derek.

She was.

Linda gazed at me. The way she was sitting her face was clear, the light was behind me. The living room window was to the front of the building, south-facing, same as my bedroom, so good light during the day. The bedroom was like I had left it, more or less. Every few months I came home for a weekend and it was there, the room was there. Mum didnay need it. Maybe she thought I was goni move back home. Actually she did, she did think that but thought it would be with a girl—a wife.

Linda was looking at me again. I shrugged. You think I should have stayed home. Ye do, dont ye? The youngest in the family stays and looks after the old folks.

You're quite tough, she said.

I'm not tough, you're tough. Otherwise I wouldnt have run away. That's what I did eh! I ran away. I smiled but Linda didnt.

It was a daft thing ye did. I dont think it's funny.

It isnt, it's sad.

Mum was devastated.

I know Mum was devastated.

Coming on top of Dad, it was horrible. Why on earth ye did such a thing—we couldnt understand it, we just—it was horrible. Mum was heart-broken.

Thanks.

She was. Then ye went away.

Linda was waiting but there was nothing to say. That frown now, her forehead smooth but not great, not round her eyes, lines there and like she was tired out. That was her eyelids, darkened, how she was looking at me. Oh God, I said.

Derek it was horrible! It was so horrible. Who had ever done anything like that? Not in our family. Nobody had ever, nobody had ever

Stolen something?

That's what ye did, didnt ye, that's what ye did, so yes, stole, ye stole.

Oh for fuck sake—sorry, sorry for swearing. I dont even think the word: "steal," who cares, steal or not steal, who cares.

Who cares!

What does it matter is what I'm saying. It wasnt against you or Mum, or the family, dishonouring Dad's name or some bloody thing. It wasnt anything against you or Mum or anybody else it was just what happened. It wasnay anything to do with anybody

Dad had just died

He hadnt just died. It was four years later. It wasnt anything to do with Dad.

Linda was shaking her head.

It wasnt.

Of course it was.

I smiled. It wasnay. I know ye thought that at the time.

Mum as well. Ye all did. And it's wrong. It was nothing to do with Dad. Nothing to do with anybody. It was just me, it was me. I stopped then I grinned, because it was funny. I found it funny—the thought, and it was true, I wanted to make a kind of—I dont know, movie or something, I dont know, something, so I took the stuff.

It was just so stupid. It was, it was just so stupid.

Yeh well, that's what ye said.

Well what did ye expect me to say? You stole that equipment Derek.

I nodded.

You did.

I shrugged.

Well and what else was it for goodness sake that is what you did, you stole it. It wasnt yours to take.

Oh for christ sake.

It was so so horrible and just

Oh Linda . . .

So stupid. The way everybody was, and Mum, everybody.

Yeh I know, I let ye all down, I know, yes, blah blah.

Dont you blah blah me! Linda was staring at me. I tried to smile but I wasnt able to, and she said it again. Ye let us all down.

I nodded.

Ye did.

I know.

Why did ye do it . . . ?

It was just basic.

Basic, what does that mean?

I smiled.

Oh God, said Linda.

Well ye're looking for a different answer and I dont have one. I wanted to make something, just, I dont know, I had ideas. I shrugged.

Ye didnt say that.

What?

Ye didnt say that at the time.

Didnt say what?

She shook her head.

I didnt say anything at the time. Did I? I cant remember.

Oh Derek.

Well what? There wasnay anything to say. People thought it was something else but it wasnt, it was just what I said, I had ideas and just—it was Art School stuff and I was an Art School student. It isnay a big deal. You think I'm selfish? We're back to that again, the baby of the family, wee twinkle toes, spoiled rotten. Yeh, that's how come he's the half-wit ye see today.

I shook my head. Linda smiled in reply but it was only slight, a slight smile; hardly a smile at all. I let ye down, I said, I let ye all down. Apart from Dad, because he wasnt there, because he was dead.

Oh God Derek.

Sorry, I said, and I left the room. What was there to talk about, nothing; nothing that hadnay been said. Linda was my sister—and was great—but on and on she went, on and on and on, Guardian of the Establishment. Yet another. The place was full of them. Everywhere ye look people telling ye, ye cannay do this and ye cannay do that. All one's effin life.

I sat on the edge of the bed, a photograph in my hand. Where did that come from? A group study. Study with People.

All one wants to do is whatever it is, not hurting people or fuck all, just fucking whatever it is.

The group studies were the ones. I could never do them. They were the real thing, people moving about the gether, laughing and joking and living and dying. Just doing it all, whatever it is, just doing it without these other bastards saying what it was to be. Here is what you are to do. We are telling ye to do this.

Fucking hell, ye get so sick of it.

I peered at the photograph. I needed a microscope. The mysteries of the group. The interaction. Touching and holding hands, making jokes and crying. When I was a hundred and thirty I would be mature enough to start on them. One is beyond everything. One can be beyond, beyond everything. In two days I was heading south. Tonight would have been better! If I had come in my own car this is what I would have done. Tomorrow was out the question. It couldnt have been tomorrow. Tomorrow it was Elizabeth's place. Marilyn and Linda too. More bloody rows! Female Group with Derek. Never mind, I needed rows. Thank God the kids were coming. Except they were all expecting presents. This is what happens when Uncles from England came home on holiday. The kids crowd round the suitcase. Ye see all their faces. These looks on kids' faces. I did it myself when I was wee. Expectancy! The excitement! One had to explain: funerals arent holidays.

Except they were! People came home, people visited, people blethered, had a laugh and a cry and fucking getting together, just gathering roundabout—ye never saw people otherwise, ye forgot what they were and all that stuff. The weans were entitled to ask, who are these people—family! that's who they are, close friends, the bonds of whatever the fuck it is, fellowship, humanity.

So how come Audrey wasnay there? That's what they all would say. Liz especially: Is she yer girlfriend or is she not yer girlfriend? If she is she should be here! Mum sitting up in the coffin: Elizabeth is right Derek listen to yer sister!

And Marilyn laughing in the background. Just laughing, that was Marilyn, she didnt bother. When I did the stupid thing she was the hardest to figure. She used to look at me and chuckle. Glasgow School of Art, her wee brother. How come? She just chuckled. That word too, I liked it, there was something very human about it. Marilyn chuckled. Was it to do with Dad? She looked at me and just—it was just something, reminded her. Maybe that is what it was. Old Dad, fucking great guy and he fucking died man that was so bad, so bad, jesus christ almighty.

I saw a production of the Chekov play at Art School, it was on down the road, students at the Drama School. It bore no resemblance. A good play, I liked it. But the females I had to contend with! My sisters were nobody's business. Even at the actual funeral it was rows. All that *if she was the one* stuff. The other two agreed with Liz. If Audrey was the one then she would have wanted to be here. Maybe she did want to be here. I didnay know because I didnay ask her.

She would have had to butt in. She didnt know anybody. She had never met anybody. She had never been to Scotland, all she knew was it was above Northampton. That was the joke. If she had come with me she would have been butting in. That is what she would have felt. Butting in to a funeral, who wants to butt in to a funeral?

Inviting her would have been major.

The landline phone ringing.

I left it to Linda. She could take it or not.

Mum was the only one that didnay give me rows, the only one, the only one that should have given me rows, that had the right to give me rows. Mum had the right. She could have given me rows all day long.

Linda was calling me. The phone was for me. Robert Finlay!

My old pal Fin. One of the good guys. If I fancied a beer and could make it in the evening he was up for it. I would have gone for a beer right at that very minute, if he had asked. He didnay ask because he was at his work. He was a teacher to trade, if that is what we call it, a trade. Why not? Good teachers are few and far between. Maybe he was good, maybe not. Whatever, it was great hearing from him.

Back in the kitchenette Linda was making toast and cheese for two. I knew you'd be hungry, she said.

I'm starving!

Linda sighed. I would have brought something in if you had said.

Yeah, sorry.

I did.

Sorry, I said, I was eh . . . sorry

The kitchenette was a small space and not meant for dining purposes but there was a pull-down table joined to one wall which Dad made. He did the joinery himself and it stood the test of time. He was good with his hands. I was not bad myself. Some of it I liked doing, stonework, bits and pieces, gardens and stuff, hammering nails and painting, decorating, wall-papering.

Linda pointed at the spare slice of toast. That's for you as well.

I grinned.

What is it? she said.

Feed the man.

Linda frowned.

I smiled. I'm not getting at ye. The very opposite. But Mum used to do it with me too. It's what Audrey calls it. The same when she was growing up how her mother always gave the boys the most food. She does it too, she gies me extra grub and all that then catches herself doing it.

She sounds like she's got her head screwed on.

Aye well. I shrugged.

Linda pointed at the toast. Shut up and eat. You should have brought her.

I shrugged.

Ye should have.

Yeah well.

Linda was gazing at me.

I shrugged again.

She sighed. We thought ye were staying longer.

Not with the work and all that. The next time.

The next time?

Well . . .

Where will ye stay?

And now I caught an irritation in her voice, now standing by the sink, with her back to the window. And I realized what she was talking about, there would be no place to come, not now. She left the room a moment and returned with her cigarettes. She reached to open the window then lit her cigarette, blowing the smoke directly out the window but it still seemed to fill the room, between that and the draught.

Smoking does ye damage, I said.

She didnt respond.

Ye catch a cold from the windows being open.

She was facing away from me now; arms folded, her right hand holding the cigarette, between her index and middle fingers—the way women do, so the smoke wont stain their fingers maybe, make their skin smelly. If the atmosphere between us had been different I would have asked her. I filed away the question. She was so much older than me but she was always my sister, not a surrogate mother.

Whatever she was thinking, seeing out the window to the back green. I reached for the spare slice of toast. She watched me bite and start eating. My two think ye're wonderful, she said, I dont know why, they never see ye. Mum too, it was always you, speaking about you, how ye were and whatever ye were up to.

Linda's eyes were closed. Why was it you? She gazed at me. Ye went yer own way Derek I'll say that.

Thanks.

She didnt say anything.

Later she was in Mum's room packing bags—filling bags I should say, bags, bags and bags. What was she shoving in! The kitchen damn sink! What sort of stuff was she taking! I smiled. She would have smacked me one for the very thought, and given me a cuddle a moment later. It occurred to me she really was hoping I wouldnt head south. It was nice.

But where would I stay? I couldnt stay here, if that was what Linda was thinking. Mum's house was rented from a local housing authority. Now she was gone that was that. They would never pass it on to me.

Or would they?

Maybe they would. Was there a chance I could get the titles switched? Did it apply to the family? The family home or something. Maybe I did qualify. It wasnay just Linda either, Liz and Marilyn had spoken about it at the funeral. Why did it matter so much? Families dont have to be the gether. Ye just stay in touch. Ye can all live in the same town but ye never see each other. Audrey's family saw each other all the time. I quite liked it. Ye didnt have to do anything. Different if it was yer own actual family. That strangled ye. With Audrey's folk ye sat in the garden and that was that, yes and no and yes and no, smiled at the kids and ate yer sandwiches.

People tried to talk to me but I couldnt. That was strange. Audrey told them I talked all the time so they had these expectations and sometimes I caught them looking. Her granny was still alive. She smiled at me. I liked that, somebody else's granny smiling at ye. They all treated me as a foreigner, a special kind of foreigner, the way English people do with Scottish people. Not for any reason. Just the opposite. Things were too comfortable. Sometimes one felt like walking down the harbour and grabbing a boat, heading south, south. Plymouth was good for boats. Surely they wouldnay miss one! Land lubber ahoy!

Fuck it man, just getting away, ye saw the sea and oh God ye wanted to go, just fucking go, wherever.

I got up from the stool, walked to shut the window. Across the way was a communal backgreen. A woman was hanging up washing, a toddler playing by her feet, now hanging onto her leg. The way she was doing it! the wee yin, trying to stop her mummy from moving, and her mummy with pegs in her mouth, clothes-pegs. Women with clothes-pegs, the toddlers and the backgreen, deft fingers and hands moving swiftly between the clothes basket, the line, the child here, a cat slinking to the rear, on the prowl—ye see these scenes; scenes of life, life above, below and through the walls. Fuck being rich. Who wanted to be rich!

Audrey. No. No she didnay. That was unfair. That was me looking for reasons. If ye want to go then go, dont blame it on somebody else.

I swallowed a mouthful of cold tea. A dispassionate bastard, that was me. It was nice to think so but it wasnt true. I had been too long on my own. Maybe if I had settled down and been rearing a family. Linda had been a mother for twenty years: twenty years!

Imagine Audrey. I liked Audrey. But was she the one? That was Mum: Oh but son is she *the one*? The one. Who is the one. The one unique being. The person's face, face of the person, the madonna as a woman, secret looks at the artist, shared with the artist.

Maybe she wasnay the one. Poor Audrey. But did she want to be *the one*! Naybody asks her. What about that smelly bastard, him with the holey socks, is he the one for you? And what did her family say when I wasnt there? How did they see me?

How does anybody see anybody.

Linda's taxi had arrived. I was off downstairs to help carry out the stuff. She smiled, shaking her head at me. O you, she said.

I smiled when she held out her arms and we cuddled tight. When I left the family house this time I might never see it again. This was the end of it.

Final events everywhere. Me and Linda here for the last time. I clenched the eyelids. Clenching eyelids.

But this is what I was doing and the spasms shook my shoulders. Linda would feel it but so what she would feel it, so what. Poor old Mum, it was just poor old Mum man it was terrible.

The driver had returned to his seat and closed the door. His window was down and ye could hear the radio disc jockey with one of these jolly voices—infantile load of crap, in a Scottish voice. I didnay want to go back to England either. I didnay want to go anywhere. Grab a boat and fuck off. Linda touched my chin. Rough, she said.

Did I scratch yer face?

Tommy only shaves once a week. And that's when he goes to play golf with his mates. Linda was holding my arms. Ye're not coming over this evening?

No, I'll just eh . . .

Are ye out with yer pal? You should.

Maybe.

Mum wanted ye to come home Derek ye know that. Yer girlfriend would come, too I bet ye, if ye asked. If she likes ye she would.

Yeah. I smiled. Linda let go my arms and got into the car. I closed the door. Her smile to me was self-conscious. I waved till the taxi turned a corner then stood for a minute watching two middle-aged men pass on the other side of the street, they seemed to be arguing about something. The weer one was waving his hands about, gesticulating. Football. Rangers and Celtic. It gave ye the fucking willies watching them, people getting hammered everywhere and them fighting about catholics and protestants, all waving their stupid flags.

I still had some business stuff to finish. Most of it I could do by email. The sisters had taken for granted they would be doing it but were glad when I got involved. I didnt mind at all. Mum would have liked it. I was her boy, I was always her boy. Even when I let them all down. I was still

. . . still her boy, and everybody else could go and take a fuck to themself.

What happened if ye died skint? When it came my time I would choose the flowers and the destination. Imagine leaving a message! Bury me on the beach—and there were good ones down where I was living. Audrey knew them and they were good for walks, just like Glasgow in a way, half an hour and ye were anywhere, great places, great walks and just peace and fucking quiet, no nothing, not anybody. Leave the message on a postcard, Greetings from Devon, set my ashes in a bottle and pap it out on the next wave.

Fair or not fair, if ye are dead. Dead is dead.

Mum had money in the bank and that was to be shared out among the four of us. Who knows how much. The sisters knew, I didnt. Probably not a lot but something. Good old Mum. Families squabble. Ours too but not over something like this. We would deal with it, the four of us.

Then that was that.

Who knows what lay ahead. I didnt.

Apart from that I didnay want nothing which is what I was entitled to—although the hat, I had found a hat in the bottom of the tool cupboard. It must have been Dad's.

I went through to my room and lifted it, and shoved it on. I liked how it sat on my head, just the feel of it.

I couldnt remember Dad wearing it. Maybe he bought it and never wore it. Maybe Mum bought it for him. It was Dad's and now it was mine.

Bastards.

Where did that come from? Who was I talking about when I said it? I put on the hat and out it came. A gesture of defiance. That is a hat. Funerals make ye angry. One of the things about them, the emotions, getting angry. People are nice and all that but if ye're family it's different, different different different—Dad dying so young, nay wonder ye get angry, living yer life for other people, blood-sucking capitalist bastards, I used to wonder how it would have been if he had been one of the ones that didnt live with the family, divorced or separated. Maybe that would have been easier. Unfortunately it was not like that for us. Unfortunately Dad was never not there until he was and that was forever—he was not there until forever. That was what was hard. I said it to Linda, and good old practical Linda: It was hard for us all. That was what she said, and of course it was. It was hard for everybody. Of course it was. He was a grandpa. There were kids. They were the ones, not me—somebody like me.

The sky had darkened, clouds layered, clouds full of rain, all the different ones, clouds in clouds or on clouds, what is layered, what is inbetween, are there gaps between.

I had the pad by the bedroom window and was sketching, a hand-mirror propped in front; one line, if it didnay work in one line, the continuity, a line is a line.

Full of rain. Spark spark, shade, shade—as soon as the business was done, I too, I was done, I was leaving. That was that decision made. Decisions decisions bump bump. The sisters could do what they liked, do what they liked with the house, buy it, rent it, burn it to the grun. Blow it up. Whoosh!

Here is the news. An explosion took place today in Glasgow.

And everything that was in it. The boy's three paintings. The lot.

The hat was appropriate. Quite cool. Monsieur Gauguin *s'il vous plaît*, that old time movie with Anthony Quinn. I would have to pluck up courage to wear it outside on the street. Down south would be okay. In Glasgow boys would pelt stones at it, try and knock it off. What's the opposite of an attitude problem? I couldnt remember Dad wearing it. Whose else could it be? Maybe Mum had a lover, a secret affair, some cheery old guy. It would have been good if she had.

It was a most unGlasgow hat. It would have fitted Dad's face and seemed to fit mine.

Although my face was straightforward. I sketched fast, fast. But what's a straightforward face?

Nothing startling, bits of this, bits of that, a man's face, bits of Mum, bits of Dad, bits of sisters one, two, three.

Strange looking. But it made me smile. That was hats. I stood revealed as one more arty farty bastard. I nudged it up so that it angled at one side—who was that? Some old actor, I couldnay remember, Paul Newman maybe. Mum liked him, she would have liked me wearing it.

Fucking hell but I was a strange bastard. I was. How strange people are, doing these things to one another.

Plus the unshaven chin. What did I look like? A fucking eedyit. I had always been stupid. Mum's eyes. The sisters said they were Dad's but they werent, they were Mum's. Mum's through and through. I looked in the mirror and there she was, and I laid down the pad—I couldnt do anything else. The eyes of Mum, the smile of Mum. What is in a mother's smile? What is inside, inside of it, of the smile?

Maybe I should phone Audrey. I wasnt feeling that good. Fairly awful in fact. It was true that I should have phoned home more often.

I had to go to the bathroom. Maybe I would piss blood. Maybe I was going to die tonight. Maybe this was it. Poor Audrey, waiting down there. Who would contact her? Naybody. Naybody would tell her. I would have vanished. She would have to make her own inquiries. There wasnt anybody up here. Not unless Linda did it. Maybe she would. She was a good sister. They were all good sisters. Good family. It was a good family.

I should have come home more regular. Invited her down. I never invited her down for a holiday. It never occurred to me. I never invited her anyplace.

Things are a mystery. How they happen. Ye dont know.

Nobody does. No wonder Mum looked surprised. That was how she looked. No fucking wonder. These things that happen, the weird things ye do. Who knows the effect. Probably she would have come, if I had asked her. It would have been an adventure. She would have loved that. Even the train, big windows and all the light, where do ye sit, what time of day is it, where is the sun the sun the sun. She would have come. I never asked her.

An ordinary Glasgow woman who should have lived for another fifteen years: at least.

I took off the hat. I should never have put it on in the first place, it wasnay mine to put on it was Dad's, it was my Dad's hat man and my mother had nursed it man, she nursed that hat. I should never have put it on that was wrong, that was making it something else and it wasnt something else.

I washed my face in cold water. The blood into my cheeks and the stubble. A stone-cold face; greeny white with a growth; yellow and red tulips, yellow in red tulips, red in yellow, layers and layers. I was growing a beard, maybe I was growing a beard.

If ye can block out everything

I was sitting up in bed seeing into the darkness. A moment later I lay down, clasped my hands behind my head.

I was wanting to tell her but when I felt about the bed, no, she wasnt here. Where could she be? I stared at the ceiling and saw the vision clearly, clenching my eyes and there they were the cracks and indentations, an entire landscape, craters of the moon. That was our fucking ceiling man I am telling you, the vista. What a vista! The whole spread of it. How would it be from a hovering helicopter? Probably the same.

But that was amazing. Amazing. Spectacular too I think, really, because it was like our lives, our entire lives together or better still our life together, the one life, call it the one, because two equals one in a deep relationship, deep deeper, deeply held, making it the one thing. That was our life together: unique. I hadnay realised that until right now at this precise moment in the history of the galaxy—not the universe because that is the fullest enclosure, to the extent that it is not an enclosure at all, it is the one thing and there is nothing goes roundabout that, call it God, call it another version of what existed before the BB, the Big Bang. Did she even know this? Probably she didnt. I would tell her, later, not now. She was worrying worrying worrying that new job she had, starting in the morning, a real job and she was worrying all night about it and in the toilet retching, retching! How come! It's just a job! I told her. I told her. Dont worry about these bastards you'll handle it, no question about that.

Oh but it wont last it wont last, they'll sack me and we wont manage.

Aye but we will manage. I'll make sure we'll manage. Stop worrying.

Something will happen.

No it wont.

I'll mess up.

Ye wont mess up. Ye're great! Everybody knows ye're great! Me most of all!

Oh but it'll not last.

Yes it will.

It wont and we'll be stuck again and I'll have to go to my mother.

No you wont.

I lay back again. I heard the sound now; the cistern flushing but she didnt come back. Maybe she had gone to the kitchen, maybe she was hungry. I was quite hungry myself. I waited. What was she up to? Maybe she was making a cup of tea. I felt like one myself except too much tea at night and I cannot sleep, not enough, never enough and it ends up I'm too tired, trying to work and just not able to do it, one reason or another, concentration, my concentration, I was talking to a couple of guys on the same wavelength, stressing that thing about energy and how it was so necessary, so so necessary, and ye have to dig it out from somewhere and that's what ye dont have, ye just dont have, not without working, just working at it and making it happen, making things happen.

The door opened and she entered very quietly, softly, that was her—softly, a word I like, a word for the feminine, does a guy enter softly, no, no no no; it is the softness, softness of the woman, holding her closely and feeling that, just that, the beauty of the woman. She held a glass of water, put it on the wee table and climbed in. How are ye? I said.

Fine, she said.

Are ye worrying?

No, only if, I dont know . . .

I could see her face now in the half-light, she was just beautiful, she was so so beautiful. I leaned to her and kissed her cheek, kissed the corner of her eye, and the touch of her skin, her flesh, she was so beautiful, and my thigh touching on her too and even the outline of her bosom in this light, this beautiful half-light man however could an artist capture this! It was just impossible, so so impossible, and me stretching too, skin to skin, I didnt have to touch her, skin to skin, is it touching? Is skin to skin touching, lying against, is lying against touching; touching is sensual, the sensitivity, but skin to skin, skin to skin is not necessarily sensual, not the same sensitivity, the receptivity, there is always that something, just something, that thing that transforms the sensation.

I'll just mess up. I know I will.

No ye wont.

I will.

Ye wont. I wish ye would stop worrying. I had leaned up on my elbow now, and was looking down on her and I could see she really was worrying. What's wrong? You're worrying all the time and I hate to see it. I placed my left hand on her forehead. I kept my hand there until she closed her eyelids. But opened them again: Oh it's just if something goes wrong, I think about that, if it doesnt work out and I end up—I dont know, if I just—if it goes wrong and they sack me and I'm out the door what's going to happen, oh God.

It will work out, you'll make sure it works out.

Yes but what if I dont?

Then I'll work, I'll take a job, I'll look for one and I'll get one and we'll be okay but it's just so ye dont worry ye're always worrying worrying and it's so hard, I just find it so damn bloody hard because I'm worrying about you, just worrying and I cant just, it's the concentration, it's so damn, if ye dont have it, I can never ever, I just cant, I cant just damn—it's the concentration, all the worrying, I just cannay concentrate and it's oh God Elidh it's doing my head in.

I'm so sorry.

No, dont, dont say that, it's not like, oh jesus christ, and I laid back down on the bed.

Oh God.

Sorry.

No, please dont.

Honest.

No.

It's my fault but that's the problem, I cant just—I dont know what it is.

Please dont.

But it is.

Oh God.

Dont worry.

I cant help it.

Ssh. I turned to her, I pushed my hand under her neck, around her shoulders, and she turned in to me and I repeated it, Ssh.

She closed her eyelids again.

Good times are coming, I know they're coming. That is a fact and there is nothing surer.

She smiled, still with her eyelids shut.

Hey, I said, have you ever looked at that ceiling? Open yer eyes a minute. Look, look at that ceiling! Honest. Look at the ceiling. That is a landscape and it is our landscape. Some folk would see cracks in the plasters and all old stuff there hanging down, wallpaper and whatnot, bumps and bloody mountains and molehills. I chuckled. But I'll tell ye something, that is our landscape, a proper landscape. It is a vista, and it is our vista. Right here and now it is spring, early spring. Not too early that the plants are yet to bloom, because they are blooming, some of them early, you walk into that park and you will see them bloom and grass and squirrels and all of that stuff, plants and trees, bushes, stiff breezes and kids playing in the playpark, look at that and it's all there and so are we, we are in there in among the population, the entire population, all careering about and laughing, everybody laughing.

You're weird.

I beg yer pardon.

What are they laughing about?

Are ye joking! This vista! Look at it! Look at it! Dear oh dear!

Dont screech.

Pardon! I'm not screeching christ it's as plain as the nose on yer face—on my face, the nose that's bumping into ye when he kisses yer lips, this guy here lying beside ye. What else is there but laughing because that is how it is and that is how it is going to be. Everything. Everything ye need. It's all there! We dont need to go anywhere else at all. This is our world. It's us and us who have made it, and we're making it, at this very moment. This is us. Every trade known to man; plumber to doctor to electrician to artist: all of them. It's all here. People all made it and that's what they're doing, it's us. In this population everyone steps forward. Up they come and on they go. And I know the message! The message is us! Me and you. We'll save them! Saving ourselves. We'll save them saving ourselves. That is the message right up there on that ceiling, that is it, is it our ceiling and our landscape, that is our life, that is me and you, skin on skin, flesh in flesh.

Oh God.

Naw but I'm not kidding, I'm not kidding. Plus the machinery, all the factories. Get rid of the bloodsuckers. I'm talking our world. Okay. Retaining the lot under state control. All everything. I've got the list and it's all in my brain, lodged in here and included is everything we need, right up there in that very vista, everything is there! Everything. A couple of cafe-bars, a school for the kids when we have them and we will have them, and a swimming pool, of course a swimming pool, in a leisure centre. What else? Just the rest of it. All necessary—supermarkets and whatever, it is all there.

Food! she cried.

Of course food. Continuous supplies. Grub grub and more grub. Remember that time we saw the fox?

Poor wee thing, skin and bone, trotting down by the dummy railway.

Yeah but you thought ye could feed it. How could ye feed it? It's a wild animal man? How come ye didnay know it was a wild animal! What is it about lassies! I dont understand ye. Ye go and feed the wild animal, it bites off her hand and leaves the other stuff.

She chuckled.

Honest. Dont mix it up with Noah's Ark and the Garden of Eden. If we look we'll see, but we need to really look Elidh and I dont think you always look. Sometimes ye dont. You would see it if ye looked, but ye dont always do that so ye dont see it like I do. Our heads go in the same direction and our eyelids are open but what are our eyes doing, our actual eyes? Are they doing anything? Or are they blind to what is up there, a land that is right here for the taking. Think about it. How could it happen? We're both human beings. Okay I'm a male you're a female but we arent that different and the world too. The two of us see the countryside. It is our countryside. It doesnay belong to anybody. It's all human beings. This land gives turnips, spuds and cabbage; beetroot and stuff, lettuce too. What else? Plenty else. All the vegetables. Tomatoes. How many farms do ye need in a town? Eh? Elidh . . .

Ye dont have farms in towns.

The surrounding area then, how many?

I dont know.

Call it four. The way I see it the real need is gaining control of the marshes. We have this marshy moorland. It is a drawback. I know it is. But a strength too because it gives us a barrier and barriers are crucial because the troops arrive, the army, the usual threats, Get back to work or we'll beat ye to a pulp. So the barriers because we need the dairy produce. Meat. We need a herd of beef animals. We're not all veggies. People eat sausages and all that kind of thing. Not sheep, ye need mountains for sheep. Continuous supplies through exchange. We brew the auld poitín and do it for export. A straightforward transference of ownership complete with capital equipment, labour force and all raw materials left behind as component parts of our movement.

Now I did smile. She didnt. My beautiful lady, I said, one smile and one smile only. One smile from you will brighten the gloom.

She smiled. She had this beautiful smile, she really did, and there was something about that smile and how truly it did brighten the gloom. I think she was listening but I'm not even sure, it was all such—I dont know how to describe it, or even the century, because sometimes that is what I felt. But one thing I knew was right now, right at this present moment in the span of what we term the galaxy—not the universe—actual farmland is not necessary. What does it matter about the surrounding area, the marshland and countryside and all of that. None of it matters as long as we control the supermarkets. Every week full supplies are delivered. Our able-bodied move in. Quietly, surreptitiously. Just before closing time. Before we make the declaration. Hold it as a Press Conference. Call in the cameras and microphones and have it all arranged, the cameras roll, we make the declaration. Unilateral independence. This is the determination of self, of all our selves. That is our intent and this declaration is the expression of that. Unimaginable. Except that it was! That vista was there and was a reflection of the end. What an extraordinary thing. Ye think it would be anyway but the vista had changed. Almost immediately I noticed. I was staring up now, my eyes fully open and that vista had altered, I was seeing it there in the half-light and that was what gave it the reality. Besides her breathing, she was sleeping, she needed to be. It may have summed up my visions but that didnt matter. It was actually better she didnt see because it had to be dealt with and she found that side of life difficult.

What else to say, these things needing to be dealt with, these bastards, the army and all of them, all there, plus the cops, the sarcastic shite, all with their union jack flags, wee photos of their kings and queens, their tanks and hierarchy forever, barriers and road blocks, the usual. Go and dream. These bastards. Nothing gets through with them. Nay supplies. Nay discussion, nay fuck all. Nothing gets in, nothing gets out. Nay food supplies. Nothing. Ye kidding. And try talking to them ye cannay, ye cannay talk to them, these boys and even lassies. That's all they are, boy and girls from other places and other lands, foreign parts, that's who they send in, that's who's there a

I heard the kids, our kids. She was through with them, calming, the calming influence; that was women. Women done that. No us. I couldnay. I could but I couldnay. And that means wouldnay. She worried about her weight. Imagine that. She did. A woman like her. All the power that was there, all that strength, and that was what we needed.

But this is what we had! We had that! There were thousands of us, tens of thousands. They would have needed an entire army. But they had an entire army. They were the army. So it was not on. I didnay need her to tell me. The publicity alone would have been too much for them to handle. Unless they had the media sorted out. Well obviously, cowardly bastards. A cakewalk for them. They owned the fucking media.

How much grub in twenty supermarkets but that was the question. Enough. How many to feed and over how long a period. How much can a thousand able-bodied lift in an evening, and how many to guard the door while they're inside doing the lifting? These were the questions and they were not petty. Ye need to organize and these are the very things that need organizing. An army doesnay march on nothing, on hot air, rhetorical arguments and orders received. That basic shite man, it is aye the basic needs doing, that most basic stuff. Where do ye get the food? People need to eat. How is it to be done. That is what makes a general. That was fucking Napoleon man he worked things out with his Chief of Staff, all his top ranking officers. Strategies and plans of action. Ye need that in this world. These fuckers man

and a month at the most. One week! One solitary week! That was all we needed. One week. One week was all we required because then the world gets to hear through social networks, one week, and success. So, food for a month for thirty thousand men, women and children. Now then, a family of four say, sausage & chips, stew & totties and mince & totties, fish & chips, luncheon meat & potatoes, omelette & chips so say how much? Fuck knows. People would work it out. She was brilliant at that kind of stuff, Tracy, the practicalities. Everybody can spend money. But doing it wisely? Porridge for breakfast and one loaf per household per day. However much that cost. Plus the twenty-five percent and the rest of it, the electricity and wi-fi charges and fuck knows what else, I dont know, she aye dealt with that, it doesnay matter. None of that stuff. It would be taken care of.

This one town of how many thousands, tens of thousands, hundreds of thousands, all the souls, the lost souls. That is us, souls. We are souls. Do these fuckers know that reality? That is reality. In this house are four souls, me, her and the weans. Bastards. Fuck them and their cops and robbers and the army and all what, I dont know, lying there. She was through the bedroom with the wee yins. I couldnay fucking cope man, that's the truth.

What? I dont know.

The ceiling. The shift in the light. The thing about being awake, seeing the shades of dark and grey; this ceiling of ours with all the shapes and crevices and rifts and old fucking damp patches turned into wee hill ranges beneath the wallpaper unless that was the fucking wallpaper man imagine putting wallpaper up on a ceiling!

To disguise the plaster, the ruts and the cracks.

Ye pull on the rucksack and off ye go for a walk through the hills. There is nowhere I would rather be than on top of this fucking mountain looking down into this fucking loch in the middle of the fucking highlands of stupit fucking Scotland, tramp tramp tramp the boys are marching, the rifle's barking.

Naw naw naw.

Okay.

Right: the average rent per month works out at thirty-five percent of our household income. Can ye believe it? I couldnay when she told me. Thirty-five percent. More than a third of all monies goes to the fucking landlord, the landowner bastard, the way it's been not for always, for five hundred years.

And what are the things we all need? What do we need? Pubs. Ye do need pubs. In this town quite a few. In this district alone which is a hotbed of crawling mud and slime and underbelly slugs and maggots

Quiet.

Then on top of that—christ sake all the add-ons; electricity & gas and the other items. All the other stuff. Economics is the crux. Ours is a sprawling bustling place and christ and the point the point, is roughly this, yes, well then, calmly calmly calmly, a carnival.

Yes, a carnival. I was out the bed and across to the sink, turning the tap, swallowing water straight from the guzzler, whatever ye call it, and I saw out the window the tenements across the street but way way away was the other pastures for the carnival. We would hold a carnival. A carnival would do it. On so many many fronts, if ye thought about it, every box was ticked, all the points, a complete algorithim if such a thing was possible we had it.

It was a pleasing thought, so much so I stopped it. I needed Tracy. She was through in the bedroom, with the weans. One of them must have woke through the night. All that noise from outside, it was a rammy, some kind of battle going on, young guys fighting, gangs and fuck knows what. Identity politics, they all fall for it, all the shite, and the troops all sniggering, the fucking stupit working class. That was that. That was what happened, so the weans woke up. I would send the fucking lot of them packing. Proper organization. Me involved. All of us involved. No representation. Fuck these bastards. And unbroached of course unbroached, by virtue of its very palpability, its palpability. Fucking dynamite. A simple bang. Send them all packing. Capture the fucking lot of them, the entire one hundred percent. The whole damn caboodle: dynamite the fuckers.

Ssh

Dynamite.

Ssh, okay. Dynamite. Our declaration is immediate secession from the rest of the entire caboodle.

No, not as easy as that. First things first. Cash. How the fuck is cash to be obtained? Wages. She would get paid a wage in this new job. Then it was me, I would get one too. What about the kids we would sort out the kids, the wee yins would be fine, I would talk nice to my mother or else her to hers—hers was better.

I hadnay worked in an actual job. I did my own stuff but that didnay count. Naybody paid me for what I did. It didnay matter what I did. It didnay matter if I did it. Who cared? Naybody. They all thought

Who cares what they all thought.

I didnay even know if I could do an ordinary job! How do ye say hullo to cunts? Is it all that "good morning" shite? Good morning. Good morning. Good morning. Oh good morning to you too! Did ye see the television last night? Wasnt it a laugh!

Oh for fuck sake, I couldnay handle it.

Dynamite. I needed to think, it was necessary to think. Things through, thinking through. Looking before ye leap. It was so so important.

Ye see these things. I did. The weans in the room. Her there with them, sitting with them, nursing them back to sleep. I could do it too. I did. We took turns. The trouble was me sleeping. I slept. She heard and I didnay. I didnay hear the kids. She did. How come? A gender issue man. Makes ye smile. Sometimes I smiled. Ye think about stuff. All sorts, yer life ending. My life was goni end. I was twenty-five years old. That was my age. Married with two kids, a great wife. She was a great woman and she was my wife.

That was me. Daylight. Ye get daylight. Things all change with daylight. Where was yer head? I know where mine was. My head. The law of the land as vested, plus the cops, the army, it was just what to do. The way I saw it, it was your own declaration, a personal one. Except declarations dont work in daylight. I would just gather in the lot and make a fucking bonfire, guy fawkes, where's the dynamite ya bastards for such as myself deemed the needy person, but I am a needy person.

Now, the thing to do.

I was laughing. I was laughing. Genuine laughter.

The fucking ceiling. Nay vistas now. What is that like they say, the cold light of dawn, this was the cold light of dawn: build a bonfire to heat the fucking sausages, the chipolatas, for the barbeque & dance. Circulate the populace, we are having a carnival. A carnival ceilidh, for fifty thousand souls.

The continuation of cash might be a problem. Rob the bastards. A couple of thousand bodies surrounding the banks. So what if the cops arrive? Who gives a fuck if the plot is divulged! It doesnay matter. So they bring in the troops to surround the fifty thousand. So what—apart from the short term. What is the short term? The short term. I was wondering about Tracy, it was all worked out now, her getting a job because I couldnay, I couldnt find a job anywhere, I was going everywhere and couldnay find one and then she did, through a pal. Her pal spoke to the supervisor and that was that now. She got the job. So that was me and the short term, thinking about the wee yins. I just wished it was the summer so we could go for walks, it was aye harder in the winter, stuck in the fucking house but apart from that …

All in all, that is what I was thinking, all in all in all in all, if we could get them into a nursery, the weans, so if a job did come and I could take it, that was my thinking, I had my own stuff, my own work and I could do that anytime, all hours of the day, I just sat down and did it, it didnay matter if the weans were there with the television full blast, I blocked it out, everything, I blocked out everything.

About the Author

James Kelman was born in Glasgow, June 1946, and left school in 1961. He travelled about and worked at various jobs. He lives in Glasgow with his wife, Marie, who has supported his work since 1969.

ABOUT PM PRESS

PM Press is an independent, radical publisher of books and media to educate, entertain, and inspire. Founded in 2007 by a small group of people with decades of publishing, media, and organizing experience, PM Press amplifies the voices of radical authors, artists, and activists. Our aim is to deliver bold political ideas and vital stories to people from all walks of life and arm the dreamers to demand the impossible. We have sold millions of copies of our books, most often one at a time, face to face. We're old enough to know what we're doing and young enough to know what's at stake. Join us to create a better world.

PM Press
PO Box 23912
Oakland, CA 94623
www.pmpress.org

PM Press in Europe
europe@pmpress.org
www.pmpress.org.uk

FRIENDS OF PM PRESS

These are indisputably momentous times—the financial system is melting down globally and the Empire is stumbling. Now more than ever there is a vital need for radical ideas.

In the many years since its founding—and on a mere shoestring—PM Press has risen to the formidable challenge of publishing and distributing knowledge and entertainment for the struggles ahead. With hundreds of releases to date, we have published an impressive and stimulating array of literature, art, music, politics, and culture. Using every available medium, we've succeeded in connecting those hungry for ideas and information to those putting them into practice.

Friends of PM allows you to directly help impact, amplify, and revitalize the discourse and actions of radical writers, filmmakers, and artists. It provides us with a stable foundation from which we can build upon our early successes and provides a much-needed subsidy for the materials that can't necessarily pay their own way. You can help make that happen—and receive every new title automatically delivered to your door once a month—by joining as a Friend of PM Press. And, we'll throw in a free T-shirt when you sign up.

Here are your options:

- **$30 a month** Get all books and pamphlets plus a 50% discount on all webstore purchases

- **$40 a month** Get all PM Press releases (including CDs and DVDs) plus a 50% discount on all webstore purchases

- **$100 a month** Superstar—Everything plus PM merchandise, free downloads, and a 50% discount on all webstore purchases

For those who can't afford $30 or more a month, we have **Sustainer Rates** at $15, $10 and $5. Sustainers get a free PM Press T-shirt and a 50% discount on all purchases from our website.

Your Visa or Mastercard will be billed once a month, until you tell us to stop. Or until our efforts succeed in bringing the revolution around. Or the financial meltdown of Capital makes plastic redundant. Whichever comes first.

God's Teeth and Other Phenomena

James Kelman

ISBN: 978-1-62963-939-0 (paperback)
978-1-62963-940-6 (hardcover)
$17.95/$34.95 368 pages

Jack Proctor, a celebrated older writer and curmudgeon, goes off to residency where he is to be an honored part of teaching and giving public readings but soon finds that the atmosphere of the literary world has changed since his last foray into the public sphere. Unknown to most, unable to work on his own writing, surrounded by a host of odd characters, would-be writers, antagonists, handlers, and members of the elite House of Art and Aesthetics, Proctor finds himself driven to distraction (literally in a very tiny car). This is a story of a man attempting not to go mad when forced to stop his own writing in order to coach others to write. Proctor's tour of rural places, pubs, theaters, and fancy parties, where he is to be headlining as a "Banker Prize winner," reads like a literary version of *This Is Spinal Tap*. Uproariously funny, brilliantly philosophical, gorgeously written, this is James Kelman at his best.

James Kelman was born in Glasgow, June 1946, and left school in 1961. He began work in the printing trade then moved around, working in various jobs in various places. He was living in England when he started writing: ramblings, musings, sundry phantasmagoria. He committed to it and kept at it. In 1969 he met and married Marie Connors from South Wales. They settled in Glasgow and still live in the dump, not far from their kids and grandkids. He still plugs away at the ramblings, musings, politicking and so on, supported by the same lady.

"God's Teeth and Other Phenomena *is electric. Forget all the rubbish you've been told about how to write, the requirements of the marketplace and the much vaunted 'readability' that is supposed to be sacrosanct. This is a book about how art gets made, its murky, obsessive, unedifying demands and the endless, sometimes hilarious, humiliations literary life inflicts on even its most successful names."*

—Eimear McBride, author of *A Girl is a Half-Formed Thing* and *The Lesser Bohemians*

All We Have Is the Story: Selected Interviews (1973–2022)

James Kelman

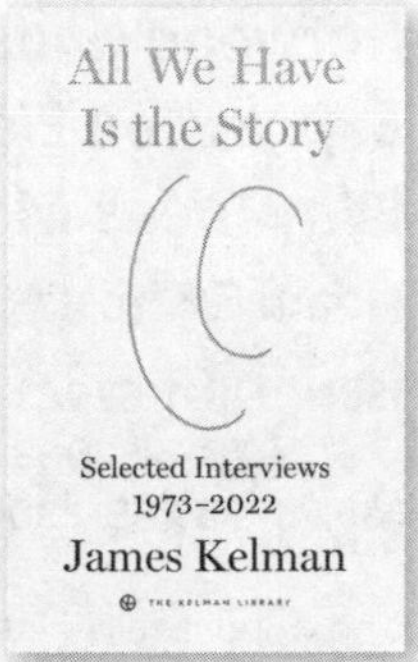

ISBN: 979-8-88744-005-7 (paperback)
979-8-88744-006-4 (hardcover)
$24.95 / $39.95 352 pages

Novelist, playwright, essayist, and master of the short story. Artist and engaged working-class intellectual; husband, father, and grandfather as well as committed revolutionary activist.

From his first publication (a short story collection *An Old Pub Near the Angel* on a tiny American press) through his latest novel (*God's Teeth and Other Phenomena*) and work with Noam Chomsky (*Between Thought and Expression Lies a Lifetime*—both published on a slightly larger American press), *All We Have Is the Story* chronicles the life and work—to date—of "Probably the most influential novelist of the post-war period." (*The Times*)

Drawing deeply on a radical tradition that is simultaneously political, philosophical, cultural, and literary, James Kelman articulates the complexities and tensions of the craft of writing; the narrative voice and grammar; imperialism and language; art and value; solidarity and empathy; class and nation-state; and, above all, that it begins and ends with the story.

"One of the things the establishment always does is isolate voices of dissent and make them specific—unique if possible. It's easy to dispense with dissent if you can say there's him in prose and him in poetry. As soon as you say there's him, him, and her there, and that guy here and that woman over there, and there's all these other writers in Africa, and then you've got Ireland, the Caribbean—suddenly there's this kind of mass dissent going on, and that becomes something dangerous, something that the establishment won't want people to relate to and go Christ, you're doing the same as me. Suddenly there's a movement going on. It's fine when it's all these disparate voices; you can contain that. The first thing to do with dissent is say 'You're on your own, you're a phenomenon.' I'm not a phenomenon at all: I'm just a part of what's been happening in prose for a long, long while." —James Kelman from a 1993 interview

Between Thought and Expression Lies a Lifetime: Why Ideas Matter

Noam Chomsky & James Kelman

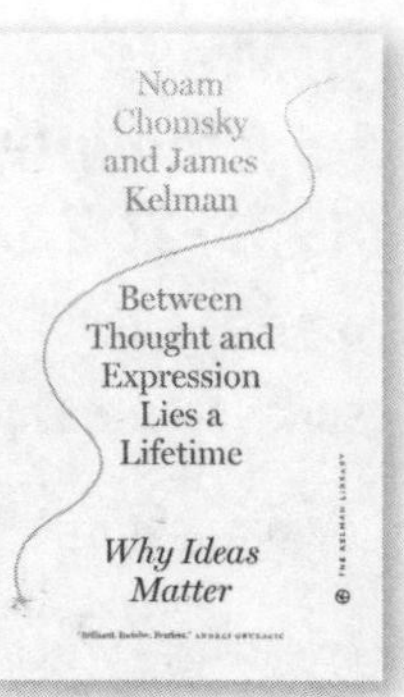

ISBN: 978-1-62963-880-5 (paperback)
978-1-62963-886-7 (hardcover)
$19.95/$39.95 304 pages

"The world is full of information. What do we do when we get the information, when we have digested the information, what do we do then? Is there a point where ye say, yes, stop, now I shall move on."

This exhilarating collection of essays, interviews, and correspondence—spanning the years 1988 through 2018, and reaching back a decade more—is about the simple concept that ideas matter. They mutate, inform, create fuel for thought, and inspire actions.

As Kelman says, the State relies on our suffocation, that we cannot hope to learn "the truth. But whether we can or not is beside the point. We must grasp the nettle, we assume control and go forward."

Between Thought and Expression Lies a Lifetime is an impassioned, elucidating, and often humorous collaboration. Philosophical and intimate, it is a call to ponder, imagine, explore, and act.

"The real reason Kelman, despite his stature and reputation, remains something of a literary outsider is not, I suspect, so much that great, radical Modernist writers aren't supposed to come from working-class Glasgow, as that great, radical Modernist writers are supposed to be dead. Dead, and wrapped up in a Penguin Classic: that's when it's safe to regret that their work was underappreciated or misunderstood (or how little they were paid) in their lifetimes. You can write what you like about Beckett or Kafka and know they're not going to come round and tell you you're talking nonsense, or confound your expectations with a new work. Kelman is still alive, still writing great books, climbing."
—James Meek, *London Review of Books*

"A true original. . . . A real artist. . . . It's now very difficult to see which of [Kelman's] peers can seriously be ranked alongside him without ironic eyebrows being raised."
—Irvine Welsh, *Guardian*

The State Is the Enemy

James Kelman

ISBN: 978-1-62963-968-0 (paperback)
978-1-62963-976-5 (hardcover)
$19.95/$39.95 256 pages

Incendiary and heartrending, the sixteen essays in *The State Is the Enemy* lay bare government brutality against the working class, immigrants, asylum seekers, ethnic minorities, and all who are deemed of "a lower order." Drawing parallels between atrocities committed against the Kurds by the Turkish State and the racist police brutality and government-sanctioned murders in the UK, James Kelman shatters the myth of Western exceptionalism, revealing the universality of terror campaigns levied against the most vulnerable, and calling on a global citizenry to stand in solidarity with victims of oppression. Kelman's case against the Turkish and British governments is not just a litany of murders, or an impassioned plea—it is a cool-headed takedown of the State and an essential primer for revolutionaries.

"One of the most influential writers of his generation."
—*The Guardian*

"James Kelman changed my life."
—Douglas Stuart, author of *Shuggie Bain*

"Probably the most influential novelist of the post-war period."
—*The Times*

"Kelman has the knack, maybe more than anyone since Joyce, of fixing in his writing the lyricism of ordinary people's speech. . . . Pure aesthete, undaunted democrat—somehow Kelman manages to reconcile his two halves."
—*Esquire* (London)

"The greatest British novelist of our time."
—*Sunday Herald*

"The greatest living British novelist."
—Amit Chaudhuri, author of *A New World*

"What an enviably, devilishly wonderful writer is James Kelman."
—John Hawkes, author of *The Blood Oranges*

RUIN

Cara Hoffman

ISBN: 978-1-62963-929-1 (paperback)
978-1-62963-931-4 (hardcover)
$14.95/$25.95 128 pages

A little girl who disguises herself as an old man, an addict who collects dollhouse furniture, a crime reporter confronted by a talking dog, a painter trying to prove the non-existence of god, and lovers in a penal colony who communicate through technical drawings—these are just a few of the characters who live among the ruins. Cara Hoffman's short fictions are brutal, surreal, hilarious, and transgressive, celebrating the sharp beauty of outsiders and the infinitely creative ways humans muster psychic resistance under oppressive conditions. *RUIN* is both bracingly timely and eerily timeless in its examination of an American state in free-fall: unsparing in its disregard for broken, ineffectual institutions, while shining with compassion for the damaged left in their wake. The ultimate effect of these ten interconnected stories is one of invigoration and a sense of possibilities—hope for a new world extracted from the rubble of the old.

Cara Hoffman is the author of three New York Times Editors' Choice novels; the most recent, *Running*, was named a Best Book of the Year by *Esquire Magazine*. She first received national attention in 2011 with the publication of *So Much Pretty* which sparked a national dialogue on violence and retribution, and was named a Best Novel of the Year by the *New York Times Book Review*. Her second novel, *Be Safe I Love You*, was nominated for a Folio Prize, named one of the Five Best Modern War Novels, and awarded a Sundance Global Filmmaking Award. A MacDowell Fellow and an Edward Albee Fellow, she has lectured at Oxford University's Rhodes Global Scholars Symposium and at the Renewing the Anarchist Tradition Conference. Her work has appeared in the *New York Times*, *Paris Review*, *BOMB*, *Bookforum*, *Rolling Stone*, *Daily Beast*, and on NPR. A founding editor of the *Anarchist Review of Books*, and part of the Athens Workshop collective, she lives in Athens, Greece, with her partner.

"RUIN *is a collection of ten jewels, each multi-faceted and glittering, to be experienced with awe and joy. Cara Hoffman has seen a secret world right next to our own, just around the corner, and written us a field guide to what she's found. I love this book."*

—Sara Gran, author of *Infinite Blacktop* and *Claire Dewitt and the City of the Dead*

Everyone Has Their Reasons

Joseph Matthews

ISBN: 978-1-62963-094-6
$24.95 528 pages

On November 7, 1938, a small, slight seventeen-year-old Polish-German Jew named Herschel Grynszpan entered the German embassy in Paris and shot dead a consular official. Three days later, in supposed response, Jews across Germany were beaten, imprisoned, and killed, their homes, shops, and synagogues smashed and burned—Kristallnacht, the Night of Broken Glass.

Based on the historical record and told through his "letters" from German prisons, the novel begins in 1936, when fifteen-year-old Herschel flees Germany. Penniless and alone, he makes it to Paris where he lives hand-to-mouth, his shadow existence mixing him with the starving and the wealthy, with hustlers, radicals, and seamy sides of Paris nightlife.

In 1938, the French state rejects refugee status for Herschel and orders him out of the country. With nowhere to go, and now sought by the police, he slips underground in immigrant east Paris.

Soon after, the Nazis round up all Polish Jews in Germany—including Herschel's family—and dump them on the Poland border. Herschel's response is to shoot the German official, then wait calmly for the French police.

June 1940, Herschel is still in prison awaiting trial when the Nazi army nears Paris. He is evacuated south to another jail but escapes into the countryside amid the chaos of millions of French fleeing the invasion. After an incredible month alone on the road, Herschel seeks protection at a prison in the far south of France. Two weeks later the French state hands him to the Gestapo.

The Nazis plan a big show trial, inviting the world press to Berlin for the spectacle, to demonstrate through Herschel that Jews had provoked the war. Except that Herschel throws a last-minute wrench in the plans, bringing the Nazi propaganda machine to a grinding halt. Hitler himself postpones the trial and orders that no decision be made about Herschel's fate until the Führer personally gives an order—one way or another.

Fire on the Mountain

Terry Bisson
with an introduction
by Mumia Abu-Jamal

ISBN: 978-1-60486-087-0
$15.95 208 pages

It's 1959 in socialist Virginia. The Deep South is an independent Black nation called Nova Africa. The second Mars expedition is about to touch down on the red planet. And a pregnant scientist is climbing the Blue Ridge in search of her great-great grandfather, a teenage slave who fought with John Brown and Harriet Tubman's guerrilla army.

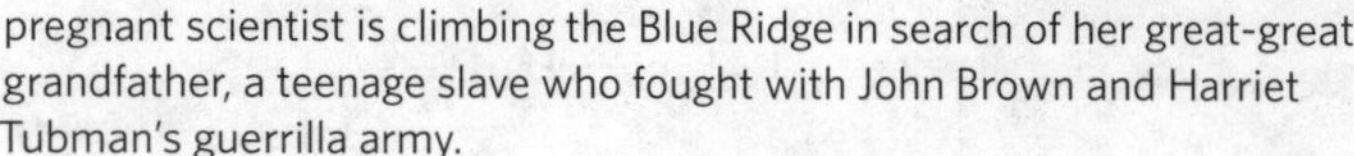

Long unavailable in the US, published in France as *Nova Africa, Fire on the Mountain* is the story of what might have happened if John Brown's raid on Harper's Ferry had succeeded—and the Civil War had been started not by the slave owners but the abolitionists.

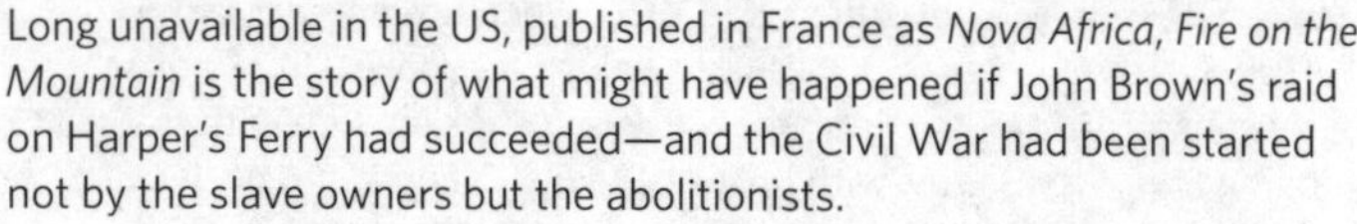

"History revisioned, turned inside out . . . Bisson's wild and wonderful imagination has taken some strange turns to arrive at such a destination."
—Madison Smartt Bell, Anisfield-Wolf Award winner and author of *Devil's Dream*

"You don't forget Bisson's characters, even well after you've finished his books. His Fire on the Mountain *does for the Civil War what Philip K. Dick's* The Man in the High Castle *did for World War Two."*
—George Alec Effinger, winner of the Hugo and Nebula awards for *Shrödinger's Kitten*, and author of the Marîd Audran trilogy

"A talent for evoking the joyful, vertiginous experiences of a world at fundamental turning points."
—*Publishers Weekly*

"Few works have moved me as deeply, as thoroughly, as Terry Bisson's Fire On The Mountain *. . . With this single poignant story, Bisson molds a world as sweet as banana cream pies, and as briny as hot tears."*
—Mumia Abu-Jamal, prisoner and author of *Live From Death Row*, from the introduction

We, the Children of Cats

Tomoyuki Hoshino
Translated by Brian Bergstrom

ISBN: 978-1-60486-591-2
$20.00 288 pages

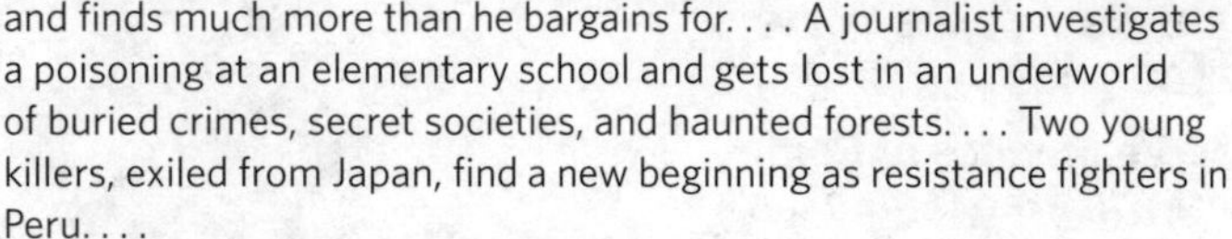

A man and woman find their genders and sexualities brought radically into question when their bodies sprout new parts, seemingly out of thin air. . . . A man travels from Japan to Latin America in search of revolutionary purpose and finds much more than he bargains for. . . . A journalist investigates a poisoning at an elementary school and gets lost in an underworld of buried crimes, secret societies, and haunted forests. . . . Two young killers, exiled from Japan, find a new beginning as resistance fighters in Peru. . . .

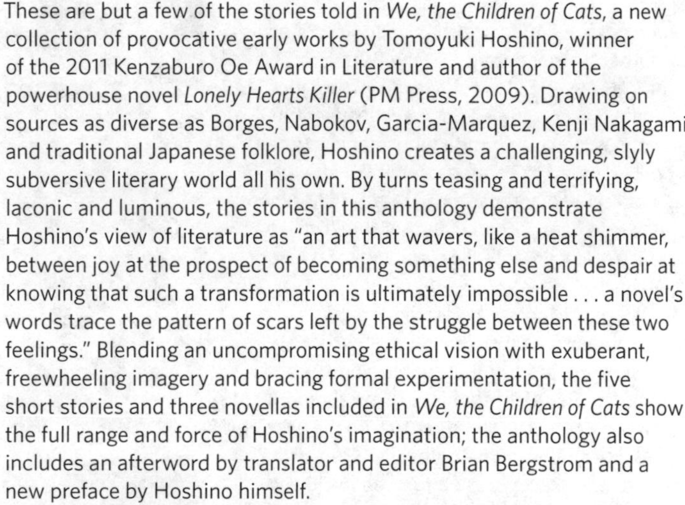

These are but a few of the stories told in *We, the Children of Cats*, a new collection of provocative early works by Tomoyuki Hoshino, winner of the 2011 Kenzaburo Oe Award in Literature and author of the powerhouse novel *Lonely Hearts Killer* (PM Press, 2009). Drawing on sources as diverse as Borges, Nabokov, Garcia-Marquez, Kenji Nakagami and traditional Japanese folklore, Hoshino creates a challenging, slyly subversive literary world all his own. By turns teasing and terrifying, laconic and luminous, the stories in this anthology demonstrate Hoshino's view of literature as "an art that wavers, like a heat shimmer, between joy at the prospect of becoming something else and despair at knowing that such a transformation is ultimately impossible . . . a novel's words trace the pattern of scars left by the struggle between these two feelings." Blending an uncompromising ethical vision with exuberant, freewheeling imagery and bracing formal experimentation, the five short stories and three novellas included in *We, the Children of Cats* show the full range and force of Hoshino's imagination; the anthology also includes an afterword by translator and editor Brian Bergstrom and a new preface by Hoshino himself.

"These wonderful stories make you laugh and cry, but mostly they astonish, co-mingling daily reality with the envelope pushed to the max and the interstice of the hard edges of life with the profoundly gentle ones."
—Helen Mitsios, editor of *New Japanese Voices: The Best Contemporary Fiction from Japan* and *Digital Geishas and Talking Frogs: The Best 21st Century Short Stories from Japan*

The Colonel Pyat Quartet

Michael Moorcock
with introductions by Alan Wall

Byzantium Endures
ISBN: 978-1-60486-491-5
$22.00 400 pages

The Laughter of Carthage
ISBN: 978-1-60486-492-2
$22.00 448 pages

Jerusalem Commands
ISBN: 978-1-60486-493-9
$22.00 448 pages

The Vengeance of Rome
ISBN: 978-1-60486-494-6
$23.00 500 pages

Moorcock's Pyat Quartet has been described as an authentic masterpiece of the 20th and 21st centuries. It's the story of Maxim Arturovitch Pyatnitski, a cocaine addict, sexual adventurer, and obsessive anti-Semite whose epic journey from Leningrad to London connects him with scoundrels and heroes from Trotsky to Makhno, and whose career echoes that of the 20th century's descent into Fascism and total war.

It is Michael Moorcock's extraordinary achievement to convert the life of Maxim Pyatnitski into epic and often hilariously comic adventure. Sustained by his dreams and profligate inventions, his determination to turn his back on the realities of his own origins, Pyat runs from crisis to crisis, every ruse a further link in a vast chain of deceit, suppression, betrayal. Yet, in his deranged self-deception, his monumentally distorted vision, this thoroughly unreliable narrator becomes a lens for focusing, through the dimensions of wild farce and chilling terror, on an uneasy brand of truth.